Praise for Sharon Gwyn Short's first novel, ANGEL'S BIDDING

"Private detective Patricia Delaney is a '90s sleuth who uses computer databases as well as old-fashioned gumshoe savvy to solve a baffling murder in the fast-paced and intriguing ANGEL'S BIDDING. Sharon Gwyn Short's debut effort is sure to win readers to this new and lively series."

> —KATHY HOGAN TROCHECK
> Author of
> *Every Crooked Nanny* and
> *To Live and Die in Dixie*

"I can think of very few debuts more promising, or more satisfying, than Sharon's (and Patricia Delaney's) in ANGEL'S BIDDING."

> —WILLIAM J. REYNOLDS
> Author of *The Naked Eye* and *Things Invisible*

"It is a pleasure to meet Patricia Delaney, a most unusual private eye."

> —NANCY PICKARD
> Author of *But I Wouldn't Want to Die There*

PAST PRETENSE

Sharon Gwyn Short

FAWCETT GOLD MEDAL • NEW YORK

A Fawcett Gold Medal Book
Published by Ballantine Books
Copyright © 1994 by Sharon Gwyn Short

All rights reserved under International and Pan-American Copyright Conventions. Published in the United States of America by Ballantine Books, a division of Random House, Inc., New York, and simultaneously in Canada by Random House of Canada Limited, Toronto.

Library of Congress Catalog Card Number: 94-94397

ISBN 0-449-14915-3

Printed in Canada

First Edition: December 1994

10 9 8 7 6 5 4 3 2 1

To Katherine and Gwendolyn,
who help me see the world anew.

"The only difference between the saint and the sinner is that every saint has a past, and every sinner has a future."

—OSCAR WILDE

Chapter 1

Gigi Lafferty startled awake, choking back the scream that rose automatically in her throat, and clutched the edge of her blanket. Then she forced herself not to move and to breathe steadily ten times. If she could get to ten, the panic of the dream would subside. And if, by the time she got to ten, Neil had not woken up, she knew he would remain asleep.

She got to ten. Her panic subsided. Neil stirred once, but did not awaken to ask her what was wrong—had she been dreaming again?—and suggest she should see someone about her dreams.

Already the substance of the dream had faded, leaving only a sense of something wrong, something or someone in pursuit. That explanation would not have satisfied Neil. And certainly she couldn't tell him that the dreams didn't matter, that she knew what troubled her sleep as well as her waking hours. The security of her marriage to Neil was based upon him believing certain things about her, and upon him not knowing certain other things.

Usually Gigi could drift back into a restless sleep, but this morning she was wide-awake. She had had a terrible time getting to sleep in the first place, because she couldn't stop thinking about her morning appointment with Patricia Delaney, an investigative consultant. Now the recollection of the appointment ensured she would stay awake. Gigi glanced at the illuminated digital clock on her nightstand: 5:09 A.M.

Slowly, carefully, Gigi moved back the covers and

1

inched to the edge of the bed. She moved quietly to the balcony; its porch door had been left partially open to allow fresh air to circulate at night, something Neil insisted was necessary for his health no matter what time of year. It was mid-September and, mercifully, unseasonably warm. Gigi dreaded winter.

Gigi stood out on the balcony, looking down at the pool. It reflected a partial moon and a few branches of the trees on the little hill just behind the pool. She considered an early-morning swim, the pool to herself, then rubbed her bare arms and decided against it. Neil would be upset if she were far away when he woke up. She opted for a soak in the Jacuzzi.

Gigi went into the master bathroom, being careful to shut the door quietly, and started the water running as hot as she could stand it in the pink Jacuzzi. Then she settled into the frothing hot water until her chin touched the surface, and closed her eyes.

Gigi's thoughts turned back to Patricia Delaney. It had been nearly fourteen years since she'd seen Patricia. She wondered what Patricia was like now. Confident, assertive, a little bullheaded, probably—she'd been like that at Poppy's Parrot. Patricia had been a bouncer at the club, where Gigi had been an exotic dancer. She remembered Patricia as an unlikely candidate for a bouncer, even unlikelier as the dancer she'd been before that. Although Patricia was nearly six feet tall and statuesque, she had a look of heartland innocence: round face scrubbed shiny clean and free of makeup; short cap of dark brown, natural curls; youthful garb of an oversized white T-shirt, jeans, and sneakers; wide green eyes a little distant, a little amused, a little too sad for someone just barely over twenty-one and obviously from a solid middle-class, Midwestern background.

Whenever they saw each other, Gigi (who had gone by the name Loretta King) was in her feather boas, satin bodice, sheer skirt, heavy makeup, tiara of paste jewels, stiletto heels—ready to go onstage, a fantasy queen in the featured act. Somehow, it always made her feel at a disadvantage to

Patricia. But Patricia always greeted her with a direct, honest smile. They became more than acquaintances, but not close enough to be considered friends. And Gigi had helped Patricia once back then; the memory of it was part of the reason she was choosing to trust her now.

Gigi wondered if Patricia would remember her. She hoped not. Only one person in her life now knew she had once been Loretta King, and Gigi needed to know if that person could really prove it, as claimed. So much, thought Gigi, so much hinged on that. She needed to know how successfully she had changed, how well she had put distance between the person she had been and the person she was now. And if Patricia did recognize her, she believed she could still trust Patricia to help her. Patricia was the only person she knew who owed her a favor.

Finding Patricia again had been an unintentional, simple act: Gigi searched the phone directory for private investigators, not knowing that Patricia had become one. She had not, in fact, even thought about Patricia in years. But when she saw Patricia Delaney's name, her heart clenched like a fist as she wondered if this could possibly be the same Patricia she had known so long ago. It was possible, she had told herself, for someone else with the same name to be in the Cincinnati area now.

But when she called Patricia's office, she knew this was the same Patricia. Even after all the time passed, even over a phone line, she recognized the voice: smooth; confident; low, slightly husky register, but well modulated with full tones; relaxed but professional. This was the same Patricia Delaney.

Gigi had called feeling confident and in control, but the sudden shock of really talking to someone from her past had made her own voice quaver, her speech falter. In response, Patricia became careful and gentle without being condescending—qualities that the Patricia of fourteen years before had not possessed.

Gigi answered a few questions, without giving details about what she wanted, and set the appointment with

Patricia. She was afraid that Patricia—or any other investigator—would refuse to meet with her if she explained exactly what she wanted over the telephone.

But Patricia would take the case. Gigi felt confident of that, just as she now felt certain that reconnecting with Patricia after all these years was somehow fated. She smiled at that thought, remembering Patricia once saying she did not believe in fate.

Gigi swished her hands through the water in the Jacuzzi, returned to the question of whether Patricia would recognize her. Gigi's hair was back to its natural deep brunette color, cut in a short, simple, but sophisticated style. She wore her makeup artfully, making her nose seem longer, her eyes deeper. And she dressed and acted the part of an upper-middle-class, somewhat pampered woman, who had been to the manor born. Which, in fact, she had been. As Loretta King, she had done everything—physically and emotionally—to distance herself from that birthright.

Now, as Gigi Lafferty, she had resumed that birthright, and her only physical reminder of her days as Loretta King was the parrot tattoo on her left shoulder. Neil found the tattoo erotic, as long as no one else saw it, and accepted Gigi's explanation that she'd gotten the tattoo on a college dare. So Gigi had never investigated the possibility of removing or permanantly covering it. She simply wore clothes that hid it from public view.

The bathroom door swung open. Gigi startled, her heart racing, her mind tense and alert. Then she saw it was just Neil. Of course. Neil. Who else did she think would come though their bathroom door?

Neil stood by the Jacuzzi, looking tired and irritated, like a little boy who has just been gotten out of bed early. Damn, she thought. She had crept out of bed quietly and carefully, but Neil, a light sleeper, could rarely stay asleep if she moved too much. Sometimes, when Gigi awoke and lay still and stiff next to him, unable to sleep, she imagined them someday buried side by side, their smooth, fleshless, bony fingers eternally reaching to each other but never touching.

"You're up early," Neil said. His voice was carefully modulated, sounding as she imagined it did when he gave orders at his company, but his mouth was puffed in a little pout.

Still, Neil was a handsome man, an advertisement for the organic personal products his company sold: medium height and build; tan and trim; hair combed back from a slightly receded hairline; temples edged in gray as casually but effectively as if a stylist had added the graying for him; eyes a light clear blue like water; quick, easy smile. Now he wore his white terry-cloth robe, letting it hang open to reveal his stomach, kept flat and solid from an hour a day on a stationary bike, his hairless chest and nearly hairless legs, his slight erection. Even after eight years of marriage, the fact that Neil walked around with his robe undone embarrassed Gigi.

"Why are you up so early?" Neil said.

"I couldn't sleep. A bad dream," she said.

"Another of those?" Neil sounded irritated. "You really ought to talk to Gregory about them."

At Gregory's name, Gigi's heart clenched, then released with a panicked fluttering. Her throat tightened. The Jacuzzi, and Neil hovering over her, suddenly seemed too confining. Gigi wanted to jump up and run from the bathroom, but of course, such a sudden movement would alarm Neil. She held herself very still.

"Yes, perhaps I will," Gigi said carefully. "He—he might be able to help."

"I can arrange it for you," Neil said.

"No, no—I will. Or maybe I should talk to someone outside of the company—"

"Suit yourself," Neil said brusquely, turning abruptly, and Gigi felt a sudden need to pull him back, to smooth the ripple of discontent.

"In fact, I'm going to see someone today," Gigi said quickly, and immediately regretted the words.

Neil turned and looked at her again. "You are? A psychologist?"

"A—a dream therapist. She—works out of her home." Gigi forced herself to smile brightly at Neil as if she really were going to a dream therapist and was eagerly anticipating the appointment. She clenched her hands. How long had she been in the Jacuzzi? Twenty minutes, twenty-five? The longest she had ever stayed in before was about twenty, and when she got out, she had crumpled to the floor, nearly passing out.

Neil frowned. "Where did you hear of her?" Neil liked to know these things.

"From—Rita." Rita Ames, who lived in their former neighborhood and worked for Neil's company, was a friend of Gigi's.

Gigi's answer seemed to satisfy Neil. Gigi was relieved when he said, "You know I can't sleep when you move around."

"I know, dear, and I'm sorry. Listen, just give me a few minutes to finish up in here, and I'll come downstairs and make you and Allen blueberry pancakes."

For a long second Neil just looked at her and again panic clutched at her—had she said the wrong thing? Allen was Neil's son from his first marriage, a twenty-six-year-old who worked for his daddy these days and had set up camp in the walkout basement. For a second she felt confused— were Allen and Neil on the outs or close these days? It was important to keep track, to know what to say. Allen loved pancakes, and the offer would seem traitorous if Neil and Allen weren't speaking just now.

"That's nice, Gigi," Neil said. He knelt down beside the tub, put his hands around her neck so that his thumbs pressed in hard at the tender spot at the bottom of her throat. For a moment she wanted to fight, to claw his hands away, but she kept still, even though as he pressed gently with his thumbs—in, out; in, out—her instinctive reaction was to gag. But she kept her throat still, her eyes wide and blinking to hold back the tears that automatically sprang to them.

Neil leaned forward and kissed Gigi's throat, his kiss covering both her throat and his thumbs. Then suddenly he released her throat. Gigi gasped and coughed, inhaling sharply, saliva and air catching in her throat. She coughed again before regaining her breath and composure. Neil held his face close to hers, his eyes in line with hers, so that all she could see was their blue flatness.

"That's nice," he repeated. His breath was warm and stale. "I'll get Allen up. We'll be waiting for you."

Gigi watched Neil as he slowly stood and left the bathroom. His actions had been, if not uncharacteristic, then at least harsher than usual when he wanted her to sense his displeasure. What did he know? How much could he, or anyone else, find out if he wanted to? That's what she needed to learn from Patricia. And once she had that figured out, she could know what to do from there.

Gigi turned off the Jacuzzi and slowly got out. She leaned with her palms into the vanity, waiting for the dizziness to pass, fighting back the urge simply to give in to it and collapse on the floor. Then she rubbed her temples with her fingertips in a slow, circular massage. It was no good, though; overheating and tiredness and tension had given her a headache. The prescription painkillers wouldn't help her this morning; lately, she kept needing more and more to kill a headache, and the pills left her disoriented and tired. Maybe a little wine while she made the pancakes; it was early for that, but it was just for her headache, she told herself, and she needed to be as alert as possible for her meeting with Patricia.

Chapter 2

Patricia Delaney undid the last screw at the back of the little gray box and carefully lifted off the lid. She looked inside the box and saw a green circuit board, embedded with computer chips and various wires held in place with tiny silver dots of soldering iron.

"Don't look like much, once you're taken apart," Patricia muttered aloud, although she was alone in her office. Patricia Delaney, Investigative Consultant, worked by, and for, herself, and so she was usually alone in her office, unless she was meeting with a client.

Which was something she was supposed to be doing right now. Except her morning's first client, a Mrs. Gigi Lafferty scheduled for 8:30 A.M., had not shown up. By nine, Patricia knew she wouldn't. Clients who didn't show up within a half hour of their appointment had changed their minds about coming at all. Perhaps instinct warned them that the information Patricia would eventually provide would frighten them or disappoint them or challenge them to either change their lives or continue a current life made somehow less satisfying.

It was usually the private—rarely the business—clients who changed their minds. Gigi Lafferty had been the former, her tone and manner on the phone when she called to make the appointment suggesting that she suspected her husband of being unfaithful. Patricia didn't care for those kinds of cases, preferring to concentrate on business cases, so she wasn't entirely disappointed that Mrs. Lafferty failed to show up. Those things happened in her line of work, and she was used to it.

And it gave her the extra time in the morning to enjoy working on her computer, which she had scheduled for the evening, so now her evening would be free to spend however she wished—a rare luxury. She usually took work home or, if it was Tuesday night, played drums in a rock-and-roll band. This was Monday, second week of September. Maybe tonight she'd catch one of the last Reds' home games of the season. Maybe she'd do nothing but sit on her back porch with her beagle, Sammie, and stare off into the woods.

Now her brow furrowed in concentration at the task at hand; she was installing a faster-speed internal modem in her computer. As an investigator, Patricia specialized in gathering information for her clients, much of it from databases on other computers. The modem was a device that let her computer send and get data to and from other computers—a feat of modern technology that enabled Patricia to put bread on her table, beer in her refrigerator, and kibble in her beagle's food dish.

Patricia also did work the computer couldn't substitute for, such as interviews and the occasional tailing. She billed herself as an investigative consultant—the title did not altogether please her, but it was vague yet impressive enough to put her mostly suburban clientele at ease with hiring an investigator.

It was too cool in the office. She went over to the window-unit air conditioner and adjusted the knob; the air shut off completely. Patricia laughed. All summer, a particularly hot one in metro Cincinnati, she'd been after the landlord to fix the air conditioner, which had lamely wheezed out tepid air. She'd finally fixed it herself, more or less; now it either huffed out glacial air or did nothing.

Patricia looked out the window. It was unseasonably hot. Sunlight glinted off the cars parked below in the lot of her building; heat shimmered near the surface of the parking lot. It looked and felt more like July than September, but

across the street in the closed gas-station lot someone had
set up a vegetable stand and was trying to sell off the last
of the summer's harvest of tomatoes, corn, zucchini, green
beans, cucumbers, and so on. Patricia turned the air back on
as she watched a brunette woman in a fuchsia knit suit get
out of a BMW and hurry toward Patricia's building.

Patricia wondered idly where the woman was hurrying.
The doughnut shop on the first floor? The accountant
across the hall? Patricia had one of the four office suites on
the second floor of a two-story building that anchored the
west end of a strip mall called Prosperity Plaza, one of
those ever-hopeful, ever-cheery names that pop up in the
suburbs, the kind of name that amused her, since the white
building was in desperate need of another coat of paint.
Patricia's other neighbors on the second floor were a family
counselor and an independent insurance agent.

Despite the faulty air-conditioning, and the orange, yellow, and green shag carpet that brought to mind a spilled
taco, Patricia liked her office. She had redone the interior
inexpensively with fresh white paint, miniblinds, plants, a
vase of fresh flowers on her desk, comfortable chairs. She
was an amateur photographer, and one of her favorite photographs, of a waterfall, taken during a weekend back-
packing trip, hung on the wall opposite her desk. The office
was roomy, the rent was reasonable, and her clients preferred coming to a building that did not obviously house an
investigator. Her clients could park out front and go up to
the building casually, as if they just wanted a half dozen of
Alliston's best doughnuts.

The office door, already partially open, was pushed open
further. Patricia turned. The woman with the brunette puff
of hair and the fuchsia knit suit was standing in front of her
desk, eyeing the parts of Patricia's computer. Apparently,
she had not been in search of the area's best doughnuts after all.

"That looks complicated." The woman was amused. She
looked up, her mouth cocked to one side in a half smile.
Tiny beads of sweat were on her upper lip and forehead,

ruining her carefully applied makeup. "I'm Mrs. Lafferty. Gigi Lafferty."

Patricia, who was eager to get back to work on her computer, was tempted to tell the woman she'd have to reschedule. But she reminded herself that this was, after all, a client, a potential one at least. She moved back to her desk, reached across, and shook Gigi's hand. It was small, limp, and shaking slightly. The woman was nervous.

"Nice to meet you, Mrs. Lafferty. Would you like some coffee or tea while I clear my desk? As you can see, I'm in the middle of some work—"

Gigi Lafferty's highly arched eyebrows collapsed into a frown. Wrong thing to say, thought Patricia; the woman thinks I'm criticizing her for interrupting, but she hasn't even apologized for being late.

"I'll be with you in just a minute," Patricia said, more abruptly than she meant to, and moved the keyboard and monitor from her chair to the floor.

Patricia had, she realized as she settled in the chair and busied herself with getting notepad and pen out from under the clutter of cables and screwdrivers, taken an instant dislike to the woman. She rarely liked or disliked someone so quickly, and her emotional reaction now bothered her. She did not like to make judgments without gathering facts. She looked up at the woman and realized she was reacting partly to the woman's overly precise makeup and hair, and partly to her way of carrying herself. Gigi sat straight up, primly, her hands folded carefully over the top of the black patent-leather pocketbook in her lap. Her facial expression dared anyone to challenge her, her smile to the side, her eyes narrowed.

Usually, Patricia began with a little small talk to help her clients relax, but in this case it seemed best to go directly to the formalities.

"Mrs. Lafferty, I'd like to begin our meeting by going over a few general things. I need to find out what you need my services for, so I'll be asking you a few questions. Then I'll go over my fee schedule, my obligations to you, the procedures we'll follow for terminating our agreement. If we reach an agreement, then there is a bit of paperwork I'll ask you to fill out—"

"How thorough are you?" Gigi asked.

"As thorough as I can be, and as thorough as you want me to be. It depends on what you've come here for. I have several references, previous clients, you can feel free to call if you wish. . . ." Patricia opened a desk drawer and pulled out one of the cream-colored brochures that described Delaney Investigative Consulting and a list of recent references.

Gigi waved the brochure and list away. "No, no, I won't call anybody." Her voice took on a somewhat desperate edge. "I can't have anyone knowing that I've come to you—"

"I assure you, my services are strictly confidential," Patricia said.

"Good. I need that—confidential. I believed that would be the case with you—" Gigi paused, bit her lip, as if she wanted to bite back the words. Patricia wondered why she would necessarily think that of her. Most of the investigative services' ads emphasized confidentiality and, in fact, thoroughness. Maybe the facade of the doughnut shop in Prosperity Plaza provided more of a sense of security than Patricia had estimated.

"I need to know how thorough you can be," Gigi said.

"It depends, like I said, on what your case is, how much you need to know, what you want to know. I certainly give each case my best attention—"

"Give me an example."

Patricia leaned back in her chair. "All right. Let's say you think your husband is cheating on you—" Patricia paused, to see what kind of an effect that suggestion had on Gigi. Gigi remained still, unflinching, totally focused on Patricia as if she were almost fascinated by her. If Gigi's husband was fooling around with someone, the idea did not seem to unduly startle Gigi.

"In that case," Patricia continued, "I'd want to know why you thought that, what behavior changes made you

suspicious, what his regular routine was, what deviations
he'd been making from that routine, and then—"

"Give me another example," Gigi said.

"It would help, Mrs. Lafferty, if I had some idea of what
you are here for."

Gigi remained silent, waiting for Patricia to come up
with another example.

That was it. Patricia wasn't going to keep creating sce-
narios, as if she were required to pull rabbits out of a hat
until she came up with one that suited the woman.

Patricia looked at Gigi pointedly. "I'm not going to give
you another example, Mrs. Lafferty. You're going to have
to tell me why you need my services, or we aren't going to
be able to work together."

Gigi fidgeted, looked away, toyed with an earring, before
finally answering. "All right, then. I want you to find out
how much someone could find out about me."

Patricia stared at the woman, incredulous.

"You don't believe me."

Patricia took a deep breath, let it out slowly. "No, Mrs.
Lafferty, I don't. You came here over an hour late, immediately began questioning my competence, and now you're
asking me, essentially, to investigate you—a request I've
never had before. I'm not sure what you want, what you
came here expecting, but I don't believe you're really ready
for an investigator's services."

"I need your help, Patricia," Gigi said, her voice edged
with desperation. "I have honestly come here to hire you to
find out what you can about me, as if—as if someone else
had come to you with the same request."

Patricia deliberated. It was an odd request, to be sure, but
for the first time Gigi both looked and sounded serious
rather than amused or mocking, making Patricia think that
perhaps the woman was not just playing games with her.

"All right. I'm intrigued. But you've got to answer a few
questions for me."

"I'll try," Gigi said.

"Fine. For starters—who might this theoretical person be who would come to me?"

Gigi didn't say anything.

"Your husband?" Patricia asked, pushing a little.

"That's right. My husband."

"And why would he want me to investigate you?" Gigi did not reply. Patricia pushed again impatiently: "An affair?"

Gigi laughed suddenly, forcefully. "No. He would never suspect that, even if it were true. He'd want to check into my past. I think he—he thinks there is something odd about my past that he needs to know."

"Is there?"

Gigi smiled, this time without a sardonic, mocking edge. It was a sad smile that acknowledged some inner hurt. "Of course. I wouldn't be here otherwise, would I?"

"No, I suppose not. I would typically ask next what that something is, but I suppose you're not going to tell me."

"If my husband were here asking you to investigate me, he wouldn't be able to tell you."

"The point of this exercise is for me to investigate you, your past, as if your husband hired me, so you can see what he would find out."

Gigi nodded. "Yes."

Patricia paused, wondering what secrets this woman's past could hold that she so wanted to keep from her husband—or from whomever it was she actually thought might investigate her. From her appearance, the woman was a well-kept, upper-middle-class wife who had never known anything but privilege. She probably did little outside the home other than participate in socially-prominent charitable activities, maybe play tennis and golf. But appearances, of course, are just that, and often mask reality. That was partly what made investigative work intriguing to Patricia.

"I hope, Mrs. Lafferty, that you are not hiding something criminal in your past," Patricia said. She was being unusually blunt, but then Gigi Lafferty's approach, to say nothing of her request, was unusual. "If you are, and I discover it,

I will ask you to turn yourself over to whatever authorities are appropriate."

Gigi nodded, looking amused at the idea. "That's fair."

"All right, then, what might your husband tell me, if he came to me with this request."

Gigi looked vaguely, momentarily uncomfortable. "I—I'm afraid I'm not sure how to answer that."

"When people come to me with a request for information, they always give me something to start with. A landlord wanting a prospective tenant checked out, for example, will give me the information from that person's application sheet—usually name, Social Security number, former address. That's enough for me to start checking out the person's history—previous addresses and places of employment, that sort of thing. Same for a prospective employee, although in that case I would also interview people who have worked with the person in the past over the phone, and check into academics as well. Sometimes a company will want its competitor or a potential partner checked out. Usually I start by looking into various databases for—"

"Databases?"

"On my computer," Patricia said, gesturing to where her computer usually sat on her desk. Now there was just the little gray box, which held the central processing unit, and it was taken apart. "There are numerous databases of information, stored in computers elsewhere, that I can get into with my computer, most of them public domain, some of them reserved for someone with a private investigator's license or a right to know."

Gigi's smile cocked another few degrees wider. "Looks really high-tech."

Patricia glanced at the jumble of disassembled parts. Now the machine did resemble a heap of gadgetry, perhaps dug out of someone's basement or attic.

Patricia frowned. She didn't like Gigi's contempt for her little gray box, especially in its disassembled state. Ridiculous to feel so protective of it, since a computer was just a machine; but still. The machine represented Patricia's livelihood.

"It's high-tech enough, Mrs. Lafferty. For example, before we met, I did a little research with it on you and your husband, just to prepare for our interview. You've been married eight years; you're his second wife; he divorced his first wife, Belinda Sue Jamison Lafferty, just six months before marrying you. Your husband, Neil, owns and runs Lafferty Products, which sells organic household and personal products. It was started eleven years ago as a privately held corporation, grosses about six million a year, and is now considered highly secure, although five years ago it was on the brink of bankruptcy. And your husband recently purchased a new home in Montgomery, for nearly six hundred thousand dollars.

"Your maiden name was Regina Marie Neumann—I don't know when or how you started going by Gigi," Patricia continued. "You're the middle child of Eugene and Angela Neumann. Your parents, who are now both dead, were prominent, wealthy people in this area during the sixties, during which time your father served two terms as a state legislator."

Gigi's eyebrows arched, and she wiggled in her seat uncomfortably.

Patricia smiled. Sometimes, people were alarmed at how much she could find out, quickly and easily, with a few taps on her computer keyboard. "That's just a scratch on the surface of what I could find out, by looking in a few databases of newspaper articles, company data, and property assets," Patricia said. "So, Mrs. Lafferty, back to our original question. What would Mr. Lafferty give me on you?"

Gigi cleared her throat, glanced down at her black patent-leather purse as if she were studying her reflection in it. "Well, he'd tell you how long we've been married, but you already know that apparently."

"How about your Social Security number? He'd have that, right?"

Gigi nodded, and gave Patricia the number.

"How about how you met? What would he tell about that?"

Gigi looked away, in the direction of the hyperactive air conditioner, focusing on the view beyond the gas station, of the trees lining the outer edge of Alliston College. "I came to Lafferty Products after my family and I had . . . had a parting of ways. At the time—"

"When was this?"

"About ten years ago. Then Lafferty Products was a small company and I was hired on as a secretary in the marketing department. Then I became a promotions coordinator."

"What does that mean, specifically?"

"I organized the twice-yearly gathering of the people who sell the products. And I put together brochures and product lists for the salespeople to give out, and to recruit more salespeople. And I dealt with the media sometimes, when there were questions."

"Like about the company nearly going belly-up?

"Yes. Like that."

"All right, go on."

Gigi shrugged. "There's nothing much more to say, really. Neil noticed me, asked me out to lunch, made it clear that he wanted to sleep with me, and I let him. Oh, he'd put it differently, I believe. He'd say that we fell in love and had an affair, but the truth is, he just wanted to sleep with me, at first, and I didn't mind. I didn't have anyone else in my life at that point. Eventually his wife found out, and did something Neil never thought she'd do, although of course I wasn't Neil's first infidelity. She left him. Neil needed a wife by his side for his professional functions, and I was looking for security at the time, so we got married."

Patricia rubbed a finger briefly over the diagonal white scar on her chin and tried not to let her distaste show. Nothing like romantic impulse as a motivation for marriage for this pair, she thought. Yet their pragmatic reasons had kept them together, and Gigi still wanted them to stay together. Patricia cleared her throat and spoke flatly.

"How did the first Mrs. Lafferty find out about your affair?"

"Neil's son, Allen, who now works for his father doing something with computers—inventory, that sort of thing— was a high-school senior at the time. He decided to surprise his dad one day, and instead got the surprise of his life when he found out what Daddy was up to in his office on his lunch hour." She gave a short, abrupt laugh. "He ran off and told Mommy, first thing. Needless to say, I'm not going to win any stepmother-of-the-year awards."

"Mmm. I guess not. Where is Neil's former wife now?"

"New Mexico, last I heard." Gigi shrugged. "Allen, who lives with us, gets an occasional postcard."

"Do you still work for Lafferty Products?" Patricia asked.

Gigi smiled. "No. Neil's very—old-fashioned that way. Likes people to know he more or less rescued me from the need to work."

Chauvinistic, thought Patricia, not old-fashioned. Old-fashioned would be opening the door for her as she went out into the world to do whatever she wished to pursue. Patricia sensed that Neil kept Gigi under his thumb, in a claustrophobic, suffocating way.

"So, what else would Neil tell me about you?"

"There's not much else to tell."

"What about before Lafferty Products?"

"Neil doesn't know much about my life before that. My parents died before I met Neil and I'm not close to my brother or sister. He doesn't care about my life outside of when I've known him. What matters is that I support him, and I don't question him."

Gigi made the statement, baldly and flatly, with no bitterness or resentment that most people might reasonably feel upon realizing that they're accepted only for what they're perceived to be, not for who they really are. It was a realization that usually led to divorce, or estrangement, or per-

haps an investigation into the spouse's life for ammunition
to take to divorce court. But here Gigi was, asking Patricia
to dig into her background, as if her husband had asked,
when apparently her husband didn't even care about his
wife's life outside of the time during which they had been
together. Patricia wondered what was really going on in
Gigi's life that had brought her here.

"He knows basically nothing of your past, your life before you were married?"

Gigi looked away. "I started to tell him once how much
I liked my grandmother, how when I'd visit she'd always
make me blueberry pancakes no matter what the time of
day. When I had those, I always knew that it would be a
special day." Gigi looked back at Patricia pointedly, and
Patricia understood that Neil had shown no interest in this
bit of childhood memory, given no encouragement for further reminiscing.

"And just what do you get out of this arrangement?"
Patricia hesitated to call it a marriage. When Patricia
thought of marriage, she thought of her parents, who knew
each other so well after forty-plus years together that in
some ways they'd started to blend.

"Security."

"And it's this security that may be threatened by your
husband's sudden interest in your past, something he
wouldn't just ask you about, but would hire someone to investigate."

"Yes. And it is my intention to safeguard my security.
But first I need to know if it can be threatened."

"And what if I come back to you and say your husband
could find out something that would jeopardize your marriage?"

Gigi shrugged. "Then at least I'd know what I'm dealing
with. I could make plans."

"Very well. I will investigate your past as thoroughly as
if your husband had made the request."

Gigi looked relieved. "Good. When will I get the results?"

"In about a week. How should I get in touch with you?"

"I'll call you."

Patricia frowned. "You don't want to set up a time now?"

"No. It's—my schedule is hard to predict. I'll call you."

"Very well. I'll ask you to fill out a form in a minute; you can give me your address and phone number then," Patricia said. "Now, I need to go over my fee structure with you. . . ."

For the next few minutes Patricia went over this information with Gigi, but she got the impression that money was of little interest to her at the moment, that she was anxious to be done with the meeting and go.

They finished, and Patricia said, "All right then, Mrs. Lafferty. Do you have any final questions?"

"No. I think we've covered everything I need to know."

Gig started to get up from her chair, but she paused and did something that took away Patricia's dislike for the woman, something that would haunt her as she recalled the moment throughout the case. It was how she would always remember Gigi, and for all that would happen, she would be grateful for the memory of at least one simple moment free of fear, terror, and doubt.

Gigi noticed for the first time the bouquet of purple and yellow mums on Patricia's desk. She touched the tips of the petals of a flower, looking as if she were a child seeing a flower for the first time. The initial gesture spoke of her vulnerability, her lingering touch spoke of gentleness. It was as if she saw something fragile and vulnerable and in it recognized a part of herself long forgotten, a part that now she wished to protect and guard. And for a second, just a second, Patricia thought there was something vaguely familiar about Gigi's face, something about the curve of her cheek as she held her mouth slightly slack and her eyes wide.

"From a lover?" Gigi asked softly.

"No," Patricia said. "I grow them in a little garden by my porch."

Gigi nodded and looked up at Patricia. "That's nice, that's good, doing something like that for yourself. They're lovely."

Patricia wanted to say something, to connect to this woman who suddenly seemed genuine for the first time, who had for a moment dropped her pretenses and enjoyed the simple loveliness of a bouquet that Patricia had thrown together and taken for granted.

But then Gigi looked away suddenly, clearing her throat, breaking the illusions of vulnerability and of familiarity.

Gigi's eyes were again carefully guarded, her mouth again cocked sideways in a defensive half smile.

"Thank you for your time. I'll look forward to seeing you next week, then."

"Yes," Patricia said, standing. "Thank you, Mrs. Lafferty." She started to come around from behind her desk.

"No need to show me the door," Gigi said. She walked to the door herself, then looked back as if she were going to say something, then paused, changing her mind, and walked out, shutting the door behind her.

Patricia sat for a moment, regarding the closed door, then the heap of computer parts on her desk. She went back to work, putting the faster modem in her computer, but now the work was just a task, and her heart and mind were no longer in it.

Chapter 3

Something—a boom, someone calling her name, a door slamming—jolted Gigi Lafferty from sleep. She opened her eyes and was immediately blinded by the midafternoon brightness.

She had fallen asleep by the pool behind the house. The morning tension at breakfast with Neil and Allen, followed by the meeting with Patricia, had upset her. She desperately needed to rest and relax, and she believed she couldn't do so on her own. Before coming out to sun by the pool, she rinsed a few sleeping pills down with a drink. The combination had worked to release her from consciousness, but that release had not given her rest.

Gigi blinked, focusing, finally able to look around. Nothing, no one. Maybe the noise had been in her dream—a merciful trick of the subconscious to deliver her from the disturbing jumble of dream images: her parents, alive, but living in this house; begging her again to reconsider the proposal of that nice, that so *very* nice boy, but this time the boy was Neil; Gregory, outside the scenario, watching her discomfort and confusion with an odd mixture of sadness and amusement, urging her instead to come with him.

Gigi shook her head. She had to stay focused. She sat up straight, struggling a bit in the process, and reached for her glass. Nothing but the melted remains of an ice cube tinged with the taste of scotch.

She lay back down on the chaise longue. She was in *her* neighborhood, not her parents', and it was one of which her parents would never have approved, built as it was with so much new money. Yet, up until recently, Gigi had never felt more secure in her adult life than since she and Neil had moved into Maplewood Estates. It was a new upper-middle-class neighborhood of half-million-dollar houses, all different, yet all blending soothingly together, fronted by lawns kept as perfectly as the nearby country club's putting greens.

Gigi dutifully attended the neighborhood watch programs with Neil, suppressing her amusement, nodding seriously along with the others as police officers talked to them about protecting their jewels and art and assets, thinking that none of them, not one of them, not even the police officers who walked and lived and worked the frightening, unprivileged streets outside Maplewood Estates, would ever understand the meaning of terror as she did.

She should feel perfectly safe here, but the dream was a gentle warning, Gigi thought, that she had to be careful, even here, lest her past come crashing into her present, doing God only knew what damage. She shouldn't trust anyone, not even Gregory, until she was sure again that she was secure from that past. And Patricia was her key to finding out just how successfully she had sealed off her past.

Patricia. Gigi did not think that Patricia had recognized her, or in any way suspected she had known her before as Loretta King, exotic dancer at Poppy's Parrot. There had been a few tense moments: when she had foolishly let slip that she knew she could trust Patricia, Patricia had looked at her curiously.

And then there had been the seconds when their eyes met after Gigi looked up from the bouquet of flowers. She feared that her eyes might have shown then that she knew Patricia; it had been foolish to relax like that in front of Patricia, to let her mind turn to the past, but the bouquet had reminded her of the flowers her aunt by marriage had grown by the lake house. Sometimes it seemed that the days she had spent at the lake house had been the only peaceful, calm times in her life.

But Patricia had not recognized her, and one thing about people that did not change over time was their ability, or lack thereof, to hide their reactions. Patricia had always been almost painfully honest.

And what if Patricia had recognized her? How would she have reacted to learning that Loretta King had become Gigi Lafferty, pampered wife of a well-off Cincinnati businessman? Shocked, surprised? Perhaps Patricia never thought of Loretta King now, never wondered what had become of her. Or perhaps, since Patricia owed her a debt of life, she lit candles for her whenever she went to mass.

Suddenly Gigi was jolted from her thoughts by a splash of cool water. She sat up, looked around, and saw a tall, lanky male figure in a too tight, too skimpy red bikini swimsuit swimming the length of the pool. It was Allen.

Gigi instinctively reached for her terry-cloth wrap, pulled it on over her swimsuit, and zipped it up, realizing that she probably had been awoken earlier by the sound of Allen coming into the house, calling her name.

Now she watched Allen swim back and forth, back and forth, under the water, hands out front, feet doing a flutter kick, only occasionally pushing himself up for air. He could hold his breath for a very long time.

Neil and Allen were built much alike, yet were so different from one another both in and out of the water. Neil had an intensely commanding presence, moved across a room with absolute confidence. Allen, on the other hand, moved with strength, but little grace.

But in the water, Allen was graceful, beautiful even, as he swam, moving with an easy, relaxed power. He seemed to have a perfect affinity for water, as if at last he were one with an element he could understand. The water gave him an eloquence and joy of movement that was missing when he was out of water, as if the water washed away his perpetual anger.

Neil, on the other hand, was clumsy in the water. He could swim, but he broke the surface of the water furiously rather than gliding through it, gasping and gulping for air desperately.

Finally Allen came to the edge of the pool, hopped out, and walked over to the lawn chair opposite Gigi. He looked at her, blinking water from his eyes, and smiled slowly, while he toweled his mat of short blond hair. Allen had his father's blue eyes and angular face. On Neil, the features were attractive and suggested confidence and power. On Allen, the effect was nullified by his lumpy half smile, which made him look like a mischievous boy waiting to be scolded.

"You're home early," Gigi said, trying to sound as if she were making a pleasant comment rather than passing judgment.

"It's too nice a day to waste inside. It'll be cold soon. Haven't you heard a bitter winter is predicted? I think I'll move to Alabama in a month."

And he was off, rambling in all sorts of directions. Gigi only half listened. Allen could never stick to one subject, a trait that exasperated Neil. Gigi suspected it was a technique Allen had developed to defend his personal space, keeping his father just a little off balance so that he couldn't thoroughly invade Allen's world.

Gigi waited until Allen paused, then said, "Does your father know you took off the afternoon?"

Allen frowned. "Yes. No. I mean, who cares? Maybe he'll notice. Maybe not. He wants me to stay in a dark little office, keep track of this, keep track of that, schedule this and that."

"I thought you liked working on the computer."

Allen gave Gigi a long, patronizing look. "Working on the computer," he mimicked. "You make it sound like a toy." He stood up suddenly, splattering her with water. He smiled down at her, his smile taunting. Then he leaned down next to her. "Do you know, I've read you can find out all kinds of things about people with a computer. Personal stuff. Maybe stuff they would rather you didn't know about them. Better than looking through their trash. Supposedly you can find out all kinds of stuff about a person by looking through their trash, too, like stuff about their sex life, what they do, but I don't like getting my hands dirty. Did you know that, Gigi?"

He drew out the syllables of her name, making it sound like the caw of a large bird. She hated the way he said her name, and she hated having him so close to her, his face near hers, his breath on her lips. She pushed on his chest.

He stumbled back, suddenly looking upset, like a little boy.

"Sorry. You were blocking my sun," Gigi said. She smiled, trying to look as if she had meant no harm.

"Right," Allen said. He walked over to the diving board. He climbed onto it, then dove into the water with a perfectly executed arc. Gigi watched him swimming back and forth and thought about what he had said about computers.

Patricia had indicated she used her computer extensively to do her investigations for people, and at the time it seemed amusing, a little pretentious even, with the computer in pieces on her desk and floor. People were always talking about modern technology and what it could do, but Gigi had always held that notion in contempt. Still, she didn't think Patricia would have any patience for anything useless in her life. What could Allen, with his computer, have already found out about her? Was he just saying that to upset her, or did he really know something?

Gigi shivered despite the heat. She hadn't really considered Allen a threat before; he had seemed so ineffectual in most things. Now she watched him doing the backstroke, one of the hardest strokes, with easy elegance, making it look so simple, so natural. Then he began swimming underwater, holding his breath for an impossibly long time.

Hadn't Neil said something once about Allen being an outstanding swimmer, winning medals, possibly going on to the Olympic swim team, being rated the best in the area, in the top ten for his age group? But Allen hadn't pursued a swimming career. For the first time Gigi wondered why. He was so perfectly good at it.

Gigi had thought she would take a swim herself before she went inside, but now she thought better of it. She suddenly felt uncomfortable at the idea of being in the water with Allen. Gigi stood up, walked around the pool, giving it wide berth, and went inside the house.

Chapter 4

For the third time that night Patricia heard the penetrating ring of a cellular telephone. Jay Bell and the Queen River Band, whom she played drums with at Dean's Tavern, had just finished the second set of the night. Although Patricia usually focused intensely on her music, twice the shrill ringing of the telephone had broken her concentration. She had not, of course, lost a beat because of it—she was too expert a musician for that—but still it bothered her.

She looked over at the table, shared by two young men, where the ringing had come from. The young men were dressed neatly in tweed jackets over turtlenecks, pressed jeans, and polished cowboy boots, appropriate for the season, if not for the season's sudden surge of hot weather. One, a redhead, was talking animatedly. From his gestures, his hands held wide apart, he could be telling the other young man a fish story. It would be a fish story of the corporate kind; the deal that almost got away, or the deal that grew in importance and significance each time its story was told.

Dean's place attracted eager young corporate types, who came there looking to get out of the city, but not wanting to go too far; a bar in Alliston, a southeastern suburb on the edge of the Cincinnati metropolis, was an ideal location, since tomorrow morning and bigger fish to catch were never far away.

Besides, Dean's Tavern was a cozy sanctuary from the daily grind. It was a refurbished train depot, circa 1880, redone with a polished wood bar and booths, dim lights

shaded by faux Tiffany stained-glass shades, and framed
turn-of-the-century ads for soaps and tonics and medicinals,
giving the impression of a supposedly gentler era. Never
mind the fact that the train tracks had long been paved over
to make way for progress.

Patricia took a long drink of her iced coffee, enhanced
with a shot of bourbon. She had to admit that it wasn't just
the young men's telephone ringing that distracted her. Gigi
was coming here, tonight, to meet her. She wasn't sure
when; Gigi wouldn't set a specific time. But Gigi had
called her office that morning, insisting that they meet that
night. During the day wouldn't do; the next morning or afternoon wouldn't do. It had to be that night. And so
Patricia, feeling she had little choice since she didn't want
to give up her night with the band, had instructed her to
come by Dean's, hoping it would be sooner rather than
later.

Now she doubted Gigi would come at all. If she did, she
would be happy with what Patricia had found. Gigi
Lafferty, based on an initial investigation, was clean. No in-
dications, on the surface at least, of financial problems.
Since the near miss of bankruptcy several years before,
Lafferty Products, according to the reports Patricia had
found in several databases of private-company profiles, had
done well. The Laffertys' property assets were considerable
and all in Neil's name. Gigi held one piece of property—a
cabin in Pikeville on Lake George in southwestern Ohio—
and the only interesting information about it was that the
deed had been transferred from an uncle and aunt, after
their deaths, to Gigi before she married Neil. Gigi held the
deed in her maiden name. Possibly Neil did not know about
the property, but that hardly seemed to warrant Gigi's request of Patricia, certainly not after all these years.

Gigi Lafferty did not have a criminal record. No involvement in dubious organizations—just low-profile activity in
a few perfectly acceptable charitable organizations, occasionally mentioned in local newspaper articles Patricia
found in newspaper databases. No publicized family scan-

dals in Gigi's present or past. No unusual activities or behavior; Patricia had followed Gigi for two days, and concluded that the woman led a routine life.

Gigi had spent most of her time in her house. She'd gone shopping one morning, then had lunch with her husband, and spent part of the other afternoon playing tennis at the Maplewood Country Club. She had not gone out at all in the evening. If she were having an affair with, say, the tennis instructor, it was in broad daylight, in full view of plenty of witnesses, in which case she wouldn't need Patricia to tell her that yes, someone could find out something naughty about her.

But there was nothing naughty about Gigi Lafferty's life, nothing corrupt, malevolent, sullied, or evil. Not even the faintest whiff of sin. Gigi Lafferty was clean. Too clean, Patricia thought.

Patricia did not assume that everyone had something in their past or present to hide; most people, she believed, probably did not. Most people led lives that were circumspectly clean and quiet.

But Gigi Lafferty had come to her with the unusual request, made adamantly yet nervously, that Patricia investigate her as if her husband, Neil, had hired her to do so. That could only mean that there was indeed something she wanted to hide, to see how easily it could be found out, perhaps in order to cover her tracks in some way or at least be prepared to deal with the ramifications. Which meant, thought Patricia, that she had missed something.

Patricia had had a few clients suddenly break down into a tearful confession of their problems, but she doubted that Gigi was that sort. Gigi would stay perpetually behind her smile, her carefully applied makeup, simply refusing to tell Patricia why this investigation was necessary. Maybe, Patricia thought, the woman was simply mildly insane, bored by her upper-middle-class suburban lifestyle, fantasizing that she had done something wrong, that she led a double life. No, there was something more than that; Patricia just couldn't identify it. Yet.

Patricia glanced down the bar at Dean, who was serving beers to a young couple, still in their office attire. Dean smiled and winked at Patricia, and Patricia smiled back. In the ten months she had been playing with the band, she and Dean had become very good friends. Patricia looked forward to Tuesday nights now not just because of the chance to play the music of her youth—now called "classic rock," a label she didn't feel did the music, or her age, any favors—but also because of the chance to see Dean. Recently, she'd been seeing him at least once a week other than Tuesday nights.

Patricia looked away from Dean before her smile became too flirtatious. She liked where their friendship was—fun times, laughs, nice talks, brief touches, friendly flirtations— but lately the flirtations had gotten a bit too intimate, the laughter and chatter a bit too comfortable.

"Nice set."

Patricia looked up at Dean. "Thanks. You didn't think the drums sounded sort of—out of it?"

"No. Why? Is the drummer sort of out of it?"

Patricia smiled thinly. "Mmm, yeah, kinda." She took another sip of the iced coffee and bourbon. She held the glass up to Dean in a half gesture of toasting him. "This helps."

"Uh-oh, the lady's turned to the juice with her troubles. . . ."

Patricia's grin grew a little. "No, I mean the fact it's cold."

"Okay, you can tell your bartender. What's bothering you?"

"Client's supposed to meet me here tonight."

Dean looked surprised. "That's unusual for you."

"Unusual client."

"So are you bothered by that, or because the client hasn't showed yet, or because of what you have to tell him? Or her?"

Patricia considered. "Her. And I'm bothered by all three." She finished off her drink.

"Another one of those?"

Patricia shook her head. "Maybe later tonight."

"After your client gets here?"

Patricia smiled. "After she's come and gone, and so has everyone else but you and me." Patricia had a habit of staying to help Dean close up on Tuesday nights.

Instant pleasure at the comment filled Dean's eyes. Patricia broke eye contact, stared into her empty glass, suddenly uncomfortable. "Anyway, forget about me. What about your day?"

"Boring, and that's with all caps, ma'am. Reviewing the books—income, expenses—trying to get ready for my big semiyearly meeting with my accountant."

"It would help if you put all that on a computer," Patricia said.

"So you've told me. And when am I supposed to find time for it?" Dean asked.

"I'll help," Patricia said. The conversation was one they'd had before, several times. Patricia was glad for the familiar, safer turf.

"When are *you* going to find time for it? You're too busy staring into your own little gray box."

"Okay, fine, I'll call your bluff. Friday."

Dean looked momentarily confused. "Friday?"

"Yeah. This Friday morning, meet me at my office at nine—I'll have coffee and Alliston's best doughnuts waiting—and we'll go over what you need for your business. We'll hit the stores at ten—"

"Forget it," Dean said quickly.

Patricia arched an eyebrow at him.

"Friday's not good," he said.

Her other eyebrow went up.

"Gotta organize the stockroom. You know, alphabetize the booze—"

Patricia laughed. "Dean, you're a hopeless technophobe. Look, do we have a date for Friday morning, or not?"

Dean's blue eyes twinkled. "Ooh, a date? I didn't know looking at little gray boxes—"

"Dean, computers. Just please, for once, say the word, com—pu—ters. Three little syllables—"

"Little gray boxes. Five syllables," Dean said, laughing.

Patricia laughed, too, rolling her eyes. "I should never have let you hear my pet phrase for the machine."

"If looking for my own box is a date, maybe I can distract you from looking at the damn things, and we can just hang around your office, and . . ."

Patricia looked at Dean wryly. "Watch it, big guy, you're about to salivate all over your counter."

"Only 'cause you're so damned beautiful, sweetheart," Dean said in his best Humphrey Bogart imitation.

Patricia ignored his flirtation. "My office, Friday, nine o'clock. I'll have the coffee on and doughnuts waiting. And we'll get down to work."

"You make it sound so businesslike," Dean said, suddenly very quiet. He was no longer smiling.

"It is," Patricia said. She looked away from the hurt in his eyes. "You've got some customers down there, ready to tear apart the counter if you don't get to them."

"Better take care of them, then," Dean said crisply.

Patricia glanced up, watching him move down the counter toward them. There was something a little jerky in his usually smooth, confident stride.

Patricia turned on her stool and got off before Dean could come back—assuming he would want to—and headed toward the table where the other members of the band were gathered, caught up, it appeared, in some animated conversation or another.

Damn, damn, damn, she thought. Why did she put the guy off like that? She liked him, found him attractive, and he obviously felt the same for her. What could be simpler than that? But it wasn't that simple. She knew the superficial reasons—the safe pat excuses of enjoying her independence, not wanting to complicate her life—but these weren't the real reasons. Those she managed to keep safely pushed down to the subconscious level, except on those nights when she couldn't sleep, when she woke up restless from the same old bad dreams, when all that she could do was go to her drums and play and play and play until the steady beats and rhythms drove the pain back down again.

And she had never been a flirt, or coy, or a person to toy with men's attraction to her; she had always despised that kind of behavior, but wasn't that just how she was acting? She wondered if Dean would come to her office on Friday after all. She half hoped he would, half hoped he would not. She couldn't blame him if he didn't.

"Hey, gang," Patricia said, pulling up a chair at the table where the other members of the band were gathered. She coughed to clear her throat. Her voice sounded rougher than she liked. "It's looking pretty animated over here. Another of Jay's high-speed boat-chase stories?"

The group laughed. Jay's boat, the *Queen of the River*—named after the fact that Cincinnati was called the Queen city and nestled the curving banks of the Ohio River—was in turn the inspiration for the band's name. It was a decent-sized house boat, big enough to sleep four people, provided they got along well.

"Gary and Jay probably don't want to hear it all again, but I was just sharing my latest tale of woe about the animal shelter," said Jasmine. She sighed and tucked a long strand of blond hair behind her ear. Jasmine was a veterinarian who spent more time than she could really afford away from her practice and family volunteering her services to the Alliston Animal Shelter. She played bass guitar in the band to relax, but right now she looked very tense.

"Seems this older lady in Newport died and left a houseful of cats and dogs," Jasmine started. "The shelter in Newport can't take them all, so we . . ."

The mention of Newport, Kentucky, which was just across the river from Cincinnati, abruptly shifted Patricia's focus from the present to the past. It had been years since she had been in Newport. Then, in college and in desperate need of money, she had danced in a place called Poppy's Parrot until she found out how much the bouncers made— twice as much as the dancers—and convinced the owner, a round, gnarly man who called himself Poppy Jones, to let her be a bouncer by flipping him, hard, to his back. Growing up with two older brothers who, through a love of roughhousing and teasing, had schooled her in the art of self-defense, had paid off. Being just an inch shy of six feet tall, and in great shape, hadn't hurt either.

It had been a difficult time in Patricia's life for reasons other than needing money, and so she usually pushed back the memories of that phase of her life as well as of Newport. Now the mention of Newport made her uneasy. She twisted in her chair, trying to get comfortable, and looked up at her friends.

Jay was grinning at her. "So glad you could rejoin us, Patricia."

"Oh, sorry, my mind was on a difficult case." Patricia stopped short, surprised at her words. She had not been thinking of Gigi Lafferty, at least not consciously. "I'm sure you'll work everything out, Jasmine," she added lamely.

"Hey, Patricia, do you know that lady?" Gary, the group's keyboardist, asked suddenly. "Just walked in, and she's staring over at you."

Patricia looked over at the door. Gigi Lafferty, in lavender dress and heels, looking like she'd just come from a semiformal banquet, stood in the doorway. She looked out of place, a woman destined for a country club, not a nightclub.

Patricia excused herself, made her way to Gigi, and led her to an empty booth. They studied each other silently for a moment. Patricia wondered what Gigi might be thinking. Fear about what Patricia might tell her? Hope? It was impossible to tell; Gigi wore her perpetual, careful smile.

Now that Gigi sat across from her, Patricia felt more irritation than relief that the woman had actually come to the bar. She wondered if her irritation showed, and then realized that she didn't care. Patricia felt that by her very presence, Gigi had somehow penetrated her personal turf, her private life, and now that loss of privacy was irredeemable. Nonsense, of course; Patricia would give her report, Gigi

would pay her for the effort, and that would be the end of
the case, Patricia reprimanded herself with a forcefulness
that belied her confidence in the thought.

"Do you want something to drink before we get started?"
Patricia asked.

"Order, and we'll get started. I don't have a lot of time."

Patricia arched an eyebrow. "Neither do I. I'm scheduled
back onstage in fifteen minutes." She gestured to Jeanne, a
college student/part-time waitress who was chatting with
the two young men with the cellular phone.

Jeanne reluctantly broke off her conversation and idled
over to the table.

"Chardonnay," Gigi said.

"Nothing for me, thanks."

"Nothing?" Gigi looked surprised.

"Nothing."

Patricia waited for Jeanne to take the order back to the
bar, then said, "I can tell you the results of what I found
before Jeanne gets back with your drink. I found nothing on
you. Nothing, at least, that would raise any eyebrows in
your circles, or get you tossed from the country club, or
give your husband an excuse to dump you for next to nothing."

Patricia waited for Gigi to make a whoop of joy, or smile
with a little more real enthusiasm, or pump her hand. But
Gigi sat stone still, her face, even under makeup and dim
lighting, going visibly pale.

"Are you—are you sure? You said you are thorough. Did
you check every possible aspect—"

"Every one that I could in a week's time."

"What I want to know, definitely know, is if my husband
had asked you to do this investigation, would your report
satisfy him that I had nothing to hide?"

"Everyone has something to hide, Mrs. Lafferty," Patricia
said. "I would be satisfied—based on the surface facts of
your life, without talking with your family members,
friends, or acquaintances, and assuming you have no

aliases—I would be satisfied that there is nothing in your life that would be upsetting to Neil."

"Or—justify blackmail?"

Patricia stared hard at the woman across from her. "I don't do investigations for people to give them ammunition for blackmail. Or to give them ammunition for getting out of blackmail. If that's what this is about . . ."

"One Chardonnay."

Patricia jumped, startled at Dean's voice. Dean smiled down at her. "Jeanne's on break. And one iced coffee with bourbon—light on the bourbon—just the way the lady likes it. On the house." Dean nodded at Gigi, then at Patricia with a quick wink. "Ladies, enjoy."

A peace offering, Patricia thought, watching him walk away. She took a sip of the coffee, trying to pull her thoughts together. She looked over at Gigi, who was staring after Dean.

"Mrs. Lafferty, if this is what this is about, if someone's trying to blackmail you, you need to go to your attorney. Surely you have an attorney who can—"

Gigi looked back at Patricia, smiling. This time her smile was genuinely pleased. "He likes you! Do you like him?"

Patricia stared at the woman, stunned at the question. What was this woman's game? "That has nothing to do with what I'm trying to tell you. Look, the bottom line is that no, I didn't find anything negative about you during a week of fairly surface-level investigation. And I emphasize that it was only a week, and only surface level. I also can't emphasize enough that if you hired me because someone is trying to blackmail you, you should see your attorney. Immediately. Now, I have the written report with me in my truck. . . ."

"That won't be necessary. You've satisfied my request."

"Fine. I suppose you're not going to tell me what this is really all about."

Gigi shook her head. "No."

The woman was in trouble, more than she could handle, Patricia thought. She sensed it. And there's nothing you can do about it, she told herself. She took a deep breath. "I consider this case closed, then. Except for my bill, which is also in my truck with the report. . . ."

Gigi sighed suddenly, loudly, and took a gulp of her wine. "Unfortunately, I do not have the means to pay you this evening. You'll have to come by my house, around three tomorrow."

"What? I thought you said you couldn't meet tomorrow."

Gigi shrugged. "That changed. And I needed the information tonight anyway. For a different appointment tomorrow."

"Mrs. Lafferty, I hope you've been listening when I've said I think you should—"

"I know, I know. I appreciate your concern. Three o'clock tomorrow, my house, then?"

"I'd rather you come to my office," Patricia said firmly.

Gigi shook her head. "I have another appointment at lunchtime that will keep me tied up at the house, and a busy afternoon."

Patricia sighed. "Mrs. Lafferty, I'm sure you can understand I prefer to conduct business at my office as much as possible."

Gigi looked at Patricia stonily. "Three o'clock. My house."

"Fine." Patricia pushed her drink aside, and started to stand up.

"Oh, and one more thing."

"Yes?"

"That young man. I hope you appreciate him. If you do, I bet you're pretty lucky." Gigi looked sad as she said it.

"Thanks for the tip."

Patricia stood up and started back to the stage, seething. Because she sensed Gigi Lafferty was in trouble, and she couldn't help her? Because she hadn't been paid, and given Gigi's attitude on the subject, she might not be? Because of Gigi's inappropriate interest in and advice on her personal life? All good reasons for anger, but none of them were quite it. . . .

An appreciative grunt came from the table of the two young men as Patricia passed. She stopped, still for a moment, then turned around slowly.

The redhead gave her a once-over before grinning wolfishly. The other one looked a little embarrassed and pushed his glasses back up on his nose.

The redhead, the one with the phone, said, "Hey, babe, I sure like how you do those drums. All that energy. Maybe after you're done—"

Patricia smiled. "Thanks. I need to make a call. Could I use your phone?"

All fumbling eagerness, the redhead offered it to her. Patricia took it. She started back toward the stage as the redhead called, "Hey—"

Patricia turned. "Oops, sorry. Where are my manners?" She dug in her pocket, got out a quarter, and flipped it at him. "Thanks for the call. I'll return your phone after the set. Babe." She glanced at the man in glasses, who was now grinning in amusement, and gave him a genuine smile.

Then she went back up to the stage. The little incident hadn't been as amusing to her as it might otherwise have been. She put the phone off to the side, settled down with her drums. The sticks felt good and solid in her hands, but while her playing was confident and competent, it didn't distract her from the real source of her anger: the nagging sense that there was something about Gigi Lafferty that she should have already figured out, but hadn't. It didn't help that seemingly unrelated thoughts of Dean and Newport kept cropping up as well.

Chapter 5

Patricia smiled as she pulled off the highway. She felt good. She had gotten up early, hiked in the woods behind her rented house with just her beagle, Sammie, for company, meditated after breakfast, then gone to the Alliston College gym for her workout, a half-mile swim in the pool and a session on the weight machines. Then she went to her office, enjoying the challenging demands and even the tedious routines of her work.

The night before, after the band had finished up its last set and she had returned the cellular phone to the young redhead, she had enjoyed a relaxed, friendly nightcap with Dean. The tension that had risen between them during the break had dissipated.

And now she was on her way to Gigi Lafferty's house to collect her pay and finally close the frustrating case. Patricia had considered not going. But she wanted, more than needed, the pay, because it was the proper closure to a completed business agreement. Besides, Gigi Lafferty was the sort who would come back to her later, with or without the pay, and make more requests for service. Patricia intended to make it clear to Gigi that she could no longer help her, except to reiterate that she should get a lawyer's advice or go to the police if, as she'd insinuated, she was being threatened with blackmail.

After her brief business call on Gigi Lafferty—and Patricia intended to keep it quite brief—she would go back to the office for a few more hours' work on more pleasurable assignments. She wasn't sure what she would do that night. Maybe do the Maine check-in, as she thought of her occasional phone calls to her parents. She had grown up in Cleveland, but her parents had retired to Maine. Rent one of the old *Thin Man* movies and pick up a LaRosa's pizza. Something relaxing and lazy, definitely.

Patricia had just driven through the small downtown area of Montgomery, replete with signs that announced the section as Olde Montgomery. The spelling of *olde*—as well as the faux gas street lamps, the signs on the curving wrought-iron stands in front of the old, renovated houses now made into antique shops and restaurants and curio shops—had her smiling in amusement, as if a misspelled adjective and a few symbols of the past were an accurate reflection of the town's history. Another day, the nostalgic effort at re-creating a past might have irritated her, especially since she had majored in history as well as English in college and knew better than to believe in a charming past that had never really existed, created solely from the imaginations of well-meaning citizens who liked to view the past as if it was a framed Currier and Ives. It was a sign of her good humor, her general sense of peace and well-being, that the "olde" section of town amused her.

She turned off onto Regency Lane into Maplewood Estates and was immediately reminded that people liked to cast a rosy glow on the future as well. A billboard-sized sign, hovering over a gray-stone entry, greeted visitors to Maplewood Estates. The sign featured a man in an impeccable suit, a woman in a flowing blouse, a small boy with freckles, and a smaller girl with pigtails, all smiling, poised before a shadowy rendition of a two-story house. Above them was the message LET YOUR DREAMS COME TRUE IN MAPLEWOOD ESTATES! LOTS STILL AVAILABLE!

Past or future, people could imagine them however they wished. Patricia supposed it was the present, the uncomfortable and sometimes uncanny convergence of the past and future, that gave the most trouble to people. But not, today, to her, she thought. A few more hours of work, and then the Maine check-in, *The Thin Man*, and LaRosa's pizza.

Near the front of the development were a few vacant
lots, as well as the wooden skeletons of houses being
fleshed out by workers. Construction debris—wooden plats,
roofing tiles, bricks, soft-drink cans—was strewn over the
dirt yards. Farther back into the development, though, the
houses were complete—mostly two stories, all brick, some
meant to be evocative of the past, some contemporary, with
roofs and walls turned at odd angles. None of the homes
were true to a particular architectural style; they drew from
a variety of styles, combining, for example, Corinthian
porch columns and Victorian gingerbread trim. They were
all meant to be different from one another, but there was
something about them that made them all seem similar.

Patricia turned left onto Crossings Boulevard and
stopped in front of number 8563. Patricia stopped her truck,
turned it off, took the keys from the ignition, got out, and
started to the house. She had studied it in detail during her
two days of trailing Gigi, and then, as now, found nothing
charming about its grandeur. The house was a mammoth,
pale brick two-story. There were two chimneys, one at the
side, one jutting out the top. The shutters on the windows
on the second story were dark blue; the windows on the
first story began at the ground level and curved at the top.
The yard was landscaped with shrubs trimmed into perfect
cones and rectangles and an island of birch trees surrounded by landscaping logs and cedar chips with clumps
of mums spaced evenly beneath the trees. A bricked entryway with a gold gate with scripted Ls in each half was apparently inspired by the entry to the development.

Neil Lafferty's taste, Patricia thought. A house meant to
impress. Patricia guessed from the little bit of research she
had done on Gigi's family origin that Gigi, if she followed
the tastes of her upbringing, would have picked something
more subdued, in an older, established neighborhood, where
the homes were just as expensive but more subtly displayed, set well back on large lawns and shadowed by
mature trees.

Patricia walked up the mosaic-patterned gray-stone driveway and walk, then swung open the gate to a small court-yard. A statuette of a woman, draped in cloth, exposing one breast, an imploring look on her face, her hand held out almost as if she were begging, stood in the middle of a small flower bed to the side.

Perhaps she should dig out the quarter the redhead had tossed back to her when she returned his phone the night before at Dean's and put it in the maiden's hand, Patricia thought flippantly.

Patricia looked around the large cherry-wood door for a doorbell. She finally settled on using the brass knocker and was surprised when she heard chimes going off inside.

A dog started barking. No one came to the door. She knocked again, and again heard the chimes. The barking grew louder, until it came from the other side of the door. She knocked once more, harder, as if the knocker worked like a regular knocker, and the door pushed open. A Shetland collie, with a red ribbon around its neck, came bounding out and began sniffing at her ankles.

"Hey boy." Patricia laughed and knelt down to scratch the dog behind his ears. He wagged his tail vigorously and gave her hand a lick.

And then Patricia forgot her natural fondness for dogs as she realized that the front door had been ajar all along.

"Mrs. Lafferty?" Patricia called. No answer. Maybe Gigi had been in a rush to go to a boutique. Or to a meeting of some sort. Or to get her nails done.

No. Something was wrong here. Maybe Gigi was passed out on a couch in one of the rooms in the mammoth house; Patricia remembered how she had gulped her wine the night before, and thought back to the alcoholic scent of her breath the morning she had come to her office.

"C'mon boy, let's get you inside before you run off," Patricia muttered to the dog.

Patricia opened the door slightly and gave the dog a gently encouraging push inside. He just whined, licked her hand, quivering and eager for more affection.

"Nothing doing, huh?" Patricia said. "All right. I'm getting your butt in, then my butt out of here."

She opened the door further, stepped in, shut the door behind her, intending to make sure the dog was safely inside, then leave quietly. But what she saw stunned and stopped her.

Something was more than just a little amiss. A picture was ripped off the wall, revealing an open safe, some of its contents spilled out onto the sofa below. An antique desk had its drawers all open and some of its contents spilled out. A small suitcase was open on the floor, a few clothes—a bra, jeans, a blouse—spilling out of it. And blood dotted the white carpet in even spaces, as if someone had had a minor wound and, in walking, dripped the blood.

Patricia's first thought was to get out, go to a neighbor's house, and call the police to report a burglary. But then the dog yelped merrily and bounced around her feet. That calmed her enough to look around a second time and reassess what she was seeing.

This was not the work of a burglar. The sculptures on either side of the two-way fireplace and the paintings were all intact. Jewelry, apparently from the safe, lay on the couch. Burglars would not have come in during the day, left behind the stuff they could sell, then, after carefully dismantling an alarm system, taken off through the front door. And the house was empty. The dog would not be so eager for Patricia's attention if anyone were here; surely the dog's yelps would have alarmed anyone who was in the house by now. It looked more like someone—a woman judging by the clothes on the floor—had wanted to leave in a hurry.

Patricia took a deep breath, slowly, in and out, to calm herself. She followed the drops of blood to a staircase, then up the staircase and into what appeared to be the master suite. Usually, it was probably a spotless room, but more women's clothes were strewn about the bed and floor.

Patricia went into the master bath. Cabinets and drawers were left open, their contents in disarray. A bottle of makeup had fallen into the Jacuzzi and broken, its creamy tan contents splattered in the Jacuzzi tub.

Patricia stepped out of the master bath back into the bedroom and noticed that the sliding-glass doors to a balcony were open. She stepped outside, wanting to get away from the mess and collect her thoughts, and decide what to do next. For a few minutes she stared at the trees on a small hill at the back of the Laffertys' property.

And then she looked down from the trees to the fenced-in pool and froze for a second at what she saw. A woman was floating facedown in the pool. Her dark hair floated out like the wispy tentacles of a strange sea creature. The water was tinged red around her head.

Patricia ran down the steps that led from the balcony to the pool area, not thinking but reacting. At the pool's edge, she dove into the water, swam to Gigi, hauled her out, and automatically began efforts to resuscitate her, ripping back her blouse to pump down on her chest, breathing into her mouth and nose. She kept on, and on, cursing between breaths until finally she accepted that she was too late. Gigi had been dead before Patricia ever found her.

Patricia moved back from the lifeless body and looked at it, intending to gather enough objective observations to make a sensible report to the police.

She stared for a long moment at the woman's face. This woman was not Gigi Lafferty. Seeing her floating facedown in the water, in the panic of the situation, she had assumed it was Gigi. But this woman was definitely not her client.

And then Patricia saw the tattoo of a multicolored parrot on the woman's left shoulder, revealed by her ripped blouse. Patricia's throat clenched, making it hard for her to breathe, as if she had been slammed very hard in the gut. She had seen such a tattoo once before—the same exact tattoo, in the same place, on a dancer named Loretta King, a dancer she had known long ago and briefly at Poppy's Parrot. In fact, Patricia had gotten a similar tattoo, at Loretta's encouragement, opting, however, for the more discreet location of her right buttock.

Patricia shut her eyes and clenched her fists to her face. A low moan escaped from her lips. Of course. Of course. The hair, the face, the clothes, the circumstances, had been different. But Gigi and Loretta were the same person. The memory of Loretta came back suddenly, slamming violently from old memory to her consciousness. The way Gigi carried herself, her voice, her manner of speaking—these things matched her memory of Loretta. These were the things that are difficult, if not impossible, for people to change. Patricia had no idea who this woman was, why she had the same tattoo that Loretta had, why Gigi had once posed as Loretta, why Gigi had come to Patricia without revealing how they had once known each other, but for the moment it didn't matter. The realization that Loretta and Gigi were the same person overwhelmed, for the moment, Patricia's ability to consider other questions.

The only thing she understood was why Gigi had come to her for help, trusting her just a little, though not enough to really tell her why and how she needed help. Gigi, as the dancer Loretta King, had saved Patricia from certain death.

Chapter 6

Detective Nancy Grey—slightly overweight, short brunette hair touched with silver—had the concerned look of a suburban mother herding her brood into the minivan in time to get to the scouts' den meeting. She was half-perched on the edge of the table in the Montgomery Police Department's interrogation room, leaning a little too closely for Patricia's comfort.

Detective Jack Rubrick—midwaist and midlife paunch stretching a light blue shirt over brown pants and belt, tie loosened, receding hairline giving ample exposure to a frown that gathered up his forehead—was slouched against the door, arms crossed, glaring at Patricia.

Good cop, bad cop—suburban style, thought Patricia, hiding a small smile by taking a sip of water from the paper cup.

Patricia ran her hand through her short crop of dark brown curls, still damp. During the rush of activity that commenced after the police arrived at the Laffertys', someone—she couldn't remember who—had been thoughtful enough to provide her a blanket in which she had wrapped herself. She had been grateful for the dryness and comfort that the blanket had provided. She briefly had chills, due to slight shock at the situation rather than actual coldness; the weather still had not caught up with the calendar.

Now, in the too warm, too small interrogation room, the blanket gave the effect of being in a sauna. What Patricia really wanted was to go home, take a hot shower, and then

47

get as thoroughly dry as all the fluffy towels in her linen closet would let her—but that wasn't going to happen until the detectives were satisfied with her story, or at least satisfied that they weren't going to get anything better out of her.

"Tell me—how long have you known Gigi Lafferty?"

Patricia sighed. She had already answered that question once for Detective Rubrick. "As I said before"—she glanced at Rubrick—"one week."

"But in the statement you gave to the officer at the Laffertys'—and I admit I've only had a chance to glance over it—you talked about knowing her before."

"As I tried to explain then—and I probably didn't do a very good job considering I was"—Patricia paused and cleared her throat—"a little shaken up, I've only known Gigi Lafferty for one week. But I believe that I knew her once before, a long time ago, when she went by the name Loretta King. I just didn't realize it until I saw the tattoo. . . ."

"And how long have you known Jessica Taylor?" Jack Rubrick growled.

Patricia flicked him a tired, irritated look. "Since I hauled her out of the pool. Which means not at all. I do not know the woman. I have never heard of the woman. I didn't know her name until you told me."

"So what's her connection with Mrs. Lafferty?"

"Well, now, Detective Rubrick, if I'd never heard of the poor thing until today, how would I know what her connection is with Mrs. Lafferty? The only thing I know that connects the two is the tattoo."

"Now, Jack, why don't we let Patricia tell us about these—tattoos," Nancy said. She said the word as if it were distasteful to her. Patricia imagined her later at the dinner table saying to her husband, "Women, sporting tattoos; really, how vulgar!" But all the while Nancy smiled at Patricia compassionately, her expression urging, Come on, you can talk to me, ignore the old grump at the door. Patricia glared at her, thinking, I hope you really do have to herd a bunch of screaming little scouts around in a minivan tonight. I hope one's a whiner, one's a biter, one gets carsick. . . .

"Patricia. You were telling us about the tattoos," Nancy urged.

"When I saw the tattoo on this Jessica's shoulder, after I tried to revive her, I knew I'd seen this tattoo before. In fact, I have a similar one. I got it years ago when I worked at a club, no longer in business, called Poppy's Parrot in Newport," Patricia said. "And then I remembered the woman who talked me into getting a tattoo one night."

Patricia shrugged. "I was in a wild, crazy stage in life, so I didn't need much convincing. I thought what the hell, I'll get one similar to that. A parrot. Sort of a memento of working at the club. The woman was named Loretta King, a dancer at the club. Anyway, seeing the tattoo on this Jessica reminded me of Loretta—"

"Because of the similar tattoo," said Nancy.

"Yes. The same tattoo, on the left shoulder. And remembering Loretta made me realize that she and Gigi were—are—the same person, that Gigi had, for whatever reason, taken on the identity of Loretta for a while."

"Okay, so you and Gigi—who then went as Loretta King—were dancers at this club—how many years ago?"

"Fourteen years ago. I was a dancer a little while, but not when I knew Loretta. By the time she came to the club, I was a bouncer."

Detective Nancy Grey's eyebrows shot up. Patricia smiled. Add the bouncer bit to the tattoos and the Greys would certainly have interesting dinner conversation tonight.

"Bouncing paid better than dancing," Patricia said.

Jack cleared his throat. "Right. Let me get what you're telling us straight."

What you're telling us, though Patricia. In other words, we know you could be making all this up. Great. Now they were going to think she was an accessory in this mess, somehow.

"You knew Mrs. Lafferty, as Gigi Lafferty, for just a week, during which time you were hired to investigate her background for anything suspicious," Jack said. "She didn't give you a reason for the request, and you didn't find anything." Jack paused and stared at Patricia.

"Right," Patricia said tiredly.

"Yet you also knew Mrs. Lafferty, as Loretta King, for, what—a year?"

"A few months."

"A few months, about fourteen years ago. And you didn't connect Loretta King to Gigi Lafferty until you hauled Jessica Taylor—whom you don't know—out of Mrs. Lafferty's pool. And the only thing that made you make the connection was a tattoo on Taylor's left shoulder, which was the same as one on Loretta King's shoulder, and similar to one you have." Another pause and glare. It was a facial dance Jack had down well. Pause, glare, two, three, four . . .

"Am I right, Ms. Delaney?"

"Yes, yes, you're right. Look, I know it's a bizarre scenario, but it's the truth. Bits of the truth. Like you, I'd love to fill in the gaps and get the whole truth."

"And nothing but. Right." Jack turned away in disgust.

Patricia looked at Nancy. Good cop's turn, she thought. As if on cue, Nancy smiled.

"I'm a little surprised you didn't recognize Gigi as Loretta when she came to your office."

"Why? Think you could recognize everyone you knew briefly—very briefly—but hadn't seen for fourteen years? People can change a lot in fourteen years, especially when those years take them from postadolescence to early midlife. Besides, the two contexts I knew Gigi in . . ." Patricia shook her head. "As Loretta, she was a tramp, or trying to act the role of one. It didn't come entirely naturally, but she had the outrageous makeup, the wildly done bleached-blond hair, the trashy clothes. She claimed to come from a poor background, but she spoke too precisely, carried herself too well to be from the poor side of town, so I figured her for a kid trying escape something—maybe a rotten home, maybe a stodgy one. Who knows?"

Patricia paused, pushed the blanket back from her shoulders.

"And as Gigi?"

"Gigi is the wife of a successful businessman, well taken care of, obviously from an affluent background. My research into her background bears that out—and she looks the role. Everything about her—hair, makeup, clothes, the way she carries herself, the way she talks—is subtle, refined. The kind of woman who would dismiss Loretta as trash."

"But you say she *was* this Loretta you're talking about!" Jack was doing his best to sound irritated, disbelieving. But Patricia could tell he was interested in what she was saying; he was forming a theory. Hope it's in my favor, she thought—without much actual hope. "How can you be sure? Did you see the tattoo on Gigi Lafferty? You yourself said that fourteen years—"

"I don't inspect my clients for tattoos or other bodily marks, detective," Patricia said. "But now I know Gigi and Loretta were the same person. Some things about a person don't change. Mannerisms. The way they carry themselves. The way they talk. The tattoo I saw on this Jessica triggered my memory of Loretta's tattoo, and the realization that Loretta and Gigi are the same person."

"But during the week you worked with her you never suspected . . ." Nancy Grey's voice trailed off, incredulous.

"Something about Gigi, and the case, bothered me. I wrote it off as being the fact that her request was so unusual." Patricia shrugged, further releasing her shoulders and upper body from the warmth of the blanket. "Maybe subconsciously I realized who Gigi was. Maybe I would have realized consciously in time. I don't know. I was planning, today, to get my pay and have nothing more to do with Gigi."

"Why?" Jack's question was simple, but he made it sound accusatory.

"She wouldn't tell me why she wanted this investigation of her background done."

"Any theories?"

"She was concerned her husband wants to leave her, and might try to use anything he could to get out of leaving her financially comfortable. Blackmail also comes to mind. She hinted at it, and obviously she had something to hide, or she wouldn't want to make sure nothing could be found out about her by your average detective." Patricia paused to venture a grin. "Or your above-average detective."

Jack sneered and snorted a derisive half laugh, making clear his opinion of Patricia's self-assessment, while Nancy didn't betray any reaction.

"Anyway," Patricia continued, deciding to let Jack's sneer slide, "I'd say now, knowing that apparently Gigi knew this Jessica back in our Poppy's Parrot days, and knowing that Gigi's husband is quite conventional, maybe Jessica showed up to turn up the heat on Gigi about her past, threaten her with exposure to a husband who would surely be displeased, and Gigi simply wanted to make sure that Jessica couldn't prove anything before paying her off. I got the impression that Gigi didn't have easy access to her husband's money, unless he wanted to lavish it on her."

Jack moved to the table, pulling up a chair and leaning close across the table to Patricia. Nancy stood up and moved to the door. Uh-oh, thought Patricia. Bad cop takes over. She sighed tiredly. All she wanted was a shower and some rest.

"So if she wanted to make sure her past as a temporary sleaze queen couldn't be discovered, why come to you, someone who could possibly remember her from those days?"

Patricia shrugged. "Ultimate test, I guess. If I didn't recognize her . . ." But that wasn't enough of a reason. There was more. And Patricia couldn't share it with these detectives. Doing so would provide them with a motive for her to work closely with Gigi, maybe nailing down a suspicion that she was working in league with Gigi, somehow involved in Jessica Taylor's death. The fact that "bad cop" had taken over was enough to make her guess that they must be thinking in that direction. They weren't buying her innocent-detective-takes-on-client-who-happens-to-be-from-her-past story, even though it was true.

"Now tell me why Gigi Lafferty came to you," Jack said.

Patricia frowned. "I just did."

"No, you gave me a story about her wanting her past investigated. But there's more, isn't there?"

Patricia stared at him, forcing her eyes and face to remain blank. Yes, she thought, but not something that I'm telling you. Not something that you'd understand.

"Look, we have a woman floating in the Laffertys' pool who you admit Gigi had reason to believe would blackmail her. . . ."

"I didn't admit that. I gave you a theory. A theory, detective, from a private citizen, remember? Just a theory. Not an admission, not a statement of truth."

"Okay, we have a dead woman who you *theorize* might be blackmailing Gigi, and you just happen to know Gigi from the time period where she was doing naughty things under an assumed name that she *theoretically* is being blackmailed over by said dead woman. That's the *theory*. The facts are that you found said dead woman, and Gigi's missing, and her house is torn up like she left in a damned hurry. So just where do you think this *theory* might lead now, Ms. Delaney?"

Patricia pressed her lips together for a moment, considering whether to answer or to call Jay Bell, leader of her rock-and-roll band by night, her attorney by day. "I don't spend much time on theories," she said.

"Okay, then, let's try for another fact. Who is one of the first suspects at the scene of the murder?"

Patricia stared at Jack, the implication registering. The answer, of course, is the person who finds the body, especially if the discoverer is alone. But surely they can't suspect . . . No, Patricia thought, they don't. They suspect

Gigi, maybe me as an accomplice. They were trying to scare her.

"Come on, Ms. Delaney, as an above-average private investigator, I'm sure you can answer that one."

Patricia relaxed her face. "If you want me to answer any more questions, I'll have to call my attorney."

Jack and Nancy exchanged a glance that Patricia interpreted as Uh-oh, we've pushed this one too far. But they couldn't change tactics now.

Nancy cleared her throat and approached the table. "You'll have to forgive my partner. Sometimes he can get a little—overenthusiastic. If you'd just tell us where you think Gigi might have gone?"

Patricia looked at Nancy, blinked once, then again. Nancy smiled encouragingly. Patricia smiled back. "If you want me to answer any more questions, I'll have to call my attorney."

Nancy reddened, glanced quickly at Jack, who said, "Tell us where you think Gigi's gone." Patricia did not answer; she kept looking at Nancy. Did she turn red like that if one of the little scouts told a nasty joke or made nasty imitation body sounds at the back of the minivan? Patricia wondered idly. Or was this a different red, reserved for recalcitrant witnesses? No, recalcitrant wasn't the right word, Patricia thought; she felt more indifferent now. She was tired, and she really was not going to answer any more questions until she called Jay. Knowing she wasn't going to say anything but one sentence over and over gave her a sense of relief.

"How much is Gigi paying you to cover for her?" barked Rubrick.

Patricia turned her weary gaze on him. "If you want me to answer any more questions, I'll have to call my attorney."

Nancy sighed. "Very well. You've given us enough for now." Then, suddenly, she leaned forward, hands on edge of table, and shoved her face close to Patricia's, so that their noses were nearly touching. The den mother finally loses her patience, thought Patricia.

"But I think you ought to keep in mind how this looks for you," Nancy said. "We'll be in touch again. And if Gigi contacts you, you'd better be in touch with us. If I were you, Ms. Delaney, and I really had gotten innocently involved with Gigi Lafferty, I wouldn't want to protect her. Because from my perspective, if you're not her accomplice, then you're sure being set up to look like you are."

Chapter 7

The view from Neil Lafferty's office window was of the warehouse, a low white frame structure, in which the organic shampoos, powders, deodorants, and soaps were packaged and labeled, then shipped out each day.

Neil rarely ventured through Lafferty Products' warehouse, but he had designed his office so his window framed a picturelike view of it. The security system had cameras on all the entrances to the warehouse, but he had adamantly wanted the window view as well.

Neil had fired the first builder for drawing up plans that did not incorporate the view he had requested, and had the second builder tear down and restart work on his office building because the view of the warehouse was not perfectly framed by his window. Neil had envisioned himself standing at his window at times of success, quietly contemplating the wealth he had created for himself and others through his own ingenuity.

Neil stood at his window now, but it was not a time of success. Two police detectives waited for his answer. His smile casual and ready, Neil turned to them.

"I have no idea why my wife would need a private investigator."

"The investigator told us she had been hired to check into your wife's past," Jack Rubrick said.

"By my wife?"

"Yes. Unusual, but it indicates that Mrs. Lafferty was concerned that something from her past, if discovered, might be used against her now. In fact, might be revealed to you if she didn't pay for silence."

Neil's smile settled into a politely pleasant, but somewhat impatient expression. It was an expression that would remain until the detectives left.

"I know of nothing—shall we say—unsavory in Mrs. Lafferty's past. If I had, I wouldn't have married her."

Nancy Grey cleared her throat. "Perhaps that is what concerned Mrs. Lafferty. This Jessica Taylor and your wife worked together in the past—as strippers in a joint in Newport. Were you aware of that?"

Neil grasped the back of his chair very hard. He intended to cast his bid for elected office next year and knew he couldn't afford any negative press.

"Mr. Lafferty, were you aware of that?"

"No."

"Mrs. Lafferty then went by the name of Loretta King. Did you know that?"

"No. How could I?"

"The investigator she hired worked in the same joint but as a bouncer, for the most part, although she claims she never knew Jessica."

"Fascinating."

"Hmm, yes. How did Mrs. Lafferty say she knew Jessica?"

"College acquaintance."

"And you never questioned that?"

"No reason to."

"You hired Ms. Taylor on the strength of Mrs. Lafferty saying they were college acquaintances," Nancy said.

"We needed someone to do data entry. Jessica seemed sharp enough, and Gigi was adamant about helping her."

"Do you have any idea why Jessica might have been at your house during her lunch hour?"

During other lunch hours, yes, Neil understood perfectly why. But the detectives were only interested in that day's particular lunch hour, the time frame during which Jessica was murdered. No reason to give them more than they asked for, and only that much in carefully couched terms.

"No, I don't."

"Would Jessica's going to lunch at your house with your wife have been a common occurrence, Mr. Lafferty?"

Neil's smile tensed ever so slightly. "I'm not in the habit of tracking what my employees do during their lunch hour."

Detective Grey smiled at that and, still smiling, asked, "And what were you doing during that time frame, Mr. Lafferty?"

"Working. At my desk. Which I ought to be doing now."

Detective Jack Rubrick stood suddenly. "Very well. Just one more question, though. Have you heard from your wife?"

"No. If I do, I will contact you immediately."

Jack's eyebrows arched slightly, and he exchanged glances with Nancy. Perhaps, thought Neil, they thought that he answered so quickly to hide a desire to protect his wife. Or perhaps they were just surprised at his willingness to give her up to them. He decided to reassure them.

"Believe me," he said, his hands relaxing just a bit on the back of his chair, "I want to know her whereabouts just as much as you do."

Nancy nodded abruptly. "We appreciate the cooperation." Neil glanced at her. Was there a sarcastic edge to her voice? "We'll be in touch." The detectives left, shutting his door behind them.

Neil let go of his chair, turned, and stared back out at the warehouse.

How long should he give them, he wondered, before he called Dee Anne, his secretary, and got a rundown on what they'd asked her? For surely they were questioning her now on his whereabouts around lunch hour.

And he knew she wouldn't be able to either confirm or deny that he had worked through lunch. He didn't have the computer knowledge his son did, but Allen had shown him how to use the electronic mail system, which included a calendar function that he could view, and he demanded that all of his direct reports keep their calendars up to date. Dee Anne was particularly scrupulous about it. He had checked her calendar just before he left, and saw that she had a dental appointment scheduled through the lunch hour.

Damn Jessica! Neil thought violently, suddenly. He had given her strict instructions not to go to his house unless he told her to. Why couldn't she have listened?

He turned suddenly from the window, crashing both fists down on his desk, one fist coming down on a glass globe paperweight, sending papers flying.

He had gathered up most of the papers before he realized his hand was stinging and bleeding from the broken glass of the paperweight. He muttered an oath, then cursed out loud when he saw the bright drops of blood on the floor. For the second time that day he got out a handkerchief, and tried to clean up blood from white carpet.

Chapter 8

Patricia opened the door a crack, and a dog started whining and pawing to get out. Inside the house, the phone was ringing. Patricia closed her eyes. This was how the nightmare had started this afternoon—an eternity ago. Patricia at a door, a dog eager for attention on the other side. Then she had crossed the threshold from just another day to a day made in hell.

But this is your door, your home, your dog, Patricia reminded herself. Inside, the phone stopped ringing. Patricia pushed the door open, and Sammie, her beagle, pawed for attention.

Patricia laughed. She was carrying a pizza box, on top of which was a video and the day's mail. "I told you I'd be right back. I got a Mama LaRosa's deluxe, with anchovies. So let me get settled in, and we'll eat."

After leaving the police station in Montgomery, Patricia had gone home for a long, hot shower and a change into dry clothes, then spent a few minutes trying to decide what to do next. Return to her office, reread every scrap in her file on Gigi, try to make sense of what had happened? Patricia rejected that option as too draining for the moment—and besides, this was police business. She was done with the case. Done, not involved, none of her business anymore, she told herself firmly with the overenthusiastic conviction of one who is trying to banish a nagging sense of doubt.

Then she had considered seeking comfort from Dean. But that struck her as too complex at the moment. She would have to reexplain everything, maybe even get into things from the past she wasn't comfortable facing by herself, let alone sharing with someone else. The same foreboding that made her doubt she could so easily wash her hands of Gigi told her that she'd have to face those sticky things from the past sooner or later.

But it could be later. Tonight, she finally had decided, she was opting to carry through on her original plans. A quiet evening at home, alone with Sammie, a pizza loaded with all the goodies, and the soothing patter of the Nick and Nora Charles characters in *The Thin Man*. Simple, as normal as pumpkin pie on Thanksgiving. Virtuous, even.

Patricia dumped the mail by the answering machine on the desk in the living room, ignoring the machine's blinking red light. She had ignored the mail and messages on her first stop home; they could wait a little longer. She took the pizza into the kitchen and deposited it on the kitchen counter. Sammie whined. Patricia turned and looked at him. "Okay. If you're as hungry as me, you're nearly starving."

One slice of pizza, cut up, in the dog's bowl for Sammie, a few slices for her plus a nice glass of dry red wine. She settled at the desk in the living room and finally started to relax. She wiggled her toes in her dry, cotton athletic socks and noted the lavender soap's scent still in her hair and on her body. It was blessed relief not to smell chlorine, not to feel the clammy dampness—unpleasant reminders of the day's horrors. She grinned to herself. Home sweet home. Blessed nightly, boring routine. She nibbled on pizza and sipped the wine as she sorted through the day's mail.

Her house was actually a rented cottage that had been a carriage house at the turn of the century, on the estate of Lina and Joseph Carswell. The cottage, used as a mother-in-law suite until Joseph's mother died a few years before, had one main bedroom, a tiny spare room, a bathroom, a combo kitchen and dining area, and a living room that featured a stone fireplace and a patio just through the double patio doors.

The cottage, which Patricia discovered for rent by chance

during an afternoon country drive just outside the limits of
Alliston, was the one thing she considered that she'd gotten
by luck in her life. And she loved it. It was just a fifteen-
minute drive from her office in Alliston, but she was out in
the country. The landlords didn't mind that she'd wanted to
do a bit of redecorating, didn't care if she had a dog, didn't
care if she grew a few flowers and vegetables by the cottage's patio, didn't care if she roamed their expansive,
mostly wooded grounds. She could bang her drums as
loudly as she wanted and not disturb anyone around her, or
sit in total silence and not be disturbed. The perfect rental
situation.

Patricia had opted for a simple decor: fresh coats of
white paint let the oak-beamed ceiling and the stone fireplace and hardwood floors show themselves off. A large,
deep-red area rug set off her blue-and-red-striped couch, the
coffee table, and the white wicker rocker in the living
room. The deep-red vertical blinds over the patio doors
matched the rug. An antique floor lamp with a fringed
white shade that had once been her grandmother's lit the
room. On either side of the patio door stood large ficus
trees.

The room included an entertainment unit with television,
CD player, and stereo equipment. One wall was filled with
bookshelves and the desk where she sat now. A white ab-
stract sculpture sat by the fireplace, Patricia's one good
piece of art, which she had purchased at a college friend's
gallery in Mount Adams three years before as a celebration
gift to herself for starting her business. Over the mantel was
one of her own photographs, a black-and-white of sequoias
taken two years before on a hiking-and-camping vacation in
California.

Patricia finished off the pizza and wine, then sorted
through the mail, mostly junk, a few bills, the *Atlantic
Monthly*. Then she glanced at the blinking red eye on the
answering machine and decided she might as well sort
through her messages, too.

Strange. Twenty messages, nearly using up the tape. But

every message was a blank—just silence, then the click of someone hanging up.

Patricia stared at the machine, as if the now steady red eye and the rewound tape would offer up an explanation. Okay, she told herself. A really pushy salesperson, who wishes to speak to the resident in person. Maybe a jilted lover who, in the heat of passion, has the digits of his or her beloved's phone number transposed and is too nervous to leave a message but can't resist calling. Maybe she just needed a new answering machine.

Nope, I'm not figuring it out tonight, Patricia thought. She carried her plate and glass back to the kitchen and poured herself another glass of dry red wine. Sammie was snoring contentedly by his now empty food bowl. Patricia grinned. Time for the oh-so-civilized detecting antics in *The Thin Man*.

The phone rang. Patricia froze in place. Let it ring, let the answering machine kick in. Another ring. No, this was a normal night, right? She was determined that it would be. On a normal night, she'd answer the phone. Another ring. She pushed herself toward the phone. Go ahead, talk with Dean. Or maybe it's your mom and dad. Maybe that jilted lover who needs reminding of beloved's actual phone number.

Patricia picked up the phone. "Hello," she said. Her voice sounded strangled. Throat too dry. She took a sip of wine.

"Patricia? Is this Patricia Delaney?"

Patricia closed her eyes. "May I ask who's calling?"

She was stalling with social formalities. She knew too well who it was.

"Patricia, please, it's—me." The voice dropped to a whisper. "Gigi. You've got to help me. I've been calling and calling, only I didn't want to leave a message, I was afraid. . . ."

"Gigi, listen to me. Do you know where I was?"

Silence.

"I think you do," Patricia continued. "I think you know

what I discovered at your house. I think you can guess I spent the afternoon with the police."

Nancy's last comment, about being set up, came back to Patricia. It was convenient, wasn't it, that Gigi couldn't pay Patricia until 3:00 P.M. today, that the payment had to be at the house, that the door was left ajar. And that Patricia had found the body of someone who could be blackmailing Gigi with her past.

"Patricia, listen, I need your help—"

"You need to go home and call an attorney. I don't know what's going on here, but the police certainly are curious."

Silence. Was she hanging up? Patricia waited for the click, the tone of a dead line, half hoping for, yet half dreading the sound.

Then finally, firmly, voice weary but resolute: "No, Patricia. I can't go home yet. I need your help. And you owe me. Big time. Surely by now you remember, you know who I was at one time."

It was Patricia's turn to be silent.

"I thought so. So you know you owe me."

Patricia swallowed, nodded, as if Gigi could see the acknowledgment. Of course, thought Patricia, it would come down to this. It had to. It was a rule of the universe, sort of like spiritual physics. A favor that big can't go unrepaid. And no matter how painful the repaying, not doing so would have worse repercussions.

Patricia swallowed again. "What do you want?"

"I want you to meet me tomorrow, ten P.M., at Yeatman's Cove Park near Riverfront Stadium. You know where I mean?"

"Yes."

"Good. The Reds have a game that night, so a lot of people should be around then. Safer that way."

Safe from what? Patricia wanted to ask—no, scream. What is going on here? What am I going to be asked to do? But she kept her silence.

"Fine. Thursday night, ten P.M., Yeatman's Cove."

"That's right," Gigi said. Then there was a pause. Then the connection breaking, the dead line.

Patricia hung up her phone and sighed. She went back to her bedroom to get her sneakers. So much for a relaxing evening. She was returning to her office, to start some new research on Gigi Lafferty. There were some things she needed to know before she met with her. And she didn't have much time to find them out.

Chapter 9

By 7:00 A.M., Patricia had arisen from one hour and fifty minutes' worth of sleep on a blanket spread on the floor of her office. Shortly thereafter, she had her first cup of coffee—leftover brew reheated in the microwave, but she was too tired to notice the acrid, stale taste.

Then Patricia drove over to the Alliston College gymnasium, where she had a community membership that gave her access to the indoor track, pool, weight room, sauna, and locker room. She chose to forgo her usual half mile in the pool, but did extra reps on the weight machines as penance. That was followed by a quick shower and a change into a white cotton blouse, khaki pants, and khaki espadrilles, which she had packed along with towels and assorted toiletries before leaving her house the night before.

Patricia headed back to her office, where she had her second cup of reheated coffee as she straightened up her office from the night's work and examined her calendar for appointments she might need to rearrange or cancel. About halfway through the process, her brain, up until now on automatic pilot, began to engage along with her taste buds, and she nearly spit up a mouthful of the coffee on her white blouse. She choked it down, however, and poured the rest on a geranium sitting in her windowsill.

Patricia updated her answering machine to state she would be out of the office for the day, but would gladly return calls as soon as possible, packed up her briefcase and purse, closed up her office, and headed down to the Prosperity Plaza parking lot toward her truck. On the way she stopped in the Alliston Doughnut Shop, which truthfully bragged on a hand-lettered sign in the window about carrying the suburb's best doughnuts and muffins. There she dutifully ignored the doughnuts and purchased a "Sunshine muffin," which contained carrots and bran and raisins and nuts and promised to give long-lasting morning energy to the consumer, and her third cup of coffee. On her way out, though, she caught a whiff of fresh doughnuts being put in the display case and, knowing she was doomed, let herself glance at them. They were Bavarian cream-filled, chocolate-iced with a dollop of whipped cream and a half cherry on top—her favorite. She bought one and ate it by the time she got to her Chevy S-10 pickup.

Patricia didn't start on her third cup of coffee until she was comfortably on the highway, on the way to Newport just across the Ohio River and state line in Kentucky. At that point, for the first time since awakening, she started mentally reviewing her previous night's research.

Besides learning more about Gigi's family of origin, she realized she needed to go back to the place, and the person, that had originally connected her to Gigi, under the name Loretta King, and Loretta to Jessica Taylor. She also knew she needed to know more about Jessica Taylor, but had not been able to find anything about her by looking in databases of local information.

She had more luck with Joey "Poppy" Jones. In a news database, Patricia found a few brief local articles mentioning the fire that had destroyed Poppy's Parrot years before. Arson had been suspected but never proven—a fact that Patricia had not known before and surprised her. The site had become a vacant lot, then a parking lot for a comics bookstore for several years. A more recent article, written in the past year, featured Joey Jones, reformed drinker, sinner, and dance-hall operator, who ran the Sacred Light Sanctuary of Hope, a combo shelter and worship hall for homeless people. The shelter was built on the very lot, which Joey had repurchased with donations, that had once been the address for the dance club he had operated, as he was quoted as saying, "in my former life."

Patricia was still mentally sifting through the additional information she had found on Gigi's family of origin as she tried to figure out what about Gigi's life as a young woman had made her flee her upper-class surroundings for the raw, dangerous world of Poppy's Parrot.

The wonders of the electronic age for the modern detective, she thought. She could be up most of the night, searching databases of public information, chasing bits of data on the information highway, finding it much easier and quicker than if she had to track it down in hard copy or microfiche at its various sources of origination. But at this point in her investigation, all that information had the same effect no matter how she found it: it generated more questions than before she acquired it; more teasing possibilities that might make sense but weren't yet verifiable; more ifs and maybes—and no answers. Now Patricia yawned as she pulled off an actual highway into Newport.

Patricia parked her truck along the curb on a street in the small downtown section of Newport, several blocks away from Poppy's Sacred Light Sanctuary of Hope, got out, and began walking toward Poppy's. Where she had parked, the two-story buildings clustered close together on the steep rises of streets overlooking the banks of the Ohio River. A bit of litter skittered over the streets in a low wind, but this section of town was relatively cleaned up. Most of the turn-of-the-century buildings had been freshly repainted and housed antique stores or boutiques. The town had certainly been cleaned up and sanitized and made tourist-and-civic-organization suitable since she had worked on this side of the river.

Cincinnati, which was zealous about keeping its city clean of more than just clutter, made sure that its citizens and visitors couldn't get certain pornography magazines or attend sleaze shows within its borders. Its sphere of influence had touched Newport, which had had a shady reputation of gamblers and questionable establishments in years past, when it had been known as "Sin City," the shadow side of Cincinnati.

But now Newport's dark-sidedness had been Disneyfied, thought Patricia as she passed a bright pink-and-purple building with a marquee that advertised MADAME LABELLE'S CABARET! A life-size cardboard cutout of a dance-hall girl revealed just a touch of thigh. Next to Madame LaBelle's stood the River Valley Café. A family of four—the poster family from the entryway to the Laffertys' plat sprung to life, thought Patricia—came out of the café. The boy and girl giggled as Mom insisted Dad stand next to the dance-hall girl while she took "their" photo. Dad smiled, somewhat embarrassed, but put an arm around the flapper girl, hesitating, however, to touch her shoulder.

Patricia smiled as she moved past the tableau. The red-light district goes G-rated—bring the whole family, she thought. Oh well, her life had gone mostly G-rated, too, and Patricia preferred it that way. Maybe she'd have lunch later at the River Valley Café.

Poppy's end of town was outside the tourist zone, and it showed. The buildings were still turn-of-the-century, but recent abuse and neglect masked their historical charm, unlike the buildings so carefully restored just a few blocks away. A tired-looking man, clothes grungy, eyes hungry, came out of a small white building. Patricia's heart quickened as she realized he was coming out of Poppy's Sacred Light Sanctuary of Hope.

She stopped in front of the building. For a second Patricia had to close her eyes and force herself to keep from pitching forward. Fourteen years; it had been fourteen years since she'd been back in Newport, if she didn't count passing by it on the highway. Fourteen years since the night of the fire here, awakening to choking, stinging smoke. Patricia had known ever since she realized who Gigi really was that by stepping into Gigi's past, she was stepping back into her own, where she would have to think about and face things that until now she had successfully put behind her.

She had known that fact, but until now, she had never squarely faced it, or understood its potential impact on her present life.

Patricia opened her eyes, forcing herself to focus on the white building. Not Poppy's Parrot anymore. That establishment, with the bright red-and-green Christmas lights framing the doorway year-round and the large red-and-green parrot on the front door, the words GIRLS! GIRLS! GIRLS! cawing from its mouth, was gone. This building, painted purest white, boasted only a roughly hewn, hand-painted sign that read THE SACRED LIGHT SANCTUARY OF HOPE. ALL WELCOME. SPECIAL SERVICES NIGHTLY, 8:00 P.M.

But it was still Poppy's territory, Patricia thought. Always had been. Always would be. His message or business or building might change, but here he'd always be, watching the stream of humanity flowing by just as surely as the broad river flowed nearby, fishing what he could from it—a desire for an instant's pleasure? a desire for an eternity's redemption?—to trade on for his own needs.

Patricia crossed the street and entered the building. She had to blink for a few minutes to adjust to the sudden change from morning brightness to interior darkness. When her eyes cleared, she saw a small box marked DONATIONS on a table in the corner.

Next to the donation box on the floor was a box of dingy, dirty-smelling clothes. Patricia dropped a quarter in the donation box, rather hoping that it was the same one the redhead at Dean's Tavern had given back to her after she returned the phone. It would be impossible to know now, but somehow it seemed ironically appropriate to think so.

Wonder what this place is a cover for, she thought. Poppy would never have a place like this purely out of the charity of his heart.

Patricia pushed open the next set of doors, stepped through, then gasped. Poppy's Parrot had been reincarnated. This building had nearly the same layout as the original building. She felt dizzy for a moment, as though she had

gone back to Poppy's Parrot in an alternative universe; the
building was the same, although its purpose was different.

A stage like the one for the dancers at Poppy's Parrot
was at the front of the large room. But now there was a
simple podium and a green neon cross, alight and casting a
strange green fluorescent glow over the otherwise unlit,
gray interior. Chairs and tables were folded up and stacked
along the walls; otherwise the room was empty except for
three men, huddled in restless sleep as far away as possible
from one another. The one nearest Patricia moaned.

Patricia tiptoed past the men, around the stage, and
through another door. Since Poppy had, it appeared, rebuilt
his club exactly as it had been before the fire, she knew exactly where his office was.

She started up a narrow flight of stairs. Dressing rooms
and Poppy's office had been upstairs in the old building. On
this building's stairs were stacked boxes of castaway cloth-
ing and canned foods, leaving little room for walking.

Patricia paused, gasped for breath, fighting a gagging
sensation in her throat, her eyes watering and stinging. But
it wasn't the claustrophobic stacks of boxes or the un-
washed smell that bothered her.

It was the memory, previously unexamined, pushed as far
back in her mind as she could make it go, come back to her
suddenly. The place was on fire, she was choking, someone
was screaming at her to wake up—the dancer named
Loretta, a young woman she barely knew, was dragging her
down the stairs—

Patricia leaned against a pile of boxes, closed her eyes
tightly, forced herself to breathe deeply. This is a different building, she told herself repeatedly, until her breathing was again calm and even. Then she continued up the
stairs.

The door immediately to the left at the top, as Patricia
had anticipated, was to Poppy's office, only now the
door was marked JOEY JONES instead of Poppy. Patricia
pushed the door open without knocking. Poppy sat with

his back to the door, his thin, frantic voice cawing into the telephone.

Patricia settled into a lumpy chair, avoiding the spring that had broken through, and stuck her feet up on the filing cabinet, watching with amusement while Poppy screeched into the phone a nearly indecipherable string of orders—the goods were here, ready; he'd already done his part—all the while brandishing a cigar in circles. What was he up to, indeed? thought Patricia. Maybe she'd take a peek in those boxes on the stairway on her way out to see if she could discover what "goods" he was talking about.

Poppy slammed down the phone, then whirled around in his chair, about to launch out of it, when he saw Patricia and stopped. He grabbed open a drawer and started to pull something out, when slowly recognition began to register on his face. He fell back in his chair and popped his cigar back into his nearly toothless mouth and began gumming on it.

Poppy hadn't changed much. He looked like a squashed giant. His squat, square frame was overly muscled, his small face overly fleshed, especially his nose and chin and cheeks, which were exaggerated, rosy globes. His eyes were glinting black specks set within deep sockets, his mouth a cocked slash between a nose and chin that almost met, his forehead knobby beneath the green-and-red yarn cap that either covered baldness or all of his hair—Patricia had never found out which. Same yarn cap? she wondered. Or a facsimile of the original, like this building? Either way, it was indubitably Poppy.

Patricia grinned. Grotesque but lovable in a demented kind of way, that was Poppy, perpetually Poppy.

"Remember me?" she said. "I'm the woman who flipped you to get promoted from dancer to bouncer fourteen years ago."

Poppy yanked the cigar from his mouth and peered at Patricia. He nodded slowly, and slammed the drawer shut. He had been, she thought, about to pull out a gun until he realized who she was. Knowing Poppy, he still might.

"Delaney." He popped the cigar back in his mouth and said around it, "I ain't hiring dancers or bouncers no more."

Then he slid his eyes up her body, blatantly appraising, then stopped at her eyes. He sighed. "It's a shame, though. You still look good. Maybe better. Just a bit older. Warier. Gone upscale, but lookin' good." He sighed lustily again.

Patricia kept her eyes evenly on him. "I'm not looking for work."

"Then what brings the lovely Delaney my way? Sin-sick and world-weary? I don't think you'd mix with the clientele here—though they'd sure appreciate you—but charitable donations are always welcome, especially from those who want to flood their darkness with my light. . . ." Poppy's grin cracked open further.

Patricia laughed. "You haven't changed, Poppy. You're as disgusting as ever."

"Joey Jones, now. Changed my name and changed my life. Why, I have found an inner truth—"

"Poppy, you're still Poppy. And the only thing you've changed is your game. You've found a new racket. I'd have thought you'd have had more imagination than to pick this one. Doesn't seem too profitable. Makes me wonder what you're covering up. Always were after the fast buck, Poppy."

For just a second Poppy looked like he might break into a pout. Then he laughed. He pawed around on the desk, then produced a quarter, which he held up between thumb and forefinger as if he were a magician who had just produced it from behind Patricia's ear. "Sin and salvation, different sides of the same coin. Call it."

Patricia arched an eyebrow. "Sin," she said without hesitation.

Poppy flipped the coin in the air, caught it, and slapped it onto his arm. He studied it, frowned, shook his head, and tossed the coin back on the desk.

"Well? Which side came up?"

Poppy shook his head. "Doesn't matter. Spends just as well no matter how you call it, or which side lands faceup. Ah, Delaney, let's have a drink to the old times." He stubbed his cigar into an overflowing ashtray, pulled a bottle of gin out from under his desk, opened it, and held it out for her to take.

Patricia shook her head. "No, thanks."

"Ah. Gave it up?"

"No. Just started running my own life."

"Ah, Delaney my dear, we all look to something outside of ourselves—if not this"—he took a long drink straight from the bottle, then wiped the back of his hand across his mouth—"then something. Ahh. What are you looking to these days?"

Patricia shrugged. "I'm into finding answers these days. But you're right, sometimes you have to go outside yourself to find them. That's why I'm here."

"Ah, yes, my Sacred Light Sanctuary offers—"

"No, I don't mean the spiritual kind of answers, or whatever you want to call it. I mean answers about the past."

Poppy took another swig, then put the bottle back on the table with a thump. "The past is gone. Done."

"Not in this case, it isn't. I just had a little visit from Loretta King. But she isn't really called Loretta these days, only was when she worked for you. She's a respectable upper-middle-class businessman's wife, gone missing, because somehow another of your former employees, a Jessica Taylor, turned up murdered in her backyard swimming pool."

Poppy stared past Patricia. "Loretta. Jessica. Hmm. Lovely names, lovely ladies I'm sure, but as I said, the past . . ."

Patricia moved her feet off the filing cabinet and stomped them down hard on the floor. "Is your hearing going bad, Poppy? This Jessica turned up murdered in Loretta's pool. And Loretta's gone missing. And the only connection between them is that they used to work for you. Don't you think the police would find that interesting? Don't you think the police would be all over this place like flies if I passed on that tidbit of information?"

Patricia settled back in her chair. Never mind that she already had, and the police seemed so convinced she must be involved in some conspiracy with Gigi that they hadn't seemed to hear her. Or maybe they just didn't believe her. But Poppy didn't know that.

"Now then, Poppy, I wonder what the police would find going on here behind your charitable front if I did send them your way? Something interesting?"

This time Poppy's face did contort into a pout, and then the left corner of his mouth started twitching involuntarily. That was proof enough to Patricia that he was hiding something. Whenever his mouth began ticking like that, it meant he was either lying or covering up. She had figured out that much about him the first weeks she knew him. It was probably why he had never been able to rise above the merely shady side of life to truly profitable criminal activity.

"Since when did you get so cozy with the law?" Poppy asked.

"Since I decided my calling in life was to be a private investigator." Patricia spread her hands in an exaggerated gesture of sincerity. "As such, and as someone Loretta has come to for help, I seek only to do what is right."

Poppy snorted and downed some more gin, then capped the bottle and tucked it back in its hiding place. "I'll bet. What do you want to know? It's been a long time, a long time, Delaney, since they worked for me. And I haven't seen them since the fire."

"Loretta never got back in touch with you?"

Poppy looked away. "No," he said.

"And Jessica? She never got in touch with you either?"

"No, she didn't," Poppy said firmly.

Patricia sighed. "Come on, Poppy, when did Jessica or Loretta contact you?"

Poppy didn't answer. He stared resolutely away from Patricia.

She wasn't, Patricia realized, going to find out when or why Jessica or Loretta had gotten in contact with him. Not just yet, anyway.

"All right, then," she said. "What was the connection between Jessica and Loretta? Back when they worked for you?"

Poppy shrugged. "Friends, I guess. They hung around together between shows, usually left together." He frowned. "Jessica was trouble. Only one of my dancers who really ever gave me trouble."

"What kind of trouble?"

"Late to work, didn't show up a few times. Or showed up drunk or strung out. Had a rough boyfriend who showed up, caused trouble during a few shows, hassling the dancers as they left after the shows, that kind of thing. Tried to rough me up, tear up the place after I fired Jessica."

Patricia frowned. "Jessica doesn't sound like Gigi's type of friend, even then. And I don't recall ever hearing her mention Jessica."

"Ah, Delaney. Things are always more complex than they seem. After the fire, Loretta—you say she's going by 'Gigi' now?"

Patricia relaxed her frown. "No, she *is* Gigi. She was going by Loretta then. As you say, things are always more complex than they seem."

Poppy grinned. "Loretta—Gigi—connected up with Jessica after the fire. Did a little prostituting in the area."

Patricia's eyebrows shot up. Now, that might be blackmail material that Gigi would definitely want kept from Neil or her current associates. "Any proof of that?"

"Ah, it's true. I—ah—know people who know these things. But they were never arrested. Would have been sooner or later, but they ran off one night to Las Vegas."

"How interesting. By themselves?"

Poppy nodded.

"Then what?"

Poppy shrugged and looked away. "That's the last I heard of them, Delaney, until you came in here."

Patricia didn't have to see his face to know the left corner of his mouth was twitching.

Which one had contacted him? she wondered. Gigi? Jessica? Both? Together or separately? Poppy wasn't going to tell her now. He'd probably only told her as much as he had to, to keep her from pushing for this information. Well, she'd find out one way or another which one of the women had contacted him, and why, maybe from Poppy himself at another time, maybe some other way. Meanwhile he had given her a new lead to follow up on. Patricia wanted to know what Gigi and Jessica had done in Las Vegas, why they had gone there together, and why and when they had come back separately.

"You said her name," Poppy said suddenly.

"Who?" Patricia said.

"Loretta's. Her real name."

"Gigi."

"And what did you say her last name was?"

Patricia grinned. "I didn't. But since you can read about this in the newspapers if you want, I'll tell you. It's Lafferty."

"Lafferty," Poppy repeated thoughtfully, and nodded slowly.

Interesting, thought Patricia. The name Lafferty meant something to him.

Patricia studied Poppy for a moment, decided not to push for more, at least not now. She stood up abruptly. "Thanks." She tossed a business card at him. "Call me if you happen to remember anything else—anything at all about those two. Or maybe I'll call you."

Poppy nodded. He pawed around on his desk, found the quarter, tossed it at her. She caught it.

"In case you need to make a wish."

"Or a choice?"

Poppy grinned. "You don't need help making choices."

Patricia looked at the quarter in the palm of her hand. "And I don't believe in making wishes." She tucked the quarter in her pocket. Ironic, she thought. She'd just gotten rid of that previous quarter. "But then, you never know."

She walked out of the office, then quickly down the claustrophobic stairs. She paused long enough to look under the clothes in one of the boxes and discovered electronic components hidden under the clothes. The "goods" Poppy had mentioned? Patricia grinned to herself. Maybe Poppy was doing his own kind of trafficking on the information highway.

Patricia left quickly. It took until she was back to her truck before her eyes adjusted to the daylight after Poppy's dark sanctuary. She started back to her office in Alliston, eager to start digging for more information about Gigi's connection with Jessica, using what Poppy had given her to go on. And she was eager to go over the information she had found on the Neumanns, Gigi's family of origin, to try to piece together why someone with Gigi's background had wanted to escape to Poppy's dark world and had sought the companionship of someone like Jessica, who was clearly bad news. If Poppy said Jessica Taylor was trouble, then she was the big, serious, ugly kind of trouble.

It was easy enough to understand why Gigi had taken an assumed name at Poppy's; her parents had been prominent in the political and business communities of Cincinnati fourteen years ago. Maybe she didn't want to be found out by them; maybe she didn't want to embarrass them. Her father, Eugene, had served two terms as a state congressman in the early sixties, then ran a successful business. Gigi had escaped from a privileged, pampered life, as numerous articles in the news database indicated—Gigi and her family members were prominently and frequently mentioned in connection with art balls, social affairs, tennis and golf tournaments for charity, even a debutante ball for both Gigi and her sister, Allison. Many young women might have found such a privileged world exciting and fun; lots of families would have made it seem so. But the fact that Gigi had run as far socially from that world as she could get indicated that she had not found it so pleasant, that perhaps her family had not made it pleasant.

Yct, running from her family, then to Las Vegas, seemed as extreme as running now secmed. Unless then, Gigi had a greater reason to run than merely tiring of her family's social standing. Unless now, Gigi's reason to run was because she had killed Jessica, as the police seemed to believe.

Suppose Gigi had killed Jessica, thought Patricia. The motive would appear to be to keep Jessica from revealing her past, or to keep from paying Jessica hush money. But wouldn't it have been easier just to pay the money? And if it wasn't easier to pay for Jessica's silence, or if Gigi found that choice particularly unpalatable and she had killed Jessica, why did she contact Patricia afterward? It seemed to Patricia that if Gigi had killed Jessica, she'd keep running, avoiding contact with anyone. Patricia shook her head as she crossed the bridge back into Cincinnati.

She needed more to go on, and she hoped Poppy had given her enough by telling her Jessica and Gigi had taken off for Las Vegas after the club burned. The first thing she would do after she got back to the office, Patricia decided, would be to get on the computer and log into the electronic bulletin board she belonged to for private detectives across the country, see if a detective in Las Vegas could help her out. And, of course, she'd start checking public records for Nevada, see if just possibly Jessica had stayed there and only recently come back to Cincinnati.

No, Patricia thought, turning off the highway at the Alliston exit, that would be the second thing she would do. First she'd contact Jay Bell, her friend and bandleader and lawyer, and ask him to meet her at Dean's Tavern before her appointed time to meet Gigi. And she'd make it clear to him she wanted him to come as her lawyer. Patricia had a feeling she was getting into waters a little murkier and deeper than she wanted to handle without someone knowing she might need to be thrown a rope.

Chapter 10

The more you know, the less you understand.

Patricia laughed out loud at the words from the *Tao Te Ching* that came up on her computer screen. She had programmed her computer to display sayings whenever she turned the machine on. The sayings, from her readings of spiritual texts of various beliefs, were those that struck her as particularly meaningful. And every now and then the saying that appeared seemed especially appropriate to her situation.

"Well put, little gray box," Patricia muttered. "But I'm still hoping to know more."

It was time for her to meet with the private investigator from Las Vegas, electronically, at least, on a computer bulletin board for private investigators. She had contacted the investigator, Marty Navox, earlier on the board. He had posted a message for her to meet him in a "room" on the board for a private "chat," meaning they could type and send messages to one another without any of the other board users viewing their messages.

Patricia signed on to the bulletin board and keyed into the chat room. A line of text at the top of the screen indicated Marty was waiting for her.

Delaney here, Patricia tapped. *Were you able to learn anything about Taylor or King?* Since Loretta King was a made-up name for Gigi, Patricia hadn't been able to find anything in her searches on that name.

Took some doing, but I checked with my contacts in the casinos around here, he typed back. *Seems a Loretta King*

*worked as a waitress in one of the casino restaurants. Ca-
sino restaurant manager vaguely remembered her, but her
employee records were still around. Got lucky. Someone
owed me a favor; showed me her records.* The words
scrolled fairly quickly across Patricia's computer. She was
glad she'd put in a faster modem that enabled her to send
and receive data more quickly; watching words appear
slowly on the computer screen was one of her pet peeves.

Reliable employee, Marty's message continued, in the
clipped language that computer communicators often use in
an effort to save time, on-line costs, and keystrokes. *But
suddenly stopped showing up for work one day. July 12,
eleven years ago.*

The message stopped. The cursor blinked on Patricia's
computer, letting her know her machine was ready for her
to input her reply. *Connection to Jessica Taylor?*

*Roommates. Casino restaurant manager gave me name
of apartment from employee records. Found apt. mgr. Liked
King okay, nothing nice to say about Taylor. Taylor and a
Tommy Malone arrested for manslaughter. Tried rolling a
businessman in the apt., it turned ugly.*

King arrested? Patricia tapped.

*No, but disappeared. Searched local newspaper data-
base; found article detailing arrest. Send it?*

Yes. Thanks.

Good luck. I'll send bill too. :) The symbol :), a smiling
face when viewed sideways, was an emoticon—a symbol
of an expression often used by computer bulletin-board
users to represent the facial expressions they might have if
they were communicating in person. Text scrolling on a
computer screen offered neither tone of voice nor body language to give the written messages context. Emoticons
were a shorthand attempt to make up for that.

Patricia left the chat area of the bulletin board and returned to the main screen. After a few minutes a message
appeared indicating she'd received a text file in her electronic mailbox; the article, Patricia knew, that Marty had
promised. She'd check for his bill later.

A few computer commands and a few seconds later Patricia was perusing the article Marty had sent to her computer. It seemed Jessica and Tommy Malone had been arrested for manslaughter—an attempt to roll a businessman looking for a good time away from his Idaho family had gotten out of hand. The police had learned about the killing through an anonymous tip. Patricia could guess who the tip had come from; no wonder Gigi, as Loretta, had suddenly disappeared from the job and apartment in Las Vegas.

How had Gigi been involved in the murder? Patricia wondered. She tapped into a news database to see what else she could learn about the case. Tonight she was meeting with Gigi. Maybe Gigi would have an explanation that would make sense of everything, but for now the *Tao*'s message, courtesy of her little gray box, was right. Patricia knew more facts, but she felt as though she understood even less about this case.

It was a quiet night in Dean's Tavern. No Queen River band, no karaoke, not even the Reds game on the big-screen television. It was, after all, a home game, so it wasn't carried locally on television; Dean had it on the radio, though, with the big screen tuned in to a muted stock-car racing event. The few patrons seemed more preoccupied with their sandwich baskets and drinks than conversation or anything else around them. Maybe the crowd was thin just because it was a Thursday night. Maybe most of the people who would normally come here were at the Reds baseball game and would come after.

Patricia ran her finger slowly around the rim of her glass, which contained a barely touched ice coffee and bourbon. Gigi wanted to meet Patricia in the cover of the postgame crowds near the stadium. Which might make Gigi feel more protected, but it made Patricia, somehow, feel more vulnerable.

Maybe she should have asked Gigi to meet her here at Dean's Tavern, she thought idly. The last time she had been here had been the last time she had seen Gigi. Now here she was again, talking about Gigi while she waited to go meet her. Maybe there was a cockeyed symmetry to the universe after all, she thought. She pushed her glass away, suddenly, and looked up.

"So what do you think?"

Jay Bell, acting in the capacity of Patricia's lawyer and having heard everything Patricia had experienced or learned since Gigi Lafferty came into her office two weeks before, assumed a serious look. "I think you are up the creek without a paddle. In a swamp without an outboard. Out to sea—"

Patricia rolled her eyes. Leave it to Jay to know all the waterway clichés and make up a few more to assess a situation. She reminded herself that although he didn't like being an attorney, he was a good one. And even acting as her lawyer, he was still her friend. "Please," she said. "I'm not in a hopeless situation. Just a—an unusual one."

"You're right. It's not hopeless. As long as you stay away from Gigi Lafferty. Forget she's your client. Forget you knew her fourteen years ago. The woman's gone AWOL, while someone else from that time and place in your past shows up murdered in the Lafferty pool. And you, whom Gigi has hired, happen to find the body in the pool. Hmmph. No wonder the police were all over you during that interrogation. I'm amazed you didn't have to call me then."

Patricia took a sip of her bourbon and coffee, and glanced at her watch: 8:15 P.M. She'd agreed to meet Gigi at Yeatman's Cove near Riverfront Stadium at ten, so she'd want to get there by 9:45, which meant leaving here by . . .

Jay leaned across the table toward Patricia, grabbed her hand, and squeezed it hard. "Listen to me, will you? Gigi Lafferty is trouble. You know what's going to happen? Eventually, the police will find her, bring her in, probably charge her with murder. She may even confess; hell, from what you've told me, she's probably guilty."

"Circumstantial evidence, Jay."

Jay snorted. "As far as you know. How much would you

care to bet that before the week's over, the autopsy report on Taylor reveals physical evidence that she struggled with Gigi?"

Patricia smiled. "I don't believe in gambling, Jay. You know that."

"Right. You're gambling with your reputation, your license, maybe your life here. The police are looking for hard evidence to tie Gigi with Jessica's murder, and they'll probably find it. Gigi's looking guilty, and you're not looking much better by association. If I'm the prosecutor, I'm looking at you as an accessory."

"Say it gets that far. But you're my defender. How do you defend me?"

Jay leaned back in his seat, studied Patricia for a minute. "By saying my very intelligent, very savvy client dropped Mrs. Lafferty as a client as soon as she learned Mrs. Lafferty had disappeared, had in fact, apparently, fled a murder scene. By pointing out that my very intelligent, very savvy client, in fact, let the officers of the law involved in the case know each and every time Mrs. Lafferty contacted her. Even, perhaps, cooperated with them in helping find her."

Patricia stared at Jay evenly. For a moment they were locked in a silent contest, each waiting for the other to speak first. Then Jay cleared his throat. "You know, you really are very intelligent. And savvy. So why do I have the feeling you're going to ignore my advice?"

"It was good, lawyerly advice, Jay. You verified where I stand, from a legal perspective, which is what I wanted from you. Send me your bill."

Jay scowled. "Oh, come on. I'm not going to bill you for this."

"I asked you to meet me here as my lawyer, Jay. You'd better bill me."

Jay crossed his arms. "I don't feel I've gathered enough information from you to consider this a full consultation. If you'll tell me why you are apparently going to ignore my advice, I'll consider that you took me into your confidence

as my client, and I can begin preparing for the day I have
to show up with you in court to defend you because of
some bizarre need on your part to protect this Lafferty
woman."

Patricia grinned. "That's what I like about you, you're
stubborn." She gestured to a waitress who was delivering a
pitcher of beer at the next booth. "But I'm not telling you
on an empty stomach. I haven't had anything since breakfast." The morning's Sunshine Muffin from Alliston's
Doughnut Shop was still on the seat of her truck.

The waitress came and took Patricia's order for a cheese-
burger and onion rings. Jay and Patricia killed the brief
amount of time it took for the food to be delivered chatting
about the band, the weather, the Reds. Dean delivered the
food, then joined them, since there were so few customers.
His waitress and waiter could easily handle the bar without
him. While Patricia ate, Jay and Dean started talking about
Jay's favorite subject, his boat, the *Queen of the River.*

Patricia mopped up the last of the ketchup with the last
onion ring, ate it, rinsed it down with the rest of her iced
coffee. Jay and Dean's conversation ended abruptly.

"All right, Patricia, your turn," Jay said. "What about
this Lafferty case is making you put your butt on the line
for a client?"

"Okay, back to work for me," Dean said, starting to slide
out of the booth.

Patricia put a hand on his arm. "Not so fast. I think—I
think you should hear this, too."

Dean glanced at Jay, then back at Patricia. "I assumed
this was business. . . ."

"It is. But you ought to hear it, too." Patricia took a
deep breath, then let it out slowly. Maybe she should tell
Jay and Dean individually; the reasons they needed to hear
what she had to say were so different. With Jay, it was
business. With Dean, personal. But this was going to be
hard enough once. Patricia wasn't sure she could bring herself to repeat it.

"Remember Gigi Lafferty, the client I met here Tuesday?

I think I mentioned her to you." Dean nodded. Patricia filled him in quickly on the rest of the story, including her agreement to meet Gigi later. Then she paused. That was the easy part. Now the hard part. She took a deep breath and continued. "Gigi—Loretta back then—was more than an acquaintance. She saved my life. Literally. If it weren't for her, I would have died in the fire at Poppy's Parrot fourteen years ago."

Patricia looked away from her companions, her eyes stinging as if they were suddenly again assaulted by smoke. "I had passed out in the upstairs bathroom during an afterhours party. Drinking too much. Loretta knew where I was because she had led me up to the bathroom. I was too sick to make it on my own. Fortunately, Loretta came up there and dragged me out. She saved my life."

Patricia looked back at her companions, first at Jay, then at Dean. She was fully back in the present, her face suddenly cool as if she had come out of a very hot room. "So, you see, now that Gigi is in trouble"—she was not aware that seconds before she'd been referring to Gigi by her assumed name of so long ago—"I have to at least find out if I can help her, I have to at least try to help her until I know that I can no longer trust her."

Jay gave a long, low whistle. "I don't know how much that story would help you in court, but—"

Dean frowned at Jay, and Jay silenced abruptly. Dean put his hands protectively over Patricia's. "Why, Patricia? Why were you drinking that much? That doesn't sound like you."

Patricia started to look away again, but Dean gently nudged her chin so that she was looking at him, directly in his eyes. He returned his hands to hers, and looked at her, waiting. His open, blue eyes seemed to say he'd wait as long as Patricia needed him to.

She took a deep breath and forced herself to speak evenly. "I had lost someone very important to me a month before. A man named Bobby Harrison. We were engaged to be married. He committed suicide, and I blamed myself for it. I'd been using alcohol since the day of his burial to zap my mind from dealing with it."

Patricia waited for Dean to respond. Somehow, she didn't dare take her eyes from his. Finally he nodded. "I can understand why you want to repay this Gigi now. But it sounds like she's in a world of trouble, and you have to take care of yourself. Listen to your lawyer. I'll come back later and we can talk some more, if you like."

He stood abruptly and left the booth. Patricia looked over at Jay. She tried to smile, gave up, and just shrugged. "So now you know the whole story."

Jay shook his head. "Not the whole story, I'm sure. No one can ever know all of someone else's story. But you were right to tell me. And Dean." He paused, studied her for a minute, then smiled gently. "Patricia, I've given you my advice as your lawyer, and I stand by it. This is as a friend. Do what you think you have to do, but keep me informed. Keep Dean informed. Don't try to be so brave on your own, my friend. Lots of us"—he paused to glance in the direction that Dean had gone—"particularly that gentleman—care a lot about you. And it doesn't make you a lesser person to admit you need help every now and then."

Patricia nodded. Jay tossed some cash on the table and picked up his briefcase. "Call me tomorrow, okay?"

"As your client or friend?"

Jay stood and grinned. "Both. And don't be late for band practice next Monday, either." He headed for the door.

Patricia laughed, feeling her throat catch as she did so, but still the laughter felt good, a release of tension and emotion.

For a few minutes she watched the few people in the bar, then looked at her watch again. She still had time to get back to her office, review her notes of what she'd learned this afternoon after visiting Poppy.

No, she told herself sternly. She knew what her notes said. She didn't need to go back to the office. She was just trying to find a convenient excuse to avoid Dean, who, she knew, would come back over once he saw Jay had gone. She'd wait for him, she decided, at least until she really did have to leave to meet Gigi.

A few minutes later Dean came over, set a glass of clear liquid with a twist of lemon in front of her, and sat down across from her.

Patricia eyed the glass, took a sip. Soda water. "You know, I haven't been drunk since the night of the fire."

Dean smiled. "I wasn't trying to suggest you've got a drinking problem. But I thought you'd want to be as clear-headed as possible for your meeting tonight."

Patricia nodded. She took a long drink of the water. "Thanks. I thought you might try to talk me out of going."

Dean shook his head. "You have to do what you have to do. And I know you. It wouldn't do any good anyway." He paused, as if he were studying her. "You haven't gotten over him, have you? Bobby."

"I'm not still in love with him, harboring some romantic fantasy that we'll float into each other's arms in the after-life, if that's what you mean."

"That's not what I mean. I mean, you still blame yourself, a part of you still does anyway, for his death."

Patricia shrugged. "I talked to a counselor a year after-ward, worked through all the guilt, the anger, self-pity. That helped."

"You may have talked about it, but you didn't get rid of it. Not entirely."

"Look, what makes you so damned knowledgeable about psychology all of a sudden?"

"Life."

Patricia glared at Dean, suddenly angry, waiting for him to elaborate. He held her gaze, still looking as if he were studying her.

"That's it? You're alive, walking on the planet earth, so you are qualified to know all about human psychology," Patricia said. "Sweet Saint Peter, if that's all the qualifica-tions you need to be a psychologist, I should have just saved my hard-earned money and visited an orangutan at the Cinci Zoo."

Dean laughed, shaking his head. "See, that's just what I mean. No, I don't know all about human psychology. I know a little about how people tick, because I pay attention to them. And I pay attention to you. And that's so typical of you. I try to get close, I try to tell you something about what I'm thinking about you, about us, and you put up a wall. You make a joke. You get defensive, witty, clever. At least now I know why. I thought maybe you just didn't like me."

"Oh, Dean. I'm tired. Do we have to go into this? Yes, I like you. Yes, I enjoy being with you—"

"Stop it, Patricia!" Dean was suddenly scowling, his eyebrows knitted fiercely. "I don't really give a damn how tired you are. I want you to get one thing clear. I'm sorry about what happened to your fiancé. I'm sorry that it has made it hard for you to trust in relationships. But I'm tired of this wall you put up. At least now I know why it's there. But one way or another, you're going to have to get over the damn thing, or break through it, or blow it up—at least if you want our relationship to progress."

"What's wrong with our relationship the way it is?"

Dean sighed. "It's straddling a wall, Patricia. Your damned wall. I'm willing to move forward with you, see where we go. If that won't work, if it's too much, I'm willing to be your friend. At least try to be. But I'm not willing to sit here on the edge anymore. I'm not sure what you want from me, from us. I don't think you know. But do yourself a favor. Get over—I mean really get over—Bobby. Stop using what happened with him as an excuse to hide from relationships. Talk to another counselor, or an orangutan, or even, for God's sake, talk to me, Patricia."

Dean stood up, leaned over, kissed her on the forehead. "You know where to find me," he said quietly, and left.

For a while Patricia sat at the booth, not moving, not thinking. Then she closed her eyes. An image kept returning to her from her memory, an image she had not shared even with her counselor, even after using all the meditation techniques the counselor had taught her so that she could supposedly relax and trust enough to share everything. And yet, she had not been able to share the memory. It was too painful, too real, each time she considered it. But she knew she would have to share the pain of the memory, someday, with someone, perhaps with Dean, if the wall he all too accurately described was ever to come down.

It was the memory of herself, as if she viewed herself from the air, lying on Poppy's Parrot's bathroom floor as the choking smoke closed in, filling her lungs and throat and eyes. But she was awake. Just before Gigi came in, she had come to. And she had understood, intuitively, with the survival instinct that had served humanity for aeons, that she needed to give in to the instinct and flee if she was to live. But she had paused. She had, for an instant, been able to remove herself from the survival instinct, and to coldly consider whether or not she wanted to escape the fire consuming the building, and live, or stay there and let it consume her.

Patricia never decided. Gigi came in just as that instant was ebbing into the next, when she would have decided one way or another. Gigi had saved her life. But Gigi had also taken the decision away from her. And so Patricia had never known the judgment she would have passed on her own life.

Chapter 11

A narrow dirt road, barely maintained and nearly impassable in times of snow or heavy rain, led one half mile off of the state route in southwestern Ohio to the fishing cabin on Lake George. The state route itself was at least thirty miles from the nearest highway; Lake George and the private property surrounding it were ten miles from Pikeville, the nearest town, whose population of about 350 eked out a living selling supplies to the lake's summer residents and commuting to various jobs in bigger towns. A thicket of trees surrounded the cabin, blocking its view from the state route or from neighbors, who most likely had closed up their cabins and vacated them for the summer anyway.

The only clear view of the cabin was from the lake itself, and now, nearly twenty-four hours after Gigi had run from her home in sheer panic, the lake held only the reflection of the setting sun. Gigi sat at the end of the small dock that ran from her property, thinking how ironic it was that the best reason to come here in her situation was because the cabin was so physically isolated; yet she had run here without questioning for so many other reasons besides that one.

One was that she felt more comfortable here than anywhere else, and always had. The cabin had belonged to her father's much older brother, Maxwell, and his wife Edwina. They had not had any children, for reasons that were unnamed but somehow known to be forbidden from discussion, but they had eagerly welcomed their nieces and nephew on summer visits, especially Gigi, as if they understood that as the middle child—not the firstborn son, destined to follow his father's brilliant political and business career, or the youngest daughter, her mother's little princess—Gigi was somehow forgotten unless she acted up in such a way that embarrassed her parents.

Of course, this was understood without being discussed, as was so much else in Gigi's family, and her parents were relieved to be able to send her, occasionally with her siblings, to visit Uncle Maxwell and Aunt Edwina. She understood she was being gotten out of the way, and she didn't mind. This was her refuge.

At least, it was her refuge until the weekend she came here just before running to Newport, Kentucky, and began a life pattern of running. Even Maxwell and Edwina, as loving and sympathetic as they had always been, had firmly taken her parents' side. As far as they were concerned, Gigi could not break her engagement to a young man whose powerful father was poised to help her father move into the political big time. Why was she suddenly questioning the position in life for which she had always been groomed?

Breaking the engagement anyway, in the traditional way, would have meant facing her family's recriminations, would have meant facing shame for letting her parents down. So Gigi had done what deep inside she had been aching to do for years; she exploded into full-forced rebellion. She was over twenty-one; there was nothing her family could really do even if they found her. And they didn't. They never knew of her life in Newport. Sometimes she wondered if they even tried to find her.

By the time she'd gotten her job dancing at Poppy's and met Jessica, she didn't care. Jessica was the kind of young woman from the kind of background that would really appall her parents . . . there was always a party, always a good time. That was part of her appeal.

But then came the unfortunate incident of the fire at Poppy's, and her subsequent choices and actions that made Gigi a little sick to recall, and running to Las Vegas, and then, when she understood she was in very, very deeply over her head, and that even if he wanted to, her father couldn't pull her out, running from Las Vegas back to Cincinnati.

But by the time Gigi came back, it was too late to try to reconcile differences with her family. Her father had had a stroke, lingered a few years, then died; her mother, exhausted from taking care of her husband, died a few years after that. Somehow her brother turned away from the social and political destiny he was supposed to have followed, and became an engineer with a quiet family life in Virginia; her sister married a young man from their social crowd but moved to Michigan. Her aunt Edwina had passed away and her visits with Uncle Maxwell were polite but strained. And, as usual, there was never any discussion of what had happened; just the unspoken understanding that somehow Gigi had been responsible for creating the distress that caused her father to start failing in his business and political ambitions, failures that in turn caused the stroke that killed him, and by extension his wife, before their time.

Gigi stared across the now dark water; the sun had set behind the trees across the lake, and the line of trees seemed just a smudge along the dusky horizon. She had always been fascinated with imagining the scenes that might be playing out in the cabins across the lake, scenes so far removed from her own life, yet perhaps not entirely different. Should she take the houseboat, which she'd inherited along with the cabin, out on the lake? Or perhaps she should try swimming the lake? She had been able to as a kid, easily. Gigi shook her head; so much had changed since then, except the fact that now she was again running.

Gigi had inherited this place several years ago from Uncle Maxwell after he died. He left it to her, rather than having it sold off with the proceeds going with the rest of his estate to several charities. Gigi guessed he had done so out of a sense of guilt, or pity, for her. She had kept the place, not telling anyone about it, not even Neil after they met and married. She always meant to, but never did, because somehow she thought it meant telling him about her past, which she knew he would not accept, and because then the place could no longer be a refuge, visited secretly only perhaps once or twice a year, but mentally much more often than that.

Now she had to decide if she wanted to stay here, and rely on Patricia's help, or run as she had once before, but this time for good. A full day, with the cabin as home base, had given her time to prepare for either possibility and to think rationally, think carefully, think like she had when she ran to Las Vegas with Jessica so long ago.

First, after breakfast, she assessed her situation. At least financially she was covered; she still had the money she had gotten to pay off Jessica. She just needed to buy time, and that she could do only with her wits. And so she worked out a plan that she hoped, at least, was plausible for the time being, and immediately put it into action.

Gigi drove north to the outskirts of Columbus. She found a large, fashionable, suburban shopping mall that was anchored by three expensive department stores. She quickly purchased some clothes, makeup, and other necessities, since, of course, she hadn't brought anything with her from the house.

Next she found a rental-car agency, parked a few blocks away, and walked back to the agency where she rented a car under her real name. She put the rental on her Visa card and even smiled when the agent asked for her driver's license. She showed the license, took the rented car, drove it to the airport, and left it in long-term parking. Then she found a pay phone and called Neil at his office. It didn't take any effort to sound nervous as she quickly told him she had ditched their car outside of Columbus, rented another one for the day, and was planning to fly somewhere—no, no, she couldn't tell him where, although she had already paid cash for a ticket. She didn't want him to know too much, as it could be dangerous for him, but she wanted him to know she was all right. Gigi hung up before he could say anything.

Gigi took another cab back to the rental-car agency, then walked back to her own car, and started back to the cabin.

As she drove, she smiled to herself at the thought of Neil, in his posh white-carpeted office, getting her phone call. He was, she knew, immediately on the phone to the police, who by now were surely looking for her. But she thought she had done a fairly good job of setting up dead ends for them. The authorities would spend time looking for the rental car and trying to find out where she'd flown off to. Meanwhile she would be at the fishing cabin, which no one, except one person she believed she could trust completely, knew about.

Now, darkness had fallen completely over the lake: it was nearly impossible to tell where the lake ended and the trees began; where the trees ended and the sky began. Gigi stood and stretched on the dock, staring into the inky darkness all around her. If she wanted to run, she'd have to figure out where to run to; probably Mexico. But she didn't really want to run. She'd run from her parents and the life they wanted for her; run from a life turned sour in Las Vegas; run from making the effort of finding out who she really was by marrying Neil, as if to atone for her former sins by returning to a life of perfect respectability in a marriage to a man who was, in a shockingly remarkable way, just like her own father.

Gigi didn't want to keep running. She didn't necessarily want to return to Neil, or to the life they had together; a day's freedom had been enough to show her that. Maybe their life could change. Maybe they'd have to divorce. But she didn't want to run from anyone, ever again. She wanted, for once, just to be herself, whatever that meant; she wanted, more than anything, to find out what that meant.

And yet, Gigi wasn't sure if she had the strength, either, to go back to Cincinnati and face her problems in order to find out what being herself might mean.

She headed back to the cabin slowly, trying to decide what to do.

Chapter 12

Patricia sat by the Ohio River at Yeatman's Cove Park near Riverfront Stadium, thinking that Gigi wouldn't show up.

Behind her, the baseball crowd was still milling about after the game. Across the river, on the Newport side, the lights of riverfront restaurants danced on the water. Voices and laughter carried from partiers on a riverboat. Beyond that, where Patricia had been much earlier in the day visiting Poppy, was darkness and silence.

Heels clicked on the paved walkway, then stopped abruptly. Patricia looked up; it was Gigi.

Gigi grinned at Patricia as she sat down next to her.

"You looked surprised. You thought I wouldn't show up?" Gigi sounded amused.

"I wasn't sure. But then, you showed up to pull me out of a burning building, and I didn't expect that."

"Is that why you're here?"

Patricia hesitated, sensing that the wrong answer might make Gigi suddenly jump up and run away. She decided to answer truthfully.

"You know it is. That's why you came to see me in the first place. You knew that I would be unlikely to betray your confidence, whether I was able to find out about your past as an investigator or recall you on my own. You couldn't be entirely sure of that with another investigator," Patricia said.

Gigi nodded. "You're right."

"Still, you saved my life," Patricia said. "I've never been sure why."

"Are you asking?"

"Sure. We can start with that."

Gigi shrugged. "You were a decent person. And when you got sick that night, I knew something very bad was troubling you . . . and I saw a little bit of the sadness in you that had made me run away to Newport. I knew you were trying to run, too, from something, and I felt for you. And . . . I felt responsible for the fire."

"You? How could you be—"

"Poppy was always having to run out Jessica's boyfriends. One of them—I forget his actual name now but we called him Pox—was really trouble. He came in one night and practically tore up the place in a jealous rage over Jessica. I don't know what she'd done. Anyway, Poppy fired Jessica that night, and got Pox arrested. Sooner or later Jessica got back together with Pox. And then one night Poppy gave me the key to the club. Told me to meet Jessica outside the club at a particular time after hours, and not to tell anyone about it."

Gigi shook her head. "I didn't question Poppy at the time. I felt I had to have my job, my identity at Poppy's, or I'd go back to being my parents' failed daughter. That seemed worse than being nothing at the time.

"So I met Jessica outside the club after hours," Gigi continued. "Pox was with her, which surprised me. Pox wanted to look around in the basement, see how the place was wired, the fuse box, things like that. I was too frightened to tell anyone."

"You're suggesting that Poppy set up the fire that destroyed his club, with Jessica and her boyfriend's help," Patricia said, recalling the article mentioning the suspicion of arson. She felt a slow anger starting within her. She had nearly died in that fire, and had been haunted by her experience as much as by Bobby's death for fourteen years.

Gigi nodded. "Yes. It's what I believe. But I have no proof of that. I almost put the visit out of my mind. When the place went up, I was as stunned as anyone. Everyone downstairs had plenty of time to get out, but I remembered helping you upstairs to the bathroom and knew you hadn't come back down. I couldn't just let you die up there. It wasn't until a year or so later that I really pieced together what Poppy's request and Jessica's visit with Pox implied."

"Poppy set up the fire, left town to prevent anyone questioning his involvement in case arson was suspected, and later collected, I'm sure, a fair amount of insurance money," Patricia said flatly.

She stared across the river for a few moments, then looked back at Gigi. "I wanted to find you after the fire to thank you, but you disappeared pretty quickly," she said. "To Las Vegas, I've just learned, with Jessica."

Gigi looked surprised. "How did you find out? I thought when you looked in my past . . ."

"I didn't know about Jessica Taylor, then," Patricia said. She explained how she had contacted the Las Vegas investigator and researched several databases to find out what had happened after Jessica and Gigi, still posing as Loretta King, arrived in Las Vegas.

When she finished, a long silence fell between the two women. Patricia waited, kept herself from looking at Gigi.

"I guess it's not too hard to figure out that Jessica was trying to blackmail me," Gigi said finally. Her voice was carefully controlled, as if she didn't want to sound bitter but couldn't keep from doing so.

"Why don't you tell me about it?" Patricia asked gently.

Gigi sighed. "I'm not sure where to start."

"How about starting with why you went with Jessica to Las Vegas?"

"Jessica wanted to leave Cincinnati to get away from Pox. He was starting to frighten her with his insane jealousy. I went to Las Vegas with her because I didn't have any reason to stay in Cincinnati. We were roommates. We partied too much but we laughed a lot. More than I'd ever laughed before. But Jessica had this way of connecting up with men who were bad news."

Gigi paused and cleared her throat. "I came back to the apartment one night early, and found Jessica and her new boyfriend, Tommy Malone, arguing over what to do about the poor businessman they'd just killed. Jessica and Tommy had a scheme going where Jessica would pick up out-of-town businessmen, bring them back to our apartment, and then she and Tommy would roll them for all their cash and valuables. Of course they didn't protest—a complaint to the police would mean their families and companies would find out. But this one tried to protest, I guess."

Gigi's voice shook as she continued. "There was blood everywhere. Tommy had a violent streak, and I guess he got carried away. It made me sick—Jessica and Tommy arguing over whose fault it was, while this poor guy lay dead. They were arguing so loudly, they didn't even hear me come in. I took off and called the police from a phone booth, without leaving my name. I even made sure I wiped the phone, in case they decided to trace the call and check for fingerprints later.

"Then I got back in the car and drove east all through the night." Gigi stared down at the river's edge. "I read about the arrests several nights later. Jessica had stabbed the guy and Tommy had finished him off by beating him up. I know it sounds terrible, but I was relieved. I was stupid enough to think that with Jessica locked away I could walk back into being Gigi. Everyone in Vegas knew me only as Loretta King; no one there or in Newport knew of my life as Gigi. And no one who'd known me in Cincinnati knew of my life as Loretta King. So I came back here, and tried to pick up where I left off."

"Life doesn't work that way."

"No. It doesn't. My parents had died. My brother and sister had lives of their own. My friends did, too. I'd been gone over two years. So I just got a job—demonstrating makeup in a retail store. And my life went on from there. You know the rest of the story."

"But then Jessica showed back up in your life. How did she find you?"

Gigi laughed abruptly. "You know, I was so shocked to see her at my front door that it took me a while to think of asking her that. In Las Vegas, I always picked up the *Cincinnati Enquirer* at this place that had newspapers from all over the country. She always teased me about it. One day she saw me crying as I read the paper. I was reading an article about my father's death. She asked me what was bothering me, saw the article. I told her that he was the father of a friend of mine. She didn't comment, just left the room. I'd forgotten about her noticing that."

"But she didn't forget."

Gigi shook her head. "No. She told me that after that she wondered about who I was, that I always acted like I was a little finer than who I pretended to be; I'd made up an elaborate poverty-stricken, uneducated past for Loretta King, who nevertheless had great parents who had died young."

Gigi smiled thinly. "As different from my actual past as possible." She paused, shook her head. "I was playing a game really, a childish game. I never thought of it somehow boomeranging into my future. . . ."

"And Jessica saw through your story, or at least questioned it enough to check out the Gigi you'd been reading about in the newspaper?" Patricia asked.

"Yes," Gigi said. "After she got out of jail, she came back here and tracked me down under my real name, which is not hard to do. She told me I owed her for turning her in—she guessed I'd made the anonymous call. And she said she'd be very curious to find out what my husband would think about my past."

"So she started blackmailing you," Patricia said.

"Not for money, not at first anyway. She said she just wanted a fresh start, and she wouldn't tell my husband about my sordid little past if I'd help her out. Maybe get her a job at his company. I believed her. I always believed Jessica. She was so charming, so—charismatic. And maybe she even believed herself. After all, for a while things were okay. I told Neil I'd known her briefly in college, and he gave her a job. Apparently she was a good employee. I felt uncomfortable around her, but I didn't see her very often, just at a company function now and then."

"From what you've said, it's hard to imagine Jessica remaining comfortable in such a conventional role for long."

Gigi sighed. "Of course. A few months ago she started putting pressure on me to give her money. She was bored, she said, restless, she needed to move on. This kind of life wasn't for her after all. I put her off, and finally came to you. I wanted to find out if she could prove anything to Neil. If not, then I could tell her to get out of my life, which is what I really wanted. I knew if I started giving her money, she'd never go away. And I figured if she still said something to Neil, then I could tell him she was insane. As long as there was no real proof, I knew I could convince Neil to believe me. I can be pretty charming myself. That's one thing I did learn from Jessica."

"And with what I found, you pretty much figured you could tell Jessica to go to hell," Patricia said. "If I couldn't find concrete proof of your past as Loretta King, then Jessica couldn't either. And without concrete proof, she couldn't threaten you with telling Neil about your past."

Gigi nodded. "That's what I thought." She sighed. "But of course Jessica had a card up her sleeve when she came to my house at lunch, the day you were scheduled to come for your payments."

"What was this one?"

"She told me she knew that someone was sabotaging Neil's business. That she did have proof of that. That she'd sell it to me for the same amount she'd been trying to blackmail me for."

"Which was?"

"Twenty-five thousand dollars."

Patricia whistled.

"Oh, I didn't fall for it," Gigi said. "Not right away. But then she said she had proof with her. Maybe she suspected I wouldn't fall for her blackmail attempt; maybe she thought I'd pay her for both. I asked to see it."

"Did she have anything, or more excuses?"

"She showed me something she called a diskette. Said all I had to do was give it to Neil, and he could run it on his computer, and it would tell him all he needed to know. Said he'd be grateful to me. Might even save my marriage." Gigi smiled slightly. "Jessica wasn't the first woman to work for Neil who was in a position to know my marriage was in trouble."

"All right," Patricia said. "Jessica shows you a computer diskette, tells you it contains evidence of sabotage at your husband's company, evidence for which you're supposed to cough up twenty-five grand. Did she show you what was on the diskette?"

Gigi shook her head.

Patricia bit her lower lip. "Did you *ask?*"

Gigi shook her head again. "I asked her instead why she wasn't blackmailing whoever could be implicated by the diskette instead of trying to sell it to me outright."

Patricia arched her eyebrows. "Good question."

"And, of course, Jessica had an answer. The person didn't have the money she needed right away, and she needed it fast. She said she'd heard that Tommy was getting out of jail and was afraid he'd come after her. So she wanted to leave town fast." Gigi sighed. "And I realized that if Tommy came after her, he could come after me as well. Or if Jessica made up with him, he could corroborate her story of my activities in Las Vegas, and either get a lot more money than twenty-five thousand blackmailing me after all, or ruin my marriage."

"And you didn't like either possibility."

Gigi shook her head. "No, I didn't. And somehow, I thought if I could give Neil something that would save his company, be a last-minute heroine of some kind, it might help my marriage."

"Why?" asked Patricia.

"Why what?"

"Why do you want to save your marriage? You've never sounded very happy about it."

Gigi smiled thinly. "Happiness wasn't the point. Security was. I didn't want to lose the security, however shallow that sounds, that I thought I had with Neil. I didn't want to be adrift—cut off from my society of friends and associates—like I was after I came back from Vegas. I know how that sounds. Especially to someone like you, Patricia. And I've been talking with someone, a counselor, to help me move past this insane need for security, to either make things change with Neil, or to carry on without him, but I was far from being there. Now, of course, Neil will have to learn of my past, if he hasn't already, and that will automatically put an end to our marriage. Neil's puritanical that way." Gigi paused. "For everyone else, that is."

Patricia took a deep breath, then exhaled slowly. "Unfortunately, Gigi, you haven't said anything that doesn't sound like a very strong motive for murdering Jessica."

Gigi looked at Patricia suddenly, sharply. "But I didn't murder Jessica. I didn't. Patricia, you have to believe me."

"All right. Then what happened?"

"Jessica waited at the house while I went to get the money." Gigi sighed. "I had enough at the house to cover your fee when you came by at three, but certainly not enough for Jessica. I still have a savings account with some money left to me after my parents died, and there's enough in there to cover what Jessica was asking."

"Okay, so you go to get the money. That had to take you what, an hour or so?"

"Maybe an hour and a half. Traffic was heavy, and that kind of withdrawal isn't something you do at an automatic teller machine."

"So you left the house at, what?"

"Half-past noon."

"And got back around two P.M.?"

Gigi nodded. "That's about right. Maybe ten after. I didn't check my watch."

And, thought Patricia, forty-five minutes to an hour later, I pull up at my designated time. Coincidence or convenience? Had Gigi planned to kill Jessica all along, and get her, Patricia, out to take the heat?

"I'm curious, Gigi. Why did you insist I come to your house instead of coming to my office to pay me? Or simply mailing me the payment?" Patricia asked.

Gigi glanced away uncomfortably. "I didn't want to mail cash, and I couldn't write a check—Neil would eventually see the canceled check and then he'd know I was up to something. And I was supposed to meet Neil for an early dinner that night. I knew I wouldn't have time to get to your office after meeting Jessica, then back to Lafferty Products in time. And Neil would ask questions if I was late."

Patricia wanted to believe Gigi, and Gigi sounded sincere, but Patricia wasn't sure who or what to believe in this case. For now, Patricia would continue to hear Gigi out.

"All right. So you got back to the house, and then what happened?" Patricia asked.

"I found Jessica in the pool. I panicked. I thought maybe Tommy had come after her after all—I didn't know what to think. I just panicked and ran. I got in my car and started driving."

Patricia looked at Gigi curiously. "Aren't you skipping a step or two?"

Gigi frowned. "Like what?"

"Like packing clothes and makeup, dropping the suitcase, taking money and jewels from the safe."

Gigi shook her head, still frowning perplexedly. "No. I just took off."

Patricia thoughtfully rubbed the diagonal white scar on the left side of her chin. "Someone, then, went to a lot of effort to make it appear like you fled. That's what I thought, that's what the police immediately thought. You had fled, of course, but it wouldn't have been immediately apparent if it hadn't been for the clothes everywhere."

Gigi's eyes were wide. "The house was as quiet and neat as usual when I got back. I started looking for Jessica, and when I found her in the pool, I panicked and ran."

"So it wouldn't have been until after you left that who-ever killed Jessica trashed the place to make it look like you'd run." Unless Gigi was lying, Patricia reminded her-self. She felt herself believing Gigi, and she wasn't sure that was a wise idea. "Damn it, Gigi, if you'd have just gone to the police right away, you could have saved yourself—and me—a hell of a lot of trouble. If you'd called them right away, they might have been at least a lit-tle inclined to believe you." Patricia didn't quite keep the edge of irritation out of her voice. "And by the way, this doesn't look too great for me. I found the body, and by now the police know I was working for you, and why."

"Look, I didn't remember you were going to come over later. I didn't think about who might find Jessica. And I'm not saying that running was a smart thing to do. I just did it. But I didn't kill Jessica Taylor." Gigi clutched Patricia's arm suddenly, desperately. "Patricia, I didn't kill her."

"Neither did Tommy Malone."

"What?"

"Gigi, he died three years ago. In prison, during a prison gang fight. I found an article about it in one of my searches in a newspaper database. Tommy wasn't coming after you or Jessica."

Gigi slowly released her hold on Patricia's arm, closed her eyes, and weaved back. For a minute Patricia wondered if she was going to faint. But then Gigi started laughing.

"Jessica, Jessica. I always believed anything she said. She always seemed so . . . knowledgeable. So convincing. Little old gullible me. I always fall for the type. I guess this does make it look bad for me."

"Yes, it does. The police might have believed your ex-planation for running if you'd called your lawyer and con-tacted them a few hours after running. Now, no way. If you want the truth, I can't believe I'm falling for your explana-tion either."

"But you do believe me? You do believe I didn't kill her?"

Patricia sighed. "I'm not sure. I want to. Maybe because

you saved my life once. Maybe because you showed up here, and you didn't have to. If you'd killed her, surely you'd have taken that money and been far away by now."

"I thought about it. But I'm tired of running, Patricia. I want, for once, to build a life that's my own. Looks like the only way I'm going to do it is by finding out who killed Jessica. On my own, if I have to. But I'd like your help."

Patricia stared out across the river. Jay was right. The correct thing to do, by all logic, by every conventional standard, was to go directly to the police, tell them everything she knew, cooperate with them, and wash her hands of Gigi. Involvement in something like this could put her business, and maybe her life, in jeopardy. She'd worked hard to build her own life, as Gigi put it. Then again, it was quite possible she wouldn't have a life if it weren't for Gigi.

"All right," Patricia said. "All right. I think you ought to call your attorney and go to the police right now. I think that's the best possible move you can make."

"I'm not going to do that, Patricia. No one's going to believe me now, not without something to show it's possible someone else did it."

"I know. But I had to tell you that. Now I'm telling you I will devote one week to helping you. One week from tonight I'm done, and I'm going to the police with what I've got, with or without you. If I find something that shows me you probably did kill Jessica, I'm going before that. But for one week I will help you."

Gigi grasped Patricia's arm again. "Thank you, oh Patricia, I don't know how—"

"Stop it, before I change my mind. All right. You didn't kill Jessica; Tommy obviously didn't kill Jessica. Someone had to, though. Maybe it was the person who Jessica supposedly could prove was sabotaging your husband's company, assuming she was telling the truth. Someone who knows your house well enough to get in without tripping the alarm, well enough to open the safe and make it look like you'd taken things from it and your bedroom before running." Patricia paused as she considered the possibilities. "Let's start with your husband. He's the obvious choice, and you implied earlier that there was some intimacy between him and Jessica."

"Neil?" Gigi laughed abruptly. "Yes, he and Jessica were having an affair. But he had lots of affairs. And I don't think he could kill anyone."

Patricia arched her eyebrows. "The police think you could. So I'd suggest that we consider the other possibilities objectively."

Gigi stared at her for a moment.

"All right. I suppose Neil could be a possibility. But why would Neil sabotage his own company?"

"You're assuming Jessica was telling the truth about that. And there are many reasons someone might want to set up his own company—covering up illegal or unethical business practices, for one. For now we'll assume Jessica was telling the truth, since we don't have a whole lot else to go on. How did you know about her affair with Neil?"

"I found an ankle bracelet of Jessica's in our basement," Gigi said. She paused and bit her lip for a moment. "I suppose she could have tried blackmailing Neil as well. He did have political ambitions, and an affair or, as you say, illegal business practices could stand in the way of those, if revealed. But he's had other affairs." Gigi laughed shortly. "We even got counseling for it, for all the good it did. And really, it could be argued that I killed Jessica in jealousy."

"How about a spurned lover, killing her in jealousy instead? One who would know your house well?" Patricia asked.

"That would describe Rita Ames. Runs the training department for Neil's company. Actually a good friend of mine from our former neighborhood. Or was. She and Neil were having an affair before Jessica came along." Gigi laughed again. "Funny, I felt more betrayed by her than Neil. I stopped feeling betrayed by him a while ago. I guess it could be argued that Rita might have killed Jessica out of jealousy, but I just can't imagine her killing anyone. But then, I couldn't imagine her having an affair with the boss, either."

"Where would Jessica have been before she came to see you at lunchtime?"

"Well, at work, of course. She was a good and faithful employee." The irony in Gigi's voice wasn't lost on Patricia.

"At work. So anyone there could have followed her to your house. Including Rita."

"Possibly."

"And there is the connection with the company. Possibly Rita could have been sabotaging the company out of revenge—" Patricia stopped, feeling irritated. Supposition. All supposition. She needed facts. She sighed. "All right. Let's look at the company angle. Who did Jessica know there who knew your home well?"

"Well, Allen, of course."

"Neil's son?"

"Yes. He does something running computer systems for the company, and Jessica worked for him."

"Doing what?"

"Entering data of some sort." Gigi shook her head. "Sorry I can't be more specific. Allen never makes it easy to ask him about his work."

And supposedly Jessica had evidence on a computer diskette, thought Patricia. She needed some way to find that diskette. Or a copy of it. She felt certain that Jessica had made more than one copy of whatever data was on the diskette. Or if she could find a way to quietly get to the original data . . .

Patricia looked at Gigi. "Who else comes to mind who knows the company and your family well?"

Gigi hesitated, frowning. "Gregory Finster. But he had little to do with Jessica, I'm certain."

"Who's Gregory?" Patricia asked patiently, thinking Gigi didn't really understand the seriousness of her situation. She was so ready to dismiss everyone who fit the criteria Patricia was using as unlikely to commit murder.

"Gregory is director of personnel at Neil's company. And he's become something of a—close family friend," Gigi said.

"All right. You've given me some leads to at least start on. And I'll do more digging into Jessica's past, but I have the feeling that the people she knew before she went to jail are either dead or have moved on to other things. And it doesn't sound like she wasted any time between getting out of jail and getting to you."

"No, she didn't."

"Now, where can I contact you?"

Gigi hesitated.

"Look," Patricia said. "I'm trusting that you didn't kill Jessica. A lot of people would say that's a pretty big leap of faith. You can at least trust me. . . ."

"It's not that I don't trust you, it's just that . . . where I'm staying . . . it's very special to me. No one knows about it, no one at least in my present life."

Patricia looked at Gigi sharply. "Do you mean the cabin on Lake George? Used to belong to your uncle and aunt? And you have it still in your maiden name?"

Gigi drew in her breath sharply. "How did you—"

"Came up when I did my investigation on you. So be careful. People can find out where you are."

Gigi grinned. "I think I've set it up so that no one's going to look for me too close to home for a while."

"Mmm. Just be careful. I'll call you in a week. Meanwhile, if you need me, or if you think of anything else, feel free to call me."

Patricia held out her hand; Gigi accepted it with a quick shake. "Thanks, Patricia. And good luck."

Gigi stood and walked away. Patricia watched her until she was out of sight, then looked back at the river.

Good luck, Gigi had said. Maybe she should have wished Gigi good luck, too, but Patricia had never believed in relying on luck. Even as a child, visiting her grandparents' farm, she was skeptical of the family ritual of tossing a penny in the well and making a wish.

The flash of memory made her think of the coin Poppy had given her earlier. Patricia walked to the river's edge. She dug the coin out of her pocket and tossed it in the Ohio River. And on which side will the coin land this time, Poppy, she thought, sin or salvation?

And then she laughed out loud at herself. For of course the coin would not land, but turn perpetually in the river, tossed and pulled and swept on by its currents.

Chapter 13

Patricia had no trouble getting in to see Neil Lafferty the next morning. Since it was a Friday morning, she had to cancel her date with Dean to go computer shopping, but agreed to meet him at the Oktoberfest that night. She had telephoned Neil at home and briefly, almost abruptly, explained to him that she was the private investigator whom Gigi had hired, and given the recent turn of events, she thought they ought to talk. When she arrived at Lafferty Products an hour later, she was greeted in the lobby by Neil's secretary, an older, severe-looking woman named Dee Anne, who crisply wished her a good morning, escorted her to Neil's office, provided her with a fresh cup of coffee, and sent her in to see "Mr. Lafferty," as she referred to Neil in a slightly hushed, semireverent tone.

This wasn't VIP treatment, of course. Patricia suspected that Dee Anne had been instructed to get her into Neil's office as quickly as possible, without giving her a chance to talk to anyone else. Once she was in Neil's office, the door shut firmly behind her, she was greeted only by Neil's profile, as he sat behind his desk, turned to look out the window, and talked in low, nearly inaudible tones into the phone. Patricia settled into one of the visitor chairs, placed her coffee on a nearby table, and waited.

Patricia recognized the message he was sending her: you called me, but I'm calling the shots. Very well, she thought; it gave her a chance to size up Neil and his surroundings.

Neil's profile was long and angular; nose and chin both somewhat pointed, flat cheekbones, high forehead, his pale skin nearly blending into his thick blond hair, which was combed straight back from a receding hairline. His mouth was pinched as he listened, and barely moved as he talked. His suit was custom-tailored and immaculately pressed. He might, thought Patricia, have been attractive, except he did not appear to be a person who laughed or smiled readily. In fact, he looked like someone to whom other people's attempts at humor would be irritating.

The most striking thing about his office was the white carpet. It seemed to have absorbed all the rest of the color out of the room. In fact, the only color in the room was the huge mahogany desk behind which Neil sat. Even the photographs on the walls were black-and-white. The pure white carpet, used so lavishly both at home and the office, Patricia supposed, was a symbol of its owner's wealth in being able to afford the costly maintenance of always keeping it clean.

It also served to make visitors a bit nervous. Patricia eyed her coffee lamentably, knowing that she'd just let it sit and grow cold, ignoring the fact that she'd skipped her morning coffee to get here as soon as possible. For once, she liked the idea of the spilled-taco coloring of her office carpeting.

Patricia stood, then walked over to the photographs and studied them. Several were basic shots of Lafferty Products' new headquarters and warehouse. Others were of Cincinnati landmarks: the Roebling Suspension Bridge, the skyline, the Tyler Davidson Fountain at Fountain Square. One stood out from the standard compositions of the other photos; it was an architectural detail of a downtown cathedral, St. Peter in Chains Cathedral. Must have been done with a high-quality telephoto lense, Patricia thought.

All the photos were signed, she noted, by Rita Ames. The friend Gigi had mentioned, who had gone to work for Neil and been his lover until Jessica came along. Interesting, thought Patricia, that these photos were the only decorations gracing Neil's office walls. . . .

"You admire the photos."

Patricia started and turned. Neil was turned toward her, slightly smiling to one side, apparently amused at her discomfort.

"They are nicely done," she said, keeping her voice casual and light, as if they had been having a conversation all along about photography. She smiled as she returned to her chair. "I was just noticing the photographer—Rita Ames. I know many of the area's photographers, since I do some photography myself, but I haven't heard of her. Is she from this area?"

"An employee," Neil said abruptly. "Office-warming gift." Neil stretched his hands, then clasped them together. His hands, especially his fingers, were long and thin. "Let's get down to business. Starting with your price."

"My price?"

"I assume you've come here to sell me something. Information as to where my wife is. Or information and silence about something you discovered while under her employ."

"I don't deal in silence," Patricia said. "I deal in information. My silence on behalf of my clients about the information I find for them is part of my professional responsibility. So you don't need to think I'm here to extort money from you."

"I have never stooped to being blackmailed. I never would. There are enough easy ways to stop it," Neil said.

Patricia raised her eyebrows. Jessica had nearly succeeded in blackmailing Gigi, but was killed before she received her payoff. What if she was trying to blackmail Neil as well? If he wouldn't stoop to blackmail, would he stoop to murder to prevent it?

"All right," said Patricia. "I must not understand what you think I'm going to set a price for."

Neil smiled coolly, briefly. "I see I've offended your sense of integrity. The police have filled me in on my wife's . . . unfortunate youthful adventures, and told me you knew her then. Let's just say I'd like to hire you to provide me with any other information you have, especially if you've discovered something that could prove . . . unfortunate for Mrs. Lafferty, or myself, if it were made public knowledge. And to tell me where she is."

Patricia shook her head. "Sorry. Gigi is still my client. I am here on her behalf. So even if I did know where she is, I couldn't tell you."

"Would you tell the police?"

"I'm cooperating with the police as fully as I can, given the circumstances. Do you realize, Mr. Lafferty, that when the police find Gigi, she could very well be arrested for Jessica Taylor's murder?"

"I realize, Ms. Delaney, that the sooner my wife turns herself in, the less of a media circus this unfortunate incident becomes, and the better able my lawyers will be to deal with this quickly and quietly."

Patricia looked at Neil for a long moment. In her business, she tried to stay as objective as possible about people she met during her cases. But she couldn't deny her feelings; she disliked Neil.

She took a long, slow, deep breath, then said, "I'm sure that's true. And I'm sure Gigi will contact your lawyers as soon as possible, but there is a little matter that bears investigating first, which could help keep Gigi out of court, lessen the negative press you're getting, and maybe even save your company a great deal of trouble and money."

At that, Neil's eyebrows went up, his mouth pursed a little more tightly. Patricia suppressed a laugh. She thought her reply would catch his interest.

"All right," he said. "I'm listening."

"First, a question," Patricia said. "How well did you know Jessica Taylor?"

Neil didn't flinch, twist, or hesitate. "Not well. Gigi asked if I could find a job for her, and I did. I rarely saw her after that. There was no reason for me to."

Patricia rubbed her finger across the scar on her chin. If Gigi was telling the truth, then Neil was one smooth liar. Or Gigi could be lying, an uncomfortable possibility that continually hovered on the edge of Patricia's thoughts. She preferred to believe Neil was well practiced in deception.

"Jessica was attempting to blackmail your wife over past activities that Jessica knew about," Patricia said. "But Gigi didn't fall for it. Then Jessica told Gigi that she also knew that someone was sabotaging your company and that she had evidence of it. Gigi agreed to purchase the evidence. When she left to get the money, Jessica was fine. When she returned, Jessica had already been murdered."

Neil tapped his fingertips against the desk, then stopped abruptly. He clasped his hands, intertwining his fingers, and rested them on the desk.

"How do you know Jessica wasn't just making that up? Or Gigi?"

"I don't. But if Jessica was telling the truth, and someone knew she was going to tell Gigi about the sabotage, that could explain her murder. Or if Jessica knew too much about something, and was trying to blackmail someone else as well, they may have murdered Jessica and simply set Gigi up to look like the guilty party."

Neil leaned back in his chair. "Interesting," he said. "Interesting theory." He leaned forward suddenly. "How do you know I'm not the one Jessica had something on? Don't you think you're awfully bold, coming in here, saying these things?"

"I don't know that you're not the one. But I couldn't figure out a way to do what I want to do without talking to you first."

"And just what do you want to do?"

"Take Jessica's job here. For about a week. If she did discover something fishy, then filling her shoes is the perfect way for me to find out what it is. If she didn't, if she was just saying that, or Gigi was just making that up to divert me from believing that she killed Jessica, then maybe I'll be able to figure that out, too. Either way, I'm asking you for a week in Jessica's position. And your silence in letting anyone else in the company know why I'm here. My name hasn't appeared in any of the news reports about this case, and hopefully it won't. In exchange, if I do learn something that points to trouble in your company, I'll fill you in on it."

Neil pressed his fingertips together, then put them to his lips for a moment as he studied Patricia. "What makes you think I'll agree to this?"

"Because if Jessica really did know that someone is sabotaging your company, you'll want to know about it."

Neil smiled. "As tempting as it might be to have you around, Ms. Delaney, I can't agree to it."

Patricia pushed back her anger at his patronizing look and tone.

"I can be subtle in finding out what I need to know here, if you'll let me in your company for a week." Patricia allowed herself an amused grin. "Or I can be noisy—very noisy—in how I find out what I need to know. Noisy enough for the press to hear me. In fact, I think I already know quite a bit about both Gigi and you that hasn't appeared in print yet. . . ."

Neil stood suddenly, then leaned across the desk toward Patricia. "Are you trying to threaten me, my dear? Or blackmail me? Because I do not take well to either."

Patricia met Neil's gaze evenly. "I'm trying to give you an option."

Neil inhaled sharply and turned to his window. "I built this company from nothing, nothing at all but my vision, my ideas, my hard work. You know why I like looking out this window? I see the warehouse where this company's products are kept. I see the parking lot where this company's employees park their cars. Cars they buy with money I pay them. Cars they drive home to families they feed, houses they live in because I pay them. I've been named businessman of the year for companies my size two years in a row. I've been given outstanding citizen awards. I'm sure you know by now that in a year or so, I'm hoping to go into public service in local government, and a lot of people—very important people—are willing to support me."

Neil turned suddenly away from the window. His face

was bright red, his nostrils flared, his eyes burning. "And I know that when I do, people like you, hired by the media, hired by my competitors, will be digging into my life, my company. So I can assure you, I have run this business as cleanly as I can. And my life as . . . discreetly as I can. And I don't intend to have my ambitions ruined by my wife, or anyone else. So if you can find someone who is trying to hurt my company, or me, I want you to find them. So I'll give you your week. But just one week. And you'd better be damned discreet about this."

Neil grabbed the telephone receiver, pounded in a number, barked into the phone, "Get Allen up to my office right now!"

Then he glared at Patricia. "You can wait in my secretary's area until Allen gets here. He'll take care of processing you as a new employee, and get you settled into Jessica's office."

Patricia stood up. "Thank you."

"I just have one question," Neil said. "Why are you doing this for Gigi? It can't just be because she's your client. Or because you believe that she's innocent."

"She . . . was a very good friend to me. When I knew her before. I owe her," Patricia answered. It was a simplified version of the truth, but she wasn't about to share the details with this man. She didn't think he'd really understand.

She leaned over to pick up her briefcase and, as she did so, noticed for the first time the spots on the white carpet. She paused and studied the spots briefly; they looked like dried blood. There had been spots like that on the white carpeting at the Laffertys' house, she remembered.

Patricia stood up and walked out of the office without looking back at Neil, feeling his hard gaze watching her go. He could be dangerous, she thought. Maybe he was giving her a week because he thought she might truly be helpful to him. Or maybe he'd given her a week just to buy a little time for himself. If he was Jessica's killer, she had just put herself in a dangerous situation. It would be, Patricia decided, the last time she turned her back to the man, either figuratively or literally.

Chapter 14

That Allen Lafferty was Neil's son was obvious as soon
as he walked into Neil's outer office. Like Neil, he was tall
and thin; he had the same long, sharp features, same
pinched mouth, same critically focused blue eyes, same
blond hair brushed back from a high, pale forehead. The
most noticeable difference between father and son was that
Lafferty the younger dressed casually in sports pants and
jacket, but no tie.

That Allen Lafferty resented being Neil's son was also
obvious as soon as he began speaking to Dee Anne, Neil's
secretary.

"What did Dad summon me for this time?" he asked.
The question was a little sarcastic, a little tired, a little sad.

Patricia quietly gathered her purse and briefcase and
stood by the couch where she had been waiting for Allen.
She watched for Dee Anne's reaction with interest.

Apparently, Dee Anne was used to Allen's attitude. The
older woman quit typing on her personal computer's keyboard, looked up from her computer screen with a sigh, and
regarded Allen with a look over the top of her glasses that
was a combination of motherliness and exasperation.

"A temp for your department. Filling in for Jessica." Dee
Anne spoke crisply as she nodded in Patricia's direction.
"She's been waiting for you for over half an hour, since
your father—since Mr. Lafferty asked me to call for you."
Dee Anne went back to her work on the computer.

Allen turned, looked at Patricia, who immediately rushed
over with extended hand and eager grin. She had decided to

play her role as Jessica's fill-in as friendly, but not overly knowledgeable about the company or her assumed role in it. She planned to act like the kind of person who asked a lot of questions out of naïveté and overeagerness. She'd found in past situations that playing that role might net more answers than asking too many direct questions.

"I'm so glad to meet you, Mr. Lafferty, I hope—"

Allen smiled, tight-lipped. "My father is Mr. Lafferty. I'm Allen, so just call me that."

He turned and walked out through the glass double doors.

Allen Lafferty, like his father, was not going to volunteer anything easily.

"Good luck, dear," Dee Anne said without much confidence as Patricia hurried out after Allen.

Patricia caught up with Allen and walked alongside him. "Is the carpet white everywhere in this building?"

"Yes," Allen said. He walked very quickly, as if he hoped he'd lose Patricia, but she had no trouble matching his stride. "Why do you ask?"

"A cup of coffee might be nice. But this carpeting makes it kind of hard to, well, think of relaxing, you know?"

Allen laughed suddenly, sharply. "Well, well, maybe you'll work out all right after all," he said. Good, thought Patricia; it might be possible to get him to open up to her. But then he added, with a mixture of tiredness and disgust, "For one of Dad's little recruits, anyway."

Patricia grabbed his arm suddenly and stopped him. "Hey, what do you mean by that? I was just sent over here by the temp agency—"

"What temp agency?"

"Well, actually, my friend, Marcia, works for this temp agency—I can't remember its name—but anyway she called me this morning, saying she'd been sent here but Albert, that's her boyfriend, wanted her to go this week with him to Michigan, I think he's got a buddy up there with a hunting lodge or something, and Albert's really special to Marcia, and she hates all this computer stuff anyway, but I love it, I mean I took a data-entry class in college last fall because I hated working the restaurant scene—I'm getting too old for that, you know?—and I really liked it, and so I was real excited when Marcia called me this morning, and said could I fill in for her, they needed someone to temp for the woman who'd been in the news this weekend—"

Allen closed his eyes, held his hands up.

"Oops, I'm sorry, did I say too much about that woman?" Patricia asked, widening her eyes. "I mean, I guess it is kind of sensitive, her being found in your family's pool and all, and, oh damn, I'm sorry, I'm saying too much again, aren't I—"

"Okay, okay, I'm convinced," Allen said. "You're not one of Dad's little friends." He opened his eyes and looked Patricia up and down. "You'd do, but he'd never put up with your mouth. I don't care how you got this job. Just pay attention to what I tell you to do. Deal?"

"Sure, I'm just excited, that's all, that—"

Allen walked off suddenly. Patricia caught up with him again, but walked alongside him in silence to a cluster of cubicles at the other end of the floor. Allen had a small office, into which Patricia followed him.

She glanced around quickly, made note of the fact that the office was, unlike his father's, an utter mess. Files and papers were stacked everywhere, even on top of his computer screen. His desk was littered with empty soda cans, some of them knocked over. The only semi-organized spot was a small end table by the window, on which was stacked several piles of magazines.

Patricia sat down in the visitors' chair and smiled eagerly at Allen. "So I'm going to be working for you, and you'll show me everything about the computer systems. . . ."

Allen stiffened. "No one knows everything about the computer system here but me. I set it up, I designed it, I maintain and control it. You'll get access to the parts I give you, and enter what you're told."

Patricia looked a little disappointed, which wasn't entirely role-playing. Nothing was going to come easily on this case, she thought, including digging through the Lafferty Products computer system for the data supposedly on the diskette that Jessica had had.

She dutifully dug a pen and paper out of her purse. "All right. Geez, I'm just trying to learn what I can about computers and business. I hope you don't mind if I ask a few questions. Like how many people work for you?"

Allen grinned. "You."

"Me? Just me?"

"Yep. Before my father insisted we take on Jessica, I was the only one who took care of the computer system."

"Oh. That was nice of your—of Mr. Lafferty. You must have been swamped."

Allen cast a derisive glance at Patricia and snorted in a half laugh as he settled into his chair. "Right. My dear father just has a bug up his butt about me learning more about the company, not wasting my talent, following in his footsteps." He snorted again and turned on his computer.

Patricia kept her eyes turned on Allen, but watched what he was doing with the computer indirectly.

"So have you?"

"Have I what?"

"Have you learned more about the company, since you hired someone to free up your time?"

"I'm not interested in this company. I have plans of my own. And Jessica wasn't that good at even the basic tasks I gave her." Allen grinned. "She freed up just enough of my time so I could spend less time here—not something my father cared for."

Allen's computer was one of the most powerful personal computers currently on the market, Patricia noted. After the computer started up, a menu of software choices came up on the screen. Allen had not typed in a password to get this far.

"It must be kind of tense around here, I mean since Jessica was murdered and found in your family's pool. I read in the paper she knew your stepmother somehow. . . ."

Allen looked at Patricia coldly. She grew quiet, glanced at

his computer screen as she turned her eyes from him, supposedly out of sudden discomfort. The menu screen, Patricia noted mentally, had four options: word processing, electronic mail, database, and games. She suppressed a smile at that last option.

"Look, I don't know exactly how Jessica knew my stepmother. And business goes on as usual. No one around here's talking about it. You want to know what I know? Watch the evening news. Got it?"

Patricia looked back up at Allen. She wondered if he had any idea how much he looked like his father with his lips unhappily pinched together, his eyes distrustingly narrowed.

"Sorry," Patricia said with chagrin. "Sometimes my curiosity gets out of hand. I really just want to learn everything I can. . . ."

She hesitated and glanced up. Allen was staring at his computer screen. He had tapped the enter key to bring up the database and was entering a password. Damn, thought Patricia. It always amazed her when she thought about just how much data existed, unprotected and vulnerable, on computers across corporate America. But not on Allen's computer.

"Yeah, yeah, I know," Allen said. "Then pay attention. I'm giving you a brief overview of the database you'll be using. Now, the first thing you have to understand . . ."

The database Allen had set up contained Lafferty Products' inventory, customer billing, purchasing, personnel, accounts receivable, and payroll data. Allen showed Patricia the basics of how data was entered, how reports were generated. It wasn't hard to encourage him to show off his knowledge and show her more than he necessarily had to or should. For many who were computer literate, Patricia knew, it was an almost irresistible urge to show off for the computer illiterate. Techno-knowledge, the new class divider.

The truth was, Patricia was very knowledgeable of the database software he had used to create the Lafferty Products database. It was a commonly used database package, and she used an earlier version of it for her business records on her office computer. If she could copy the data off of Allen's machine—or perhaps find a backup copy of the data—she wouldn't need to use his computer to explore Lafferty Products' company records; she could do so on her own computer.

By the time Allen was done, a knot of pain had gathered in the middle of Patricia's forehead. Playing dumb was at times the most difficult, although valuable, part of her investigative skills.

She forced herself to smile. "Wow. I'm really impressed with what you've set up here. I can't believe before Jessica came, you entered all the data yourself."

Allen looked disdainful. "I didn't and I don't. This machine is networked to computers in payroll, accounts payable, and other departments. Managers there enter the appropriate data, and send it to my machine. Some areas haven't been automated yet, like the warehouse's inventory reports and personnel data. Those are still filled out manually. Jessica's job was, and yours will be, to enter that data in the system."

"Then what do you do?"

"I'm working on automating the parts of the company that still need it. And I take care of reports that managers want out of the data. Usually that means Dad." Allen smiled thinly. "He likes a detailed look at all the numbers. Frequently."

Patricia heard a tap on the door. "Come in," called Allen. The door swung open.

A handsome man, with auburn hair streaked silver at the temples, hazel eyes, and a casual easy grin, came through the door quickly, almost said something, then stopped short when he saw Patricia, looking momentarily confused. He obviously had not expected someone to be in Allen's office.

"Sorry. Didn't realize you had a visitor. Just checking to see if we're still on for lunch."

Allen glanced at his watch. His eyebrows arched suddenly. "Sorry. Didn't realize the time." He looked up and smiled at the man. It was the first time that morning that Patricia felt she had seen Allen with a genuine grin. He looked at Patricia. "This is Gregory Finster, our director of personnel."

Patricia looked back at Gregory, wondering at Allen's sudden change in tone. Up until now, Allen had disparagingly referred to Lafferty Products as "Dad's company." Now, he was introducing Gregory as "our" director. Was it out of a sudden pride in the company, somehow subconsciously inspired by Gregory? Or because of some fear of Gregory that made Allen think he had better show him respect? But Allen seemed suddenly put at ease simply by Gregory's presence, and Gigi had described Gregory as a family friend.

Patricia smiled at Gregory. "Nice to meet you."

"And you, too. You're . . . ?"

"Oh, sorry. Gregory, this is Patricia Delaney. She's a temp filling in Jessica's position."

Gregory's smile faded, and his focus on Patricia tightened. Patricia felt uneasy; something was going through his mind as he studied her, something more than simply assessing a new, temporary recruit. But she refused to let her own smile drop, or to pull her gaze from him. She had taken on the role of eager ingenue to see what she could learn, and as long as it worked for her, she wasn't giving it up.

Then Gregory smiled suddenly. "Well, Patricia, good luck in your new position." He looked at Allen. "Ready? Or do you need a few more minutes with Patricia?"

"No, we can continue after lunch. Patricia, I'll show you to your work area on our way out. You may want to drop your things off, get a little settled in, before you go to lunch yourself."

Patricia followed Gregory and Allen out. Something, she thought, had passed between Gregory and Allen, something that went beyond the usual office camaraderie. And something had gone off in Gregory's mind about her when he learned her name.

Chapter 15

Jessica's office was actually one of several cubicles outside of Allen's small office, her work space a spartan example of the modern, modular office in which walls were really large movable dividers covered in a gray nubby cloth; the desk was actually a laminated surface attached to the dividers; lamps were not necessary because overhead lighting panels in the ceiling lit the whole area; and doors were no longer available to define a worker's space as private.

The whole concept, Patricia supposed, was to make the work space easily reconfigurable as needed, and since workers were supposed to be working together and constantly sharing information, who needed doors? Patricia dumped her purse and notepad on the desk, sat down tiredly in the chair after Gregory and Allen left, and felt a momentary nostalgia for her office, even its spilled-taco carpeting, inept air conditioner, the infusion of grease and sugar smells from the doughnut shop below, and the fully functional doors that shut and locked.

Patricia flipped past the notes she had dutifully taken, but didn't really need, during Allen's explanation of her duties in filling in for Jessica. She paused. She needed to stop, take a few real notes, put in writing the questions that had been nagging at her over the past few days, questions she hadn't had time to consider fully since so much had been happening.

Jessica told Gigi that sabotage of some sort was occurring at Lafferty Products. Presume, thought Patricia, that this were true; that Gigi hadn't made up the story for some reason Patricia had yet to discern, or that Jessica hadn't made it up to con Gigi out of twenty-five grand after all.

Then, thought Patricia, consider what kind of sabotage. Patricia started a list of the kinds she'd observed before in other cases: fraud, theft, selling proprietary secrets to competitors, corporate espionage, legal violations.

Supposedly Jessica had evidence of this sabotage on a computer diskette. Patricia closed her eyes, inhaled, went back mentally to the afternoon she had hauled Jessica out of the pool. Nothing on Jessica but her clothes. No memory of a purse, satchel, briefcase. But in the confusion of the moment, and the chaos of an unfamiliar house, she could have easily missed something small like a computer diskette. She had not, after all, thoroughly searched the house as the police would have.

It would help to know whether or not the police had found the diskette. But Patricia doubted they had, if Gigi's story about coming back to a clean, quiet house and leaving it in that state were true. If someone had tossed the house to make it look as though Gigi had fled the scene, the same someone could have taken the diskette. But Jessica could have had other copies, perhaps here. Or at her apartment, thought Patricia.

Neil, Allen, Rita, Gregory, thought Patricia. They all were members of or close in some way to the Lafferty family, and they all were directly involved in Lafferty Products.

Yet anyone from Lafferty Products might have been, say, defrauding the company; been discovered by Jessica when, perhaps, she found something unusual in the company database; then learned of Jessica's knowledge through, say, her failed attempt at blackmail; then, not trusting Jessica, followed Jessica around until one afternoon she went to the Lafferty house. . . .

Patricia tossed the notepad and pen against the desk in disgust. Great, she thought. She'd narrowed down the evidence to revealing just about any kind of corporate sabotage possible, and narrowed the possibilities of whoever was perpetuating the sabotage, and thus who had a motive to murder Jessica, to anyone who worked at Lafferty Products. That was only about two hundred and fifty people.

Patricia sighed and picked up the notepad. She tore the top sheet of her jotted notes off the pad, folded it carefully, and put it in a zippered section of her purse.

All right, then, she thought. The best way to find this person would be to concentrate first on Neil, Allen, Rita, and Gregory, but also find out who else Jessica knew, whom she talked with on breaks, with whom she went out to lunch or after-work drinks. Second, presume Jessica had a second copy of the evidence or that Patricia could find it in the company computer system.

Patricia glanced around the small cubicle. Too risky a place to hide evidence like that, and the cubicle seemed mostly cleared out. Still, she thought, it never pays to overlook the obvious. Sometimes the obvious really is the solution.

She opened an overhead bin. Computer manuals, office supplies. She leafed through the manuals and looked inside the envelopes. Nothing of interest there. Another bin was empty. An in-box had forms ready to be input. A box of tissue was on the desk.

A company-issued calendar was pushpinned into one of the cloth-wrapped walls, each day neatly marked through with a hot-pink felt-tip diagonal line, as straight and neat as if Jessica had used a ruler to make the line. The days were marked through up to and including the day of Jessica's death in the Lafferty pool. So, thought Patricia with a little startle at the insight, it was a ritual, this marking through of the days, that Jessica performed in the morning. This was the first insight into Jessica that she had gotten on her own, rather than from Gigi or the Las Vegas detective or someone else. She would not have thought of Jessica as given to such a detailed ritual, or as a morning person. She took down the calendar and flipped back through it. Nothing was written in the calendar. The first day marked through was April 12. Patricia hung the calendar back up.

Patricia opened the lap drawer. Pushpins were sorted by color; paper clips were assorted by size; a few fast-food coupons were arranged alphabetically and paper-clipped together; pencils were precisely sharpened, their sharpened points all lined up in the same direction. There was one blue ballpoint pen, one black ballpoint pen, and the hot-pink felt pen Jessica had apparently used to mark off her days at Lafferty Products. Patricia picked up the felt pen, uncapped it. An overly sweet scent of peppermint came from the pen; Patricia recapped it. Everything but the pen was standard company issue and bespoke of a precise, detailed person; the felt pen was the only bit of personal whimsy Patricia had encountered. Perhaps Jessica really had been trying hard, at first, to follow a new straight-and-narrow path. Perhaps she thought that meant absolute, zealous precision in all things, and a total removal of personal mementos from her office.

Patricia opened up one more drawer, this one for hanging file folders. The folders were labeled neatly, arranged alphabetically, and contained nothing startling: time sheets, memos regarding a company picnic just passed, and a reminder of the company dress policy, stuffily worded and issued by Neil himself. A copy of Jessica's employee information form, including her current address, an apartment in Montgomery. Nothing was listed for *previous address*. Next of kin was a Naomi Taylor, grandmother, but no address was given. Education was listed as a high school in the Cincinnati area, and a year at the University of Cincinnati, where of course Gigi had told Neil she'd met Jessica, and where Jessica had never actually gone. Previous work experience was listed as *hostess*. Patricia smiled at that and jotted down the grandmother's name and Jessica's current address on her pad; then she ripped that sheet off and folded it up and put it in her purse's zippered section along with the other sheet.

She flipped through a few more file folders; they contained forms sorted by department and arranged in reverse chronological order by the date on which they were filled out. In the upper right-hand corner of each form was a precise, hot-pink check mark, implying that Jessica had either checked off each form to remind herself that she'd already entered it, or had verified her entry against a printout. The woman, Patricia thought, certainly appeared to have been precise and detail-oriented.

At the back of the file drawer, as she got to the end of the files, she noticed a small box that had been previously obscured by the file folders. Patricia opened the box and arched an eyebrow at what she saw; not that anything in it was shocking, but just that it held Jessica's few personal items that had been packed up and were ready to be removed from the office. The box contained a ceramic coffee mug, navy blue with yellow sunflowers painted on the side; a photo, 35mm, of an older woman, poorly focused, taken with a camera that imprinted the date on the print. The photo was dated just two months before in July. The woman had slouched shoulders, a stooped back, and wore a housedress and a floppy hat that shaded her eyes. But her chin and mouth were tilted proudly, almost defiantly. She held a cat. The picture was displayed in an inexpensive gold-colored frame. Patricia took the picture out of the frame, checked between the picture and cardboard backing. There were no notes, nothing written on the back of the picture. She reassembled the picture.

The only other items were a package of breath mints, a tin of aspirin, a small hairbrush and mirror, a fuchsia lipstick, and an unopened package of suntan-colored panty hose.

Had someone, upon learning of Jessica's death, packed her personal items up to be sent somewhere? But Jessica had only just been murdered, and the box was stashed behind the file folders at the back of the drawer, not sitting out in the open as if someone recently cleared her belongings off the work surface. It appeared more likely that Jessica herself had packed up her few personal items, which would indicate that she knew she would be leaving, as Gigi had said Jessica told her she needed to. Had Jessica meant to come back for the items, back to the office after being at Gigi's to collect her final payment, or had she been in such a hurry to meet Gigi and collect the money that she'd simply forgotten about them? Either way, it indicated an intent to leave the office permanently and was a small, if circumstantial, confirmation of what Gigi had told Patricia that Jessica had said.

Patricia was surprised at the sense of relief the box gave her. She wanted to believe Gigi. She did not want to discover that her actions on Gigi's behalf were entirely foolhardy.

"Mr. Lafferty requested that I come by to check on how you are doing. And to bring you a temporary badge."

Patricia started and looked up. It was Dee Anne, Neil's secretary, who was looking at her a bit suspiciously. Interesting. Was he concerned about what she was up to? How much had he told Dee Anne? Probably nothing more than what she said; it would be reasonable for an employer—many employers anyway—to show moderate concern for a new employee he'd personally brought on board, but Patricia didn't believe for a second that Neil cared at all about Patricia's comfort in settling in to her new, temporary role.

Patricia accepted the badge and clipped it to her collar. Then she picked up the coffee mug, held it up, grinned. "Looking for one of these. I'm doing fine, but I could really go for another cup of coffee."

Dee Anne smiled, a little more relaxed. "Come with me, then."

Patricia stood up and followed Dee Anne. Time to adopt the chatty, amiable persona again.

"You know," she said, "it feels kind of weird, working in Jessica's cube, I mean, I'm really, really glad to have the job, but it's just, well, strange, you know? I bet it's even weirder for everyone else around here, I mean, who knew her and stuff, I mean all her friends here." Patricia paused. Dee Anne didn't say anything, kept her chin resolutely pointed forward.

"I mean, everyone must be talking about what happened, all her friends here, aren't they?" Patricia persisted.

"Jessica wasn't here long enough to make friends with that many people." Dee Anne's terse tone indicated that Jessica really wasn't all that missed, and maybe even wasn't all that well liked.

"Well, but she was friends with the Laffertys. I mean Allen said . . ." Patricia let her voice trail off as if she were suddenly unsure of herself.

Dee Anne cast her a quizzical, long look, some of the suspicion returning to her expression. Her voice was a mixture of amusement and bitterness. "Yes. She was close friends with the Laffertys. Quite close."

Again the tone implied more than the words; perhaps Jessica's affair with Neil was common company gossip? It wouldn't take long for something like that to get around any company, what's more a company this size. Maybe there was another spurned lover besides Rita Ames. Perhaps that would be sufficient reason to murder Jessica and use Gigi as a scapegoat.

"Still," Patricia persisted, shaking her head, "it's got to be strange, a coworker dead like that, the boss's wife missing. Must be hard to keep on working, with everyone talking about it . . ."

Dee Ann cleared her throat and gave Patricia a critical look. "No one's talking about it. We're all keeping hard at work. It's what Mr. Lafferty expects."

"That's good, I mean that everyone's working hard, but it's kind of sad, don't you think?" Patricia shook her head.

"What is?"

"To die like that, and not have anybody where you work miss you." Come on, thought Patricia, give a little, Dee Anne. Neil had his secretary very well trained in terseness. She usually had an easier time than this in leading people to give her information. "I mean, didn't she go out with anybody for drinks or anything after work?"

Dee Anne smiled thinly. "I really wouldn't know. I myself generally go home straight after work. Most people do.

Occasionally, I did see her chatting with or leaving with Rita at lunch, but then Rita's job is to train employees, so they could have been friends, or maybe their talks were job-related. And of late she and Allen left after work together. I thought perhaps they—"

Dee Anne stopped and shook her head as if she suddenly realized she was saying too much.

Patricia wondered why Rita would want to spend time with Jessica, especially if Neil had broken off with Rita for Jessica. And Allen had seemed eager to dismiss Jessica as an inferior, hardly worth his notice.

"Rita?" Patricia asked. "She trains employees? There's so much I want to learn. . . ."

"Rita Ames. Manager of sales and employee training. I expect if you become a permanent employee here, you'll get to know her." Dee Anne turned into a break area, gestured at a coffeepot that was half-full of coffee. "Here's what you're looking for. Can you find your way back to Jessica's—I mean, your cubicle?"

Patricia nodded. "Yes. Thanks." She busied herself with pouring coffee.

"Very well," Dee Anne said. "I'll check on you again, periodically, to see how you're doing."

Patricia grinned broadly. "Thanks."

Dee Anne left, and Patricia remained in the break area for a few minutes sipping her coffee. She wanted Dee Anne to be well on her way back to her office, or on her way out for lunch, when she left the break area. She really had no intention of going straight back to Jessica's cube; she intended to try to find Rita Ames's office. After a few minutes she went back out into the office area.

Patricia wandered for a while, then found a secretary who directed her to Rita's office. The door was shut. Patricia knocked anyway.

"Come in," a weary female voice said.

Patricia turned the knob and entered. At least something was going easily for her today; Rita was the sort to work through lunch. Rita looked up at Patricia from behind her desk with interest but some wariness. She was an athletic-looking woman; angular, pronounced facial bones, intelligent eyes under heavy dark brows, short straight dark hair cropped close, little makeup, white blouse, simple turquoise suit, gold chain, and gold earrings. Her work was arranged neatly before her and on the credenza behind her. She had a partially eaten sandwich and a can of diet cola on the desk before her. She didn't seem at all Neil's type, or the type who would go for Neil. Patricia thought that under different circumstances she would like to truly get to know her, maybe even become friends with her.

As it was, Patricia gave a chatty introduction of herself as new-temp-on-the-block, then said, "Oh, I see I'm disturbing you at lunch, but I was really hoping to talk with you. Someone told me you had really helped Jessica a lot and I thought maybe, well, since I'm at least temporarily in her position . . ."

Rita patted mouth with a napkin, frowned slightly. "Sit down," she ordered. Patricia sat. Bringing up the Jessica connection touched a nerve, she thought.

"Who told you I helped Jessica?"

Patricia thought for a second. Saying the truth, that it was Dee Anne, would probably only serve to get Dee Anne in trouble. And Dee Anne had not been mentioned by Gigi as someone close to the Lafferty family. Why not throw out Allen and Gregory's names and see what reaction that got?

Patricia smiled. "Allen Lafferty. And a, um, Gregory Finster."

Rita's frown deepened. She licked her lips. "They said I helped Jessica?"

"Oh yes. Career advice. Taking her to lunch and all. Mentoring, I think that's what one of my professors called it in a business class." Patricia smiled brightly. "You don't have to take me to lunch, I'm not asking that, but I thought since you were willing to be so helpful to Jessica, and I'm filling her position now . . ."

"I talked to her once or twice. I gave her no more help

than I would any other employee." Rita's tone was now abrupt, dismissing.

Patricia managed to look flustered. "Oh, I'm sorry, I guess this soon after her death, you'd be a little sensitive, losing a friend like that. . . ."

"I'm sorry, of course, to hear of her death, but Jessica was not my friend. I advised her of career possibilities and the training she might need for them, as I would any other employee. She was interested in sales, so she frequently attended Gregory's motivational seminars for the sales staff, even though she wasn't, obviously, on the staff. A special courtesy for Jessica, but you might ask if you could attend if you're interested in that area." Rita smiled thinly. She was trying, Patricia understood, to get rid of her.

Patricia settled back more comfortably in her chair. "But I thought Mr. Finster was director of personnel, and you . . ."

"Run sales and training." Rita's smile became more brittle. "Oh, I do, I do. But, you see, Gregory used to work for me doing sales training until Neil promoted him a few months ago. Still, Gregory likes to keep his hand in training, especially with new people."

Rita's smiled remained forced. She was attempting, without success, to hide her bitterness over her former employee's sudden rise to a position above her own.

"Oh, well, thanks for the tip. When's the next motivational seminar?" Patricia asked.

"He's on the second day of one now. They last three days, a couple of hours in the afternoon. You'll have to ask Allen about permission to go. Now, Ms. . . . ."

"Delaney."

"Delaney. Right. I will be glad to give you more advice later." Rita looked amused. "You might want to spend a few days on your current assignment, however."

Rita was again trying to dismiss her, but Patricia remained seated. She glanced at the photos hanging around the room. Rita had been made uncomfortable by the connection with Jessica. Let's see, thought Patricia, how she would do with a connection to Neil?

Patricia looked directly at Rita and smiled. "Those are great photos. I noticed the ones you did in Mr. Lafferty's office, too. He was very complimentary of them. You must do a lot of photography."

Rita did not respond. She just stared at Patricia for a long moment. The reference to the photos seemed, at some level, to distress her more than the reference to Jessica.

Rita cleared her throat, finally. "I don't do photography anymore."

"Oh, well, thanks for your help," Patricia said. "I'm sure we'll be talking again. I tend to have lots of questions."

"Did you ever hear the saying that curiosity killed the cat?" Rita asked. Her sudden smile was not pleasant.

"I'm a dog lover myself," Patricia said brightly.

"I'd be careful anyway. Curiosity—now that's something you and Jessica seem to have in common."

"Thanks," Patricia said, and left the office. Were Rita's comments meant as warning or threat? she wondered as she worked her way through the labyrinth of gray cube walls back to Jessica's cube.

Patricia was getting the impression that in her two months at Lafferty Products, Jessica had not won many friends. Allen, Neil, and Rita seemed more than eager to distance themselves from anything more than a cordial work association with her, although others indicated that she was more closely associated with them.

Now, thought Patricia, she needed to learn more about Gregory, supposedly a Lafferty family friend and Jessica's mentor, and a man who had done nothing to befriend himself to Rita.

Chapter 16

Gregory Finster pounded his fist against the computer keyboard, then cursed under his breath as the computer beeped and displayed an error message. It could not, of course, interpret the random characters that he had entered by pounding the keyboard with frustration at the cryptic message *failed with init sense*.

Gregory pushed back from his desk, muttering, and swiveled in his chair toward the window. Then he laughed out loud at himself.

He did not really need to understand the computer. His secretary could take care of helping him with the day-to-day functions of the damned thing. And Allen, of course Allen could most certainly take care of all the rest. Allen was a self-proclaimed computer expert. Gregory did not understand enough about computers to know if that was true or not, but he knew that Allen was putting into and getting out of the Lafferty Products computer system just what Gregory wanted. He didn't have to understand how.

Through his window, Gregory watched people returning to the warehouse after lunch. He had never understood much about machines, computers, or otherwise. His own genius was with people, particularly manipulating them to get what he wanted.

Take the people going into the warehouse. Any one of them, he was certain, would do his bidding, if he had enough time to work with them, and never consider that they had been manipulated. It was just a matter of identifying what mattered most to them, and making them think he

138

could help them achieve it. And, of course, it was a matter of identifying if they had anything of worth he needed from them. Gregory did not waste his talents on people who didn't have something he wanted.

Looking back, his gift of gentle manipulation of the human psyche was something he had had all along, using it even as a child. It was a realization he first had while he studied psychology and counseling in college. His studies merely taught him the vocabulary he needed to define and sharpen his talent and to convince others of its legitimacy.

By the time he had been a counselor for two years, he was amazed at how easily he could suggest an idea or belief to someone so that he or she assumed it was his or her own, then convince that person to act on the belief.

He quickly tired of using such a skill expressly for the good of his clients. The skipped payments, the clients who suddenly dropped out of therapy, even a few lawsuits from clients who somehow came to believe his methods were less than appropriate: all these things combined to convince him that his skills were underappreciated, and certainly underrewarded.

And so he had left private practice and entered the business world. His career there was bumpy at times as well, when again he encountered the less-than-appreciative. But now, at last, his efforts were being handsomely rewarded. Soon he would again aggressively and publicly launch his persona into the business world, and this time nothing would stand in his way.

Allen had been perfect in his role to help Gregory. Would it be kinder to let him down slowly over time, or suddenly? Gregory shrugged. It didn't matter. Allen's work was nearly complete for him.

Gregory frowned as he thought of his lunch with Allen. He hadn't told Allen just yet about Patricia Delaney. He wondered if he should have shared with him that Gigi had told him about Patricia. Allen tended to overreact at times, especially about anything concerning his stepmother, and Gregory needed time to think about what Patricia's presence could mean in the long run. Certainly her being here today was an unexpected, unwelcome turn. It would help if he knew just how much Gigi had told her.

Gregory checked his watch, then sighed when he saw the time. He had half an hour before he began the motivational training class, and he really should spend the time preparing. But later tonight he would think carefully about this Delaney woman and how she fit into the human equations he had so carefully engineered. But then, thought Gregory, that was the price of his talent; sometimes it became just a little tricky to keep straight the confidences, the nuances of personality, and the motivations of all the people he puppeteered.

Chapter 17

Patricia sat near the back of the small auditorium and suppressed a yawn.

On the one hand, it seemed like a waste of her time to come to Gregory's motivational training meeting. She did not seem to be learning anything that, on the surface at least, pertained directly to her case.

On the other hand, Gregory Finster was one of the people whom Gigi had cited as being close to both Lafferty Products and the Lafferty family. Observing Gregory at the head of the auditorium, pacing in front of the podium, tie loosened, hands gesturing grandly, at least gave Patricia some insight into his character.

In a word, he was a huckster. At the turn of the century he would have hitched up a wagon and gone from town to town hawking medicinals. Now, thought Patricia, he was hawking psychobabble—a few surface-level psychological concepts, appealingly packaged for the corporate setting as self-motivational selling skills, appealingly presented by a handsome, confident man with a booming, compelling voice and a double-breasted power suit, the jacket unbuttoned and the tie loosened just so. His persona was carefully displayed to underscore his message: believe me, trust me, I'm on your side, I can help you win, just believe me, trust me. . . .

At her next thought, Patricia stifled both a yawn and a smile: was her ingrained cynicism protecting her from the huckster, or keeping her from benefiting from the full impact of his message? For certainly, most of the people around her, about fifteen altogether, seemed eagerly receptive to his message. Yet this was a group that would walk away from the street-corner preacher, laughing at his urgent appeal, or feel slightly superior as they remote-control-flipped away from an eager "product representative" on a late-night infomercial.

Poppy had called sin and salvation two sides of the same coin. It seemed, thought Patricia, that that coin could appear in many forms.

"Do you really want to believe in yourself? Do you really want to be a winner? Then you must confront your fears!" Gregory was saying.

This was a man who, on the surface, had no fear. Yet he had started, slightly, when she met him earlier in Allen's office, and had done the same thing when she had come into this auditorium. That unsettled her a little.

Suddenly Gregory was looking at her, eyes sharp, his finger pointing. "You! What fears burn inside of you? You must face those flames, walk to them, walk into them!"

Patricia stared back at him, not sure for a few tense seconds if she was really expected to answer. Certainly, she would not identify her fears in front of a group of unknown people. . . .

But then Gregory moved on, pointing his finger at another member of the audience, asking the same question. Patricia relaxed a little, realizing Gregory was using an overly dramatic technique, and overly dramatic words, to command attention to his one-man show. But for just a few seconds even Patricia had felt compelled by his manner, by his persona, to answer an intimate question in front of a group of strangers if that was what he asked of her.

Whatever she thought of Gregory's message, she realized he was not a person to be dismissed lightly. Researching him tonight, she thought, should prove illuminating.

Chapter 18

Small clusters of employees, two or three at a time, came out of Lafferty Products, said good-bye among themselves, then went their separate ways to their cars. Patricia sat in her truck watching the employees leave. She wanted to get a feel for when the buildings cleared out.

The remainder of her day at Lafferty Products had confirmed her earlier conclusion about Jessica. If Jessica had gotten close to anyone during her time at Lafferty Products, no one was willing to reveal it. Patricia had taken frequent breaks from doing the little work Allen gave her and chatted with the occupants of the nearby cubicles. While no one said anything negative about Jessica, no one expressed any real grief or regret about her demise, either. Patricia got the sense that Jessica had not gone out of her way to make friends, or to accept friendly overtures from any of her coworkers. If she really had found evidence of sabotage, she probably had done so on her own.

The most obvious place for Jessica to find evidence of sabotage would be in a discrepancy in the reports she had entered, which were for the personnel department, recently headed by Gregory Finster, purchasing, and the warehouse inventory. Purchasing was supervised by Abigail Pagado; the warehouse by Terrence McSherry. Patricia made a note to look into the backgrounds of both.

Probably whatever Jessica found would be something most people would miss, but Jessica's cubicle indicated that she was a person who paid greater attention to detail than the average person, who would pore over her own work incessantly to make sure it was accurate. It was possible that in the course of doing so, she had found something to make her raise questions.

Patricia had made copies of all the reports that Jessica had yet to enter, but what she really wanted was the data Jessica would have seen during her brief time at Lafferty Products. Since, Patricia learned, the data was cleared off her computer after it was sent to Allen's computer, that meant that Patricia needed access to what was on Allen's machine. What she wanted to do was copy his data off his machine onto a diskette and then study it on her own computer in her office, something she obviously couldn't do until his office and the surrounding cubicles were clear.

Patricia pulled her notebook out of her purse and wrote notes on what she had learned at Lafferty Products. Then she turned to another page and wrote in the upper left corner, *Naomi Taylor, Grandmother.* She wanted to talk to her as soon as she learned her address; hopefully a little research back at her office would help her there. Then on another page she wrote Jessica's home address in the upper left corner. She wanted to go by Jessica's apartment and see what she could learn, maybe talk to the landlord. Plus she wanted to see what more she could learn on her own about this Abigail Pagado, Terrence McSherry, and Gregory Finster, since they ran the areas from which Jessica had entered data. And then there was the task of simply reviewing her notes and writing them up in a coherent fashion so that, she hoped, a picture would start to emerge from the puzzle pieces she had gathered. She just hoped it wasn't a picture of herself as a chump for being led astray by Gigi.

Patricia sighed. She was tired. She had slept little in the past few days, and there was so much she needed to get done as quickly as possible. She checked her watch. She had a few hours before she had a date to meet with Dean to go to the Oktoberfest along the Ohio River in downtown Cincinnati. She had considered calling him earlier to cancel, but she didn't think that would really be a good idea. Their relationship was fragile enough; she didn't want to alienate him further. She needed, somehow, to find the strength to talk with him openly and honestly.

Patricia snapped her notebook shut abruptly and put it back in the satchel. She briefly considered writing *Dean* in the upper left-hand corner of one of her notebook pages. Dean, of course, was not a lead for this case. But somehow on this case what she had vowed to never let happen had happened: her personal and professional lives were entangled, one informing the other, just as the past was spilling over into the present, just as she needed to resolve issues from the past to get on with the present and future.

Patricia glanced around her truck's inside. It was a mess, an exception that proved the rule of her neatness and preciseness in every other area of her life. An acquaintance who was an FBI agent once told her that one could learn a great deal about a person's personality just from their car, that the details of the vehicle they drove could tell them about a person's past, childhood, likelihood of committing particular crimes, tendencies, obsessions, and so on. Patricia wondered what her apparent need to let her truck slip into a mess when everything else in her life was precise, orderly, clean, and neat said about her. She smiled ruefully at herself. That she had unresolved parts of her life? But then, she supposed everyone had. And always would.

Patricia looked at her watch again. No real time to go back in and get the data she wanted. She wanted to take her time and be careful about it. But she could get in a visit to Jessica's apartment on the way to meet Dean. She pawed through the junk—food wrappers, notes, grocery lists, her nephew's bright green toy phone, abandoned in the truck when Patricia bought it from her brother, which she jokingly referred to as her "car phone." The toy phone was another exception that proved the rule—in everyplace else in her life, she was completely high-tech, but in her truck she refused to get a real car phone, preferring the bright green toy phone as a humorous reminder not to rely too completely on technology in her work or her life. Finally she found her book of maps of the greater Cincinnati area. She thumbed through and quickly found Jessica's address, calculated the best way to get there, and pulled out of the Lafferty parking lot.

After twenty-six minutes of weaving through rush-hour traffic, Patricia pulled into the parking lot by Jessica's apartment building, a two-story, flat-roofed, square building set behind a florist's shop on a busy intersection that featured mostly fast-food joints and gas stations. Patricia parked by an old car with a flat tire that looked like it had sat in that condition for a long time. Not the fanciest address, but still, to Jessica it had to be a lot better than a correctional institution, and it was in a safe, clean, working-class area, and on the metropolitan-area bus line. It looked like for a little while, anyway, Jessica really had tried to get her life together. Patricia headed into the building, wondering what had derailed her.

Just inside the front door, in a small dark entry area, Patricia found a cluster of small mailboxes. There were three levels of units; stairs led down to a semibasement area, and up to two other floors. The place smelled of mildew. Patricia scanned the names above the mailboxes. Jessica's apartment number was two. Patricia went down the stairs, and the mildew smell worsened. The door to Jessica's apartment was open. Patricia stepped inside.

The place was small; a tiny family room held a television, a couch, a chair, and a coffee table, all of which looked new and rented. And the place was a wreck. Cushions were askew on the couch and chair, the contents of the drawer of the coffee table dumped on the floor, a houseplant turned over into the middle of the carpet, magazines strewn about.

Voices came through the doorway in the back wall that led, Patricia guessed, to a kitchenette. One of the voices belonged to Detective Nancy Grey. Patricia smiled at the recognition. Another doorway stood to the left; she decided to duck quickly into it for a quick look around before letting her presence be known.

This room was the bedroom, and it was in a similar

mess. The bed was undone. Clothes from a chest of drawers were piled in the middle of the bed. The nightstand's drawer was open and empty. A tiny bathroom went off the back of the bedroom. The cabinets were opened, jars askew; a hamper stood open and the clothes that had presumably been in it dumped on the floor next to it. As in the family room, the furniture in the bedroom looked new and rented.

Patricia considered possible reasons for the mess. Maybe the apartment was the exception that proved the rule for Jessica, or maybe her cubicle was; maybe she was really a slob? No. A messy truck or purse or briefcase or cabinet, perhaps; but someone almost obsessively precise and neat as Jessica was at her office wouldn't live with a place like this. Maybe Jessica had been in a hurry to pack, get out, and had had a hard time getting her things sorted and together. Patricia pushed open a closet door. Clothes were still hung, and a suitcase lay open, but empty, on the closet floor. Okay, thought Patricia, she'd had one hell of a party. But there were no plates or drink cans or cups around, none of the typical debris of a party. That left one explanation. The place had been tossed by someone, looking for something. The diskette Gigi had described as containing Jessica's evidence of sabotage at Lafferty Products? Gigi's story was gaining at least circumstantial credibility, thought Patricia.

"Not much of a housekeeper, was she?"

Patricia started and turned around. Detective Nancy Grey stood in the doorway with an expression that was a mixture of irritation and amusement.

"I'm not sure yet. I haven't seen the kitchenette, after all."

"It's no different from this." Nancy gave a gesture that was far more encompassing than the scope of the room. It made Patricia smile.

"Still, I want to see it."

"You're intruding on property that is being searched."

"And I'm so glad you were here—with the door left

wide-open and no police tape across it, no less. I was so afraid I'd have to disturb the neighbors to try to find the landlord to let me in."

Nancy frowned, then recovered quickly with a sharp nod. "And I'm so glad you came here. We've been trying to locate you all day."

Patricia laughed. "Touché." She watched Nancy carefully. She seemed guarded, but more open to talking with Patricia than she had to be. It was well within her rights to hustle her out of the apartment and off the premises, but so far she had not. Maybe the police had learned something that didn't cast Patricia, and Gigi, in such a bad light? Maybe something useful?

"Tell you what," Patricia said. "Let me take just a quick peek into the kitchenette, and then let's go talk."

Nancy considered a moment, then nodded. She stepped aside and let Patricia through. Patricia stepped into the kitchenette. It was in the same condition as the rest of the apartment, cabinets flung open, plates and dishes stacked on the counter, contents of the cabinets askew. A young man who was busily taking notes looked up, saw Patricia, and frowned. "Who the hell—" he started to say.

"It's okay, John," Nancy said. "I know her."

Patricia grinned. "Just going to glance around."

She scanned the kitchen for anything that wasn't out of order. She saw a spice rack tacked up over the stove. She stepped over to it. The spices were in alphabetical order. There were covers over the burners on the stove, covers decorated with a kitten with a paw held up to a butterfly. She made one step to the left and was in front of the refrigerator. A to-do list listed *laundry; dry cleaner; get stamps; birthday card, Nana.* Everything was ticked off except for the birthday card.

Patricia looked over at Nancy. "Thanks. I'm done."

Nancy arched an eyebrow. "You're sure you don't want to look inside the freezer?"

"Positive."

Nancy looked over at John. "This lady and I are going

to go have a talk pertaining to this investigation. I won't be
gone long. I will, however, be shutting the door behind me.
So if, while I'm gone, you need to come and go for some
reason, this time shut the door." She said the last three
words with emphasis, and John looked chagrined. "The
next person who wanders in may not be someone we want
to see."

Patricia suppressed a smile as she followed Nancy out,
and waited for Nancy to shut the door more firmly and
loudly than was necessary.

"New, huh?" Patricia said as they started up the stairs.

Nancy sighed. "Everyone has to start somewhere."

Outside of the apartment building they settled on a ham-
burger place called Burger Shack across the street. They
both ordered just coffee. Once they'd settled into a booth,
they looked directly at each other.

"We've found some new information that makes Gigi
Lafferty's story, as you told it to us, seem a little more
plausible," Nancy said. "We still want to talk with her, of
course. Knowing we have new information that makes us
more inclined to believe Gigi should make it easier for you
to convince her to come in and talk to us. Or you could
make it simple and tell me where she is."

"What's the information you have?"

Nancy frowned. "I'm not at liberty to disclose that,"
Nancy said. "You know that."

Patricia shrugged. "I can't tell you where she is."

"Look, crossing into a police investigation is one thing—"

"You didn't have a tape up. The door was wide-open."

"You know, if you're withholding information pertinent
to a police investigation, such as your client's whereabouts—"

"As far as I know, you don't have a warrant out yet for
Gigi Lafferty." Patricia took a sip of her coffee. It had a
burned, acrid taste, but it was decidedly a relief to drink
coffee somewhere without white carpeting. "Look, why
don't we try to help each other out here? Give me just a

brief, high-level description of this information you have, and I'll tell you what I know."

"All right," Nancy said, sighing. "Seems our victim, Jessica, had quite a gambling problem while she was back in Vegas. And it seems she didn't totally shake it once she got here. We did some checking on the comings and goings of people at her apartment, as well as her activities, and she seems to have spent considerable time over in Newport hanging out at a few establishments known to take illegal bets, mostly on sports events."

Patricia swallowed hard, forcing her expression to remain steady. Poppy had told her that neither Gigi nor Jessica had been in contact with him. She hadn't believed him, but she also hadn't believed that he was deeply involved with either woman. Jessica had been eager to get away from Cincinnati; if she was involved with illegal gambling, or in financial trouble, that could explain why. Of course, Patricia knew better, but she didn't say anything. If Poppy were going to talk with anyone, he'd talk to Patricia. Maybe it was time to pay Poppy another visit and see what further information she could get out of him. Again, Gigi's story was taking on more credibility.

"Trouble is," said Nancy, "we can't connect Jessica with anyone in Newport other than her former employer, and he swears he hasn't had anything to do with her in years."

"If we could learn more about her activities in Newport," Nancy continued, "that might lead us to someone who would have reason to harm Jessica, maybe shake her up a little, maybe someone who got carried away."

"Like a loan shark."

"Maybe. Not that we're totally dropping the possibility that your client is a suspect. Her sudden disappearance is still a concern."

"Because Jessica was trying to blackmail Gigi over her past."

"That's the theory, based on what you told us."

"Well, I'll tell you what I've learned so far. Jessica *was* trying to blackmail Gigi. But according to Gigi, Jessica was also aware of some kind of corporate sabotage going on at her husband Neil's company, and tried to sell her the evidence. She was eager to get out of Cincinnati. It's possible Jessica was trying to blackmail someone else as well."

"You didn't tell us that when we interviewed you."

"I didn't know that then."

Nancy's eyebrows shot up. "You have been in touch with Gigi, then."

Patricia shook her head. "Gigi has been in touch with me." She took another sip of the coffee. "Let's see, if we combine what we both know, it basically gives us Gigi, anyone who worked for Neil or Neil himself, and illegal betting and loan people in the area as suspects in Jessica's death." She looked directly at Nancy. "Looks a little more complicated than a few days ago, doesn't it?"

Nancy pressed her lips together. "You have to admit, things didn't look too great for you and your client. They still don't look totally rosy."

Patricia nodded. "I understand. Did you, while searching the Laffertys' house or Jessica's apartment, find a computer diskette?"

Nancy's eyebrows lifted. "You know I can't give you direct information about evidence." She bit her lower lip momentarily. "Why do you ask?"

Patricia smiled. That was as good as saying no, they hadn't found a diskette. "Supposedly it contains the evidence Jessica had of corporate sabotage at Lafferty Products. Could be an interesting lead."

"Could be."

"Well, if you do run across such a diskette, I'd be happy to put my computer skills to work and help you access whatever's on it. If you need such help. And just as a concerned private citizen."

"Not as a concerned private investigator?"

Patricia shrugged. "Just offering. And it's investigative consultant."

"Thanks for the offer," Nancy said. "But we still need to

talk to Gigi. Look, tell us where she is. We'll just talk to her, let her go."

"I'll tell her you want to talk with her if she contacts me."

Nancy frowned. "Damn it, I shared more than I should have with you. . . ."

"And I shared more with you than I had to."

Nancy nodded. "I appreciate that. You didn't have to do that."

"I might need your help at some point."

"Look, Patricia, watch how deeply you're getting in. It's our job. . . ."

Patricia grinned. "I'm keeping one eye on the shore."

She stood and left, heading back to her truck in the parking lot of Jessica's apartment building. Keeping an eye on the shore, she had said. But, Patricia thought, when and if this case came to a culminating point, there was no guarantee someone would be on the shore keeping an eye on her.

Chapter 19

The lights of the cities on either side of the Ohio River, and of houseboats and floating restaurants, made the dark ripples of the river sparkle.

Patricia sat by the river near the bridge where before she had waited for Gigi. Around her she heard the laughter, the voices, the festive sound of an oompah band, of Cincinnati celebrating its German heritage with its yearly Oktoberfest, the second largest in the world.

Yet even surrounded by the festivities and the people, Patricia felt wholly alone. Not lonely. But alone, complete within a pocket of aloneness, yet at once connected with everything around her. She had brought herself into this state of being simply by listening to the sound of the vehicles passing over the bridge by which she sat. The vehicles made the bridge's supports sing in vibrating hums that arced, peaked, and faded, one on top of another, like the rounds of some medieval chant somehow intentionally evoked now by steel strumming steel, a mantra of human achievement of which the drivers crossing the bridge were not aware.

Patricia had come to hear the hum of vehicles on the bridge numerous times in the past fourteen years, always to free her mind of troubling thoughts of Bobby. But tonight, nested in her pocket of aloneness, she understood that she could not banish the demons of her mind and spirit. She could only abide with them, no longer fighting them but never giving herself over to them. And thus, in peaceful accord with all the parts of her being, even the parts she did not like, she could be free to move on with her life.

Patricia understood that this freedom meant that she could choose to do or even not to do anything—about this case with Gigi, about her relationship with Dean.

And thus Patricia arose from her spot beside the river knowing what she wanted to do, and what she would do.

She moved through the crowd, toward Fountain Square, where she and Dean had agreed to meet.

Fountain Square was a focal point of downtown Cincinnati. The Tyler Davidson Fountain's water danced under lights turned on around it. Patricia scanned for Dean among the people gathered around the fountain. She finally spotted him leaning against its edge, his arms crossed, his pose relaxed and nonchalant. But he looked around at the faces in the crowd nervously. Patricia approached him quietly and touched his arm gently.

"Hey there," she said. "You looking for someone in particular or will I do?"

Dean looked at her, grinning with relief. "You're here!"

"You sound surprised."

"I wasn't sure if you would come."

"Why?" Patricia asked as she and Dean started wandering away from the fountain and through the crowds with no particular destination in mind.

"You shared some pretty difficult things with Jay and me last night, and I was kind of rough on you."

Patricia shook her head. "Just realistic. I *have* blamed myself for Bobby's suicide. I haven't really let go." She sighed. "I didn't realize how true that was, not consciously anyway, until I got into this case with a client from that time in my life."

"You don't have to talk about it unless you want to," Dean said.

"I don't want to. But I have to. I owe you more than the few cryptic words I gave you and Jay last night."

"Oh, Patricia, you don't owe me—"

Patricia put her hand on Dean's arm, stopping both of

them momentarily, and looked directly in his eyes. "Oh yes, I do. I do because you're my friend . . . maybe more than a friend, and I want to keep that. I want it to grow."

"The more part?"

Patricia nodded.

Dean smiled. "Me, too." He paused. "All right. Then why did Bobby kill himself? And why do you blame yourself for it?"

They started wandering again. "Bobby and I met at the University of Cincinnati's College-Conservatory of Music. He was a violinist and composer; I had already realized that a music career, which is what my parents, particularly my father, wanted for me, was not what *I* wanted for me. Bobby was very supportive. It was a difficult decision, to turn away from music as a career choice when I'd been preparing my whole life for it. I had some talent, but not the will or the temperament for it. Anyway, I dropped out of the conservatory, which led my parents to temporarily cut me off. I took a job at Poppy's Parrot as a dancer, then a bouncer, just because I needed the money. And Bobby and I moved in together and agreed we'd get married. It wasn't a decision we shared with either set of parents."

"Why was that?"

Patricia laughed ruefully. "Well, as much as my parents wanted me to have a music career, Bobby's parents didn't. They wanted him to pursue medicine, which was the family's career tradition. Neither of us were communicating a whole lot with our parents. Perhaps if we had been, things might have turned out differently. . . ."

"But maybe they wouldn't. And you can't blame them, any more than you can blame yourself."

"I know. And I don't blame them. I didn't then either. It's just . . ." Patricia paused, shook her head. "I like to believe that people generally do what they think is best at the time, based on who they are and what they know. It doesn't make much difference if later they realize they could have made a better choice. By the time they realize it, they're different people."

"Like you're a different person now than when you lived with Bobby."

Patricia grinned. "Yes, and I know what you're trying to say. I shouldn't blame myself for Bobby's choice. I've known that intellectually since the day I saw him buried. Just not emotionally. Bobby—Bobby really needed help. Not my help. I was so cocky, thinking I could handle everything by myself. But he needed a professional's help. And I failed to see that at the time. Maybe I refused to see it."

"Maybe you just didn't want to. It would be hard to admit that about someone you love."

Patricia nodded. She swallowed hard. "Bobby loved music. More than anything else. I understood that when we started living together, and it didn't really bother me. I've always been happy on my own, so in a way, I was more comfortable with him putting music first. But after I dropped out of the program, he became obsessed with it. I don't know, maybe seeing me quit triggered some subconscious feeling that maybe his parents were right, or some fear that maybe music wasn't the best choice for him either."

"Was he a good musician?"

Patricia paused, closing her eyes. She could still hear him playing the same difficult passages of a violin concerto over and over and over, as ceaselessly as the humming of the vehicles on the bridge. But his passages were, unlike the hums created by the vehicles, self-aware. So instead of rising heavenward, they inevitably fell into a dull, heavy silence, a silence that drove Bobby to fury or tears or exhaustion.

Patricia opened her eyes. "He could have made a living at it, which is no small feat or backhanded compliment. But he was not great. And he became obsessed with being great, great in a way that you have to be born with, a greatness that has to come to you naturally and which is revealed by hard work, but not created by it. Bobby couldn't accept that. He became obsessed with achieving greatness until every tiny setback, every failure, sent him into a deep depression. It finally got so that even the slightest criticism would leave him nearly immobile; he wouldn't talk for hours afterward, or leave the apartment except for classes, and eventually he began skipping those. He just quickly descended into this spiral of depression. To me, it was overwhelmingly quickly. At the time it seemed like overnight, but of course it took months."

Patricia sighed, hugging her sweater around her against the night's chill. Abruptly, the weather had caught up with the calendar. Dean slipped his arm around her quietly and gently, and Patricia did not shrug it away. "I tried to stick by him. But one night, after getting off work from Poppy's Parrot, some of the dancers asked me if I would go out with them for drinks. They'd asked before, but since Bobby started slipping into this depression, I'd always declined, gone home to check on Bobby, to see how he was. That night I didn't feel like it. I didn't feel like facing his relentless depressions, his raging in anger, almost in hatred, at the music that was supposed to evoke feelings of love and sensitivity. So I went out with them. And when I got back to our apartment . . ." She paused, took in a deep breath, and let it out slowly. "When I got back, Bobby was dead. He'd slit his wrists."

Dean drew Patricia close to him. For several moments she allowed him to hold her closely and silently. Then he started, "Patricia, I—"

Patricia pushed him away gently, and put her finger to his lips. "Don't. It's enough that you've listened. I said before that people usually make the choices they think are best based on who they are and the information they have at the time. I did it then, and I'm doing it now."

"Meaning?"

"Meaning I have a lot of work to do on this case. I have to research the backgrounds of some of my client's husband's employees. I have to go visit the grandmother of the victim I found in my client's pool. Later tonight I have to cross the river and talk with an old employer. And I have—I have a little something I have to do to say good-bye to Bobby." Patricia paused and smiled gently. "But first, I'd like to spend more time talking with you."

"Patricia, you know you can talk with me all night long if you want."

Patricia shook her head. "Not about me. I've talked all I can for one night about me. About you."

"Me? I'm not very interesting. . . ."

"I think you are. And I know there's a lot of things you've wanted to talk with me about, and I've put you off."

Dean arched his eyebrows in surprise. "Like what?"

"Like about your divorce. Your son. I know he's very important to you. I think maybe I should hear about those things after all."

Dean studied Patricia carefully, hesitantly. Then he said quietly, "Tell me the truth, Patricia. Do you really want to work on this relationship?"

Patricia smiled. "Yes."

They walked toward he river, each talking and listening by turns, like neither had with another human in a very long time.

Chapter 20

The neon green cross was alight over the stage where Poppy pranced back and forth as he gave his message, his voice crescendoing at regular intervals, then crashing suddenly and resolving itself for a time into a chant. The neon green light gave his arms and face beneath the yarn cap an odd, green sheen, as if he had been carved out of some strange wood and polished with some stranger lacquer. He scampered as he moved across the stage, like a marionette suddenly brought to life and freed, a perverse Pinocchio.

The light of the cross seeped over the stage into the first few rows of folding metal chairs, then faded out. The rest of the room was dark. A few people listened attentively to Poppy. Some slept.

Patricia stood at the back of the room, watching Poppy on the stage so similar to the one in his former establishment. Only now, the impassioned body on stage moved to a different power.

The thought amused her: Poppy on the stage now, rather than behind the stage compelling others to perform. What had he said yesterday? Sin and salvation, two sides of the same coin. Either way, whether behind or on stage, Poppy was after the coin.

Finally, Poppy's message wound down. Some of the people came forward to talk to him. Some started to leave. Some continued sleeping, curled up by the walls. Patricia started toward his office.

As she went up the stairs she forced back the choking feeling and took deep breaths. The air was stale and smelled of mildew, but it was air, she reminded herself. No smoke or fire this time.

At the top she paused, gathered her equilibrium, and walked to the door of Poppy's office. She knew from experience that he would come back here after he was done. He always had after and before the performances at Poppy's Parrot. His door was locked. She sat down outside it, put her head down between her knees, and forced herself to keep breathing, to keep the blackness at bay.

She was amazed that the fire's memory could have such an effect on her after all these years. What was it Gigi had told her about the fire when they met by the river? Patricia had not given it a lot of thought because she was so wrapped up in this case. Gigi had made it clear that in all likelihood, Poppy had arranged for the fire that had claimed his first business, the fire that had nearly claimed Patricia's life.

Now, suddenly, Patricia stood. She was angry, with a cold limitless anger that could not be denied. Angry at Bobby. Angry at herself. Angry at Poppy. She moved away from the office door, into the shadows, ready. This time she was getting all the answers she needed from Poppy.

Soon, tired, shuffling footsteps came up the steps. Poppy slowly approached his door.

Patricia lunged at him and caught him from behind in a choke hold. Poppy fought, cursed, struggled, and grabbed at her arms, but she was strengthened by her cold anger.

"I threw you once, Poppy. I'll do it again, only not so nice this time."

"Pat-Patricia—what the . . ."

"I want to know about Gigi Lafferty. And Jessica Taylor. Especially Jessica Taylor.

"I told you. . . ."

Patricia tightened her grasp around his neck. He started gagging and gasping for air. "Everything, Poppy. This time I want to know everything."

"Okay—just let me—breathe—"

Patricia lightened her hold only slightly. They moved as

if caught in some absurd dance, Patricia behind Poppy, arm around his neck, shoving him toward his office door. "Open it," she ordered.

Poppy did. She pushed him through the door and flicked the light switch. Poppy tried to lunge for his desk drawer, but Patricia, still holding him, half shoved, half swung him away from the desk. She opened the drawer and grabbed the gun as he struggled to break free of her grasp. She held the gun to his temple. He was suddenly still.

"I want you to feel this against your head for a few moments. And I want you to know I'm controlling it." For a few seconds Patricia and Poppy were perfectly still. The only sound was their breathing, labored after their struggle. Then she said quietly, "Now, I'm going to let you go, and we're going to talk quietly for a few minutes."

She held him for a few seconds more, then suddenly let go and pushed him away from her. Poppy stumbled forward, collapsed in a chair, and glared up at her, gasping for breath. Patricia leaned against his desk and casually trained the gun on him. She didn't try to hide her amusement at his discomfort.

"Why don't we start with you telling me when and why Jessica came to see you."

"What makes you think she did? I told you before she hadn't." Poppy spoke contemptuously, as if he were spitting.

"You never could lie well. It's both your downfall and probably what's saved you all of these years. I know Jessica was gambling. I know she had at least one, probably two, blackmail schemes set up. But then she wanted to leave town in a hurry. Tells me maybe she had some nasty debts to pay."

Poppy cocked his head to one side and twisted his mouth into a mocking grin. "What makes you think I'd have anything to do with that?"

"Simple. I figure it worked something like this. Jessica had a gambling problem in Las Vegas. She finishes doing her time, comes back here, figures she'll cash in on her old pal Loretta's real identity as Gigi Lafferty to get a new start in life. But the gambling itch comes back to her. No legal casinos or gambling here, other than the horse tracks and the lottery, and that just isn't going to cut it for Jessica. So who's she going to turn to to get her back in the underground gambling scene? You."

"I told you, I run a clean operation now. And a clean life. Totally charitable."

Patricia glanced down meaningfully at the gun she held and back up at Poppy. "That's why you have this? Oh, maybe it's just a toy. Maybe I should test it and find out." She held the gun out, aimed squarely at Poppy's forehead.

"Okay, okay," he said quickly, frowning, flapping his hands. "I do still have a few connections. So I did tell Jessica about where she could go for some gambling action."

"And when she started running out of ready cash?"

"I told her where she could go to borrow some."

"I take it by that you don't mean you simply gave her directions to the nearest savings and loan." Patricia lowered the gun.

"No." Poppy grinned again. "That's not what I mean. Look, I should have told you earlier. I'm sorry I didn't. But now you have the whole story, right? So you can give me back my gun, we can forget all this."

Patricia sighed. "Sorry, Poppy. It's not going to be that easy, I'm afraid."

"Why not? I told you everything—"

"You told me too easily. You know I wouldn't kill you if I didn't get information out of you. You're not really afraid of me. You're just trying to get rid of me."

"Look, I told you the truth, Patricia."

"Oh, I believe you told me the truth. I just don't believe you told me the whole truth. Here's what I think, Poppy. I think Jessica came to you for something more, something you haven't told me just yet. Something other than a few shady names. Something that really did make you uncomfortable. But Jessica's game was blackmail. She had this talent for learning the truth about people, ugly truths."

Patricia paused and studied Poppy, He looked away momentarily, uncomfortably. "It's a talent we share," she said. "Difference is, I wait until people ask me to get information for them, then I get paid for doing so, and I try to safeguard what I learn and be ethical about it. Not Jessica. She went out and learned what she could and then used her information as a personal tool for getting what she wanted.

"And you know what, Poppy? She knew all along something about you that I just learned over the past few days. The fire which burned your old place several years ago wasn't accidental. Jessica knew it was set. In fact, you hired her boyfriend at the time to set it.

"Now, Poppy, while I wouldn't kill you just because you won't tell me what you know, I might kill you for arranging that fire. Because I almost died in that fire. Because a lot of people could have died in that fire. But you didn't care. You wanted the insurance money."

Poppy looked at her for long minute. He quietly asked, "What do you want, Patricia?"

"The whole truth. About why Jessica came to see you after she was back here."

"At first, it was just to get connections regarding gambling. And borrowing money. Both illegally. I gave her a few names. I guess she got in touch with them. I don't really know."

"Names, Poppy. What are the names you gave her?"

Poppy looked scared. "I can't tell you that. You'll go to the cops, and if they find out . . ."

Patricia fired one shot a few inches to the left of Poppy. The bullet embedded into the floor.

"My God, Patricia . . ."

"Names, Poppy."

He swallowed hard. "Elroy Johnson, for the gambling. His brother Toni handles the loan side of things. I can't swear she ever contacted them. . . ."

"Fine. What else did she want?"

"The same thing I wanted several years ago from her. A connection with someone who can set up fires, make them look accidental."

Patricia was surprised, but kept her expression steady as she slowly considered this new information. "Why? Why did she want that?"

"It wasn't for her. It was for a man she was with. A man she brought with her."

"Who? Did you get his name?"

"Introduced himself as Gregory Smith. But people don't always give their real names. Jessica was the contact. He just wanted to make sure I understood that he needed someone who could do the job and make it look accidental. And I think he wanted to impress me with how much I'd get."

Patricia considered. Gregory Smith—could be Gregory Finster changing his last name. Or, as Poppy said, anyone, just using that name. Poppy would only need to know that Jessica would be the go-between for Poppy and the man, just as Poppy would be the go-between for the arsonist and Jessica.

"How much money was he talking?"

"Ten grand for me, finder's fee. Don't know how much for the firebug. That would be between them."

"Did you accept?"

Poppy looked at Patricia. "I said I'd see what I could find out for them."

"When did you meet with Jessica and this man?"

"Earlier this week. Yes. Monday night."

Two days, thought Patricia, before Jessica was murdered.

"What kind of job was this going to be? House?"

Poppy shrugged. "Didn't get many details. The man said it would be for a warehouse of some kind."

"Lafferty Products?"

"The man didn't say."

"Come on, Poppy; the name struck you as familiar when I was here before. I saw your reaction."

Poppy folded his arms and grinned. "Maybe I heard it

mentioned as they were leaving and talking to each other. But I wasn't supposed to."

"What did the man look like?"

Poppy shrugged. "Average build. Suit. Dark eyes, maybe brown, maybe gray. Hard to tell in the light in here."

"Did this average-looking man have any kind of a time frame?"

"He was in a hurry. Wanted the job done in the next month."

Patricia frowned. "Why so fast?"

Poppy shrugged again, but didn't say anything this time.

"All right Poppy, I can see you've told me all you want to."

"I've told you all I can," he said.

"Not the same as all you know."

Poppy grinned. "But close. Pretty close."

"You didn't have to."

He shrugged again. "Maybe I thought I owed you one."

That, thought Patricia, was as close to a confession—or an apology—as she was going to get out of him about the fire from several years ago.

Patricia turned and started out the door.

"Hey, Patricia."

She turned around again and looked at Poppy. "Yes?"

"Careful," he said. "If you're treading where Jessica tread, trying to find out what happened to her, you're treading on dangerous territory."

"Gee, thanks for the concern," she replied.

"Smart-ass. You always were a smart-ass. So smart, you don't think you need any concern." Poppy held out his hand. "I'd like my gun back."

She opened the chamber, dumped out the bullets, pocketed them, and tossed the empty gun back at him. He tried to catch it and missed, and scrambled after it. When he retrieved it, he looked at Patricia, red-faced.

She grinned. "I try to minimize my risks, Poppy. Let me get away with being a smart-ass from time to time."

Patricia turned, and walked out of Poppy's place.

Chapter 21

Lake George was mostly dark, brushed with only the barest glimmer of moonlight. Although the moon was nearly full, even its light was intermittent as clouds passed before it. A storm would blow up later tonight, thought Gigi. The lake's surface rippled restlessly, rocking the houseboat. The air felt charged and had that electric smell that comes with a storm. She would stay out here, she thought, until the storm kicked up in earnest.

Gigi stared across the lake. She had often stared into darkness at nothing in particular, wondering about the lives being spun out on the other side. But only once had she been on the other side.

It was the year before the trouble began with her family, before she ran off to Newport. She had gotten bored, gone into town, met some young people, a brother and sister and a female cousin who were spending part of the summer in a cottage across the lake from her aunt and uncle's cabin, and had a good time with them. They invited her to come to a party, and she accepted.

If she had been there alone or with her siblings visiting her aunt and uncle, it would probably have been okay. But it was one of the few times her parents had been visiting, too, and they were unhappy when she told them about the party, making vague comments about the people across the lake not being of their caliber, their cottages being smaller and belonging to people they preferred not to associate with, a different section of lake residents. But Gigi had defied her parents that night, for the first time in her young life, and gone anyway.

Gigi had not enjoyed the party, although it was a lively one at a cottage not all that much smaller than her aunt and uncle's. She had broken away from it, going out to stand by the lake, and stared across at her aunt and uncle's cottage. Gigi had, of course, been unable to see their cottage, just as she had been unable to see the young people's cottage from her aunt and uncle's. But she had stared across nonetheless, unable to see where her parents were, unhappy with her, perhaps discussing her behavior. She wondered then what would happen if she never went back. No, Gigi had not enjoyed the party, but she had savored her first taste of defiance.

Now she sighed and brushed the first few spatterings of raindrops from her cheeks. She had, of course, returned after the party. She had in fact returned to her family again and again, as well as its ideals, unable to break from them, somehow believing in the security on the other side of the darkness. It was why she had come back to Cincinnati after leaving Las Vegas, instead of going elsewhere to start over; why she had married a man like Neil; why she couldn't bring herself to run now.

Gigi wondered if she should have told Patricia more, told her everything. But no, she had some things she had to protect, some things that were too fragile to share, some things she had to cling to if she was ever going to break free and cross the lake again, this time for good. And it had nothing to do with what had happened to Jessica. Nothing. She was quite sure of it.

For a long time Gigi lay in the grass, staring across the darkness, letting her mind drift into similar darkness, similar nothingness. She nearly drifted into sleep, but she caught herself and started awake, looking around with a sudden, stark awareness.

And then she saw she had not started herself awake. The movement of someone toward her had. As the figure moved into the light from the inside of the cottage behind her, she felt a sudden tension, a sudden fear. And then the figure moved into the light, and she saw who it was.

Relief flooded her. Who did she think had tracked her here? Who else? Only the one person who knew of her place here.

And then she saw the other figure come out after the first and come for her with shocking suddenness and she knew, her last clear thought before the panic and hysteria and finally nothingness of the moments to follow, that she should have, most certainly should have, told Patricia everything.

Chapter 22

The necklace was a simple gold chain that held an amulet in the shape of the musical treble-clef sign. It was the only jewelry Bobby had given Patricia. He gave it to her for their engagement, since he could not afford a traditional engagement ring. The necklace had occupied a special spot in Patricia's jewelry box for fourteen years, a spot that it had not left except during a brief interlude earlier in the year when her niece Lucy had been visiting and took it temporarily. But Patricia herself had not removed it from the box in fourteen years, until tonight. It had not adorned her neck in fourteen years, either, until tonight. And tonight she wore it because she intended, quite literally, to bury it.

She was aware of it gently brushing her skin as she worked at her computer at her office. She had gone back to her house after meeting with Poppy to retrieve the necklace. But there were a few questions, first, that she wanted to get started working on. Then she'd take care of the necklace, and finally go back home for a well-deserved night's rest.

First, she wanted to find if Jessica's grandmother was local. That was the easy question to answer. Patricia had a CD-ROM disk that was an electronic version of a crisscross directory, but for addresses of people all over the United States. She had slipped the disk into the CD-ROM reader attached to her computer, and searched with the name Naomi Taylor and Cincinnati-area zip codes and quickly found a match. Soon, perhaps the next day, Patricia would telephone and, she hoped, visit Naomi Taylor. Perhaps the second diskette of evidence, which Patricia was sure existed if the original one truly did, was with the grandmother, since it didn't appear to be in Jessica's work cubicle or at her apartment. And Patricia wanted to know if Jessica had told her grandmother anything that might shed more light on Jessica's visits to Poppy, and on her sudden need to give up her blackmailing schemes and leave the Cincinnati area.

Trying to make sense of what Poppy had told her was the tougher question. Who had Jessica brought with her to see Poppy? It could have been Gregory, since the man had used that name, or it could have been Neil or Allen using his name, if the premise was true that whoever had killed Jessica was closely associated with both Lafferty Products and the Lafferty family. If that premise wasn't true, then it could have been any man Jessica might have known at Lafferty Products. And why burn down the Lafferty Products warehouse, as Poppy had implied?

Patricia tapped out the possible reasons in the word-processing file she was keeping on this case. One reason, if Neil were the man, could be Poppy's old reason—insurance money. But from Patricia's earlier research, Neil's finances seemed to be in good condition, and there were surely easier ways for him to get money if he needed it than to destroy his own business.

Another motive for destroying the warehouse could be revenge. That would implicate someone who hated Neil— certainly striking at the company would be like striking at Neil's core.

The third possibility was that another crime was being covered up, which fit with Jessica's claim of sabotage. That could mean that someone wanted to burn the warehouse either to destroy something that was there that should not be, or to cover up the fact that something was not there that should be.

Patricia leaned back from her computer, shaking her head. Theories, all theories, and any one of them could be easily dismissed or easily supported—in theory—with a few logical arguments. She needed more facts to either support or dismiss the theories, and in particular she needed to see the evidence, or a copy of it, that Jessica tried to sell Gigi.

Patricia had also researched, as much as she could through her computer, Neil, Allen, Gregory, Rita Ames, as well as Terrence McSherry and Abigail Pagado, who apparently were not close to the Lafferty family but who managed the Lafferty Products warehouse and purchasing, the areas for which Jessica had entered data in the company computer system.

About Neil she found no more than she had originally found when she researched Gigi's background. She found little more about Allen—just some old articles from a news database citing his name as a young swimming star and Olympic hopeful. He was also mentioned as attending the funeral of Terry Parker, a friend and swimteam mate who had, ironically, died in a fluke drowning during a team retreat at a lake.

After the brief article on the funeral, Allen's name did not appear in news articles again, at least not in relation to swimming. He was occasionally named in the articles citing his father's business achievement. Useful background material, Patricia thought, but hardly the stuff of blackmail and corporate sabotage six years later.

Patricia researched Terrence, Abigail and Rita as thoroughly as possible, but found nothing to indicate anything more than typical middle-class, suburban lives. While she could not look at their credit information, either legally or ethically, she could look at the header information on their credit reports and at various public records about property ownership.

All three were married and had rarely moved in the past ten years. Rita had one son, age ten; Abigail had two teenage daughters; Terrence, no children. All three owned their suburban tract homes with their spouses; the only interesting related fact Patricia found was that Rita lived in the same neighborhood that the Laffertys had lived in before they moved a little more upscale. Additionally, Rita's husband owned a boat; Abigail and her husband had a rental apartment unit. None of these Lafferty employees were mentioned prominently in the press, except for small notices about appointments to officerships in professional organizations. If any of them had a reason, personally or financially, to sabotage Lafferty Products, it wasn't readily revealing itself through public records available through Patricia's computer.

Her computer research did yield a somewhat different picture of Gregory Finster. His records showed he had moved often during the past five years, sometimes only staying a few months at a time in any given place. His name did not appear in any databases of United States' property records, making it a likely bet that he did not own and had not ever owned any property. This could suggest financial instability, but enough to motivate him to sabotage his employer? More circumstantial evidence, Patricia thought.

The portrait of him that emerged from a few articles in newspaper databases was more intriguing than that of Terrence, Abigail, Neil, Allen, or Rita. As a practicing psychologist in the Seattle area, he had been sued twice, once by a man and once by a woman, with allegations that he had coerced sexual favors from them as part of their "therapy." Nothing, however, was proven against him.

Later, when he lived in Salt Lake City, he had started a business that he called Creative Motivational Concepts. One article focused on his unique approaches to motivating corporate employees to focus on inner goals and strengths and apply those to teamwork in the workplace. A few months later, however, an article appeared that stated some participants felt he had pushed them too far. One man accused him of contributing to his stroke by pushing him to participate in outdoor "exercises" designed to establish trust of others. A woman said he had berated people in the seminar she attended into sharing personal experiences they obviously weren't comfortable revealing. And finally, another article revealed that Creative Motivational Concepts had gone out of business, while Gregory himself declared bankruptcy.

Unusual background, Patricia noted. But how could she fit that piece with all the others she had gathered? And did it even belong in this particular puzzle? That was the trouble. She had bits and pieces of facts and theories, but none of them was adding up to anything.

Patricia pushed aside the printouts of her research and rubbed her eyes. For now, she might as well head to Bobby's grave as she had planned, then return home and call it a night.

The phone rang. Patricia started. The sound, so commonplace during the day, was jarring and unexpected this late at night. She answered it hesitantly.

"Delaney Investigative Consulting, Patricia Delaney speaking. May I help you?"

There was a deep breath, then a small voice spoke. "Patricia, I need to talk with you. There—there are some things I've got to tell you."

Patricia's fist tightened around the receiver. It was Gigi Lafferty.

"Gigi, where are you? Are you at the cabin?"

"Yes."

"Are you okay?"

"Yes."

"You sound stressed, Gigi. Is something wrong?"

"No—I mean, yes, something is wrong. I've misled you Patricia. I've lied to you, and I just can't deal with it anymore. Lying, I mean, or hiding out here."

Patricia frowned. "Gigi, if you've got a confession to make, you ought to be making it to your lawyer first."

"No, Patricia. I want to talk to you. After all I've put you through in the past few days, I owe you that much. Then I'll talk to my lawyer."

"I'm not really comfortable with this, Gigi. I think you should talk to your lawyer first."

"I'm going to call him as soon as we hang up, Patricia.

He'll be here when you get here. But I just want you to know, too, why—" Gigi's voice cracked in a sudden sob.

"All right, Gigi. I'll come. It will take me about an hour to get there."

"I'll wait," Gigi said. The line went dead.

Patricia slowly hung up the telephone. Perhaps that was why all the bits and pieces she'd been collecting didn't fit. They couldn't, because she'd wanted to overlook the obvious explanation from the start. Gigi Lafferty had killed Jessica Taylor, because Jessica had been trying to blackmail her, pure and simple. And Gigi had been trying to use Patricia to cover for her, and keep her informed of the police investigation.

Patricia's throat tightened. She'd go to see Gigi, all right. She wanted a sensible, clear explanation from the woman, once and for all.

Chapter 23

The rain was coming down hard by the time Patricia pulled her truck down the lane leading to Gigi's cottage on Lake George. It was a good thing, she thought, that she was driving a truck; otherwise, in a smaller vehicle, she'd get stuck in the muddy muck the lane had become. She still might.

Patricia stopped near the cabin and turned off her truck's lights, but didn't immediately turn off the truck. She sat for a few minutes listening to the tape that had been her only companion on the drive from Alliston. It was a collection of operatic arias sung by Carlotta Moses, her father's favorite opera star, who had long ago retired from stage and song. The fact that she was listening to it now betrayed her nervousness. She only dug out the tape, which her father had given her several years before, when she needed to evoke the sense of confidence and strength he always expected of her, even in the most difficult of times.

How lovely, Patricia thought, to sit and listen to the mingling sounds of the rain slashing against her windshield and of the music until the tape came to the end. But she had business to attend to.

She turned off the tape and cut the truck's engine. She fished her flashlight out of the glove compartment, switched it on, then got out and made a dash for the front door of the cabin.

The cabin was dark. She pounded on the front door and called Gigi's name. No reply. She tried the door. It was locked.

Patricia dashed around to the back door, but it, too, was locked. No one appeared to be in or around the cabin.

She noticed, then, the music and lights from behind her. Patricia turned and saw that they came from a houseboat tied up to the dock. Apparently Gigi, for some reason, had decided to wait for her on the boat. She ran to the houseboat.

No one was on it.

Where was Gigi? Patricia wondered. She started to move to the houseboat's door when something made her pause. She was overcome by a sudden intuitive wariness.

Patricia took a long, slow breath to steady her racing mind, then forced herself to think carefully. She had driven here very quickly, at Gigi's panicked request. And now no one appeared to be here; yet the lights and music had been left on in the houseboat, attracting her to it. Someone, perhaps Gigi, had meant to draw her to it. But for what purpose?

Something, Patricia thought, was very wrong. If someone meant to attract her to the houseboat, that meant he—she? they?—would be watching the boat, would see that she had boarded, would soon be coming after her, and not for any purpose, she suspected, that would be to her benefit. And the person or persons probably were watching from the cabin. She'd already alerted whoever it was by knocking on the cabin, waving her flashlight around, and calling for Gigi, she thought grimly.

A sudden burst of light from outside the cabin caught the corner of her eye. Lightning? she wondered. She waited for several seconds. Thunder did not follow.

Patricia knelt down, then edged around the deck of the houseboat keeping herself as low as possible. She could still make out the cabin, the trees moving in the wind. The cabin was dark. Perhaps she had imagined the flash of light. But then a backyard floodlight came on and went off again. The cabin door opened. Someone, she realized, was coming toward the houseboat.

Patricia moved quickly to the back of the boat, hesitated

only briefly at the sight of the frigid, choppy water, and slid in.

The water was cold and dark. Before she could adjust to the shock of being in the freezing water, she was suddenly slapped in the face. She kicked away, then turned her flashlight in the direction of where she had been hit.

Gigi Lafferty's body dangled from the motor blades of the boat. Patricia gasped, taking in water. She forced herself to choke down the water, to remember to hold her breath. She swam back to Gigi, training her flashlight on her. Gigi had drowned. There were deep scratches and bruises around her neck. The back of her dress was caught in the motor blades. Whoever had killed her had probably expected her body to be carried away into the lake, not caught up by the boat. The force of the water, made violent by the storm, would finish rending Gigi's dress and set her adrift, fulfilling the killer's intent. Patricia had a different idea. She wanted Gigi's body to be found, and then she wanted to get away from Lake George as fast as possible.

The cold water was starting to make her panic. She forced herself to stay calm, to keep her movements deliberate. She turned off her flashlight, shoved it in her jacket pocket, hoping her light under the water hadn't already attracted attention, hoping her pursuer wasn't on the houseboat yet. It was impossible to know how much time had passed since she had gotten in the lake. She unhooked Gigi's body and swam with it to one of the ropes tying the boat to the dock. Then she bound Gigi's arms to the rope.

Patricia surfaced long enough to take a quick gulp of both air and water as the waves slapped her and to hear movement on the dock above. She went underwater again, swimming as fast as she could, keeping, she hoped, as close as possible to the edge of the lake. The lake, it seemed, wanted to pull her out to its middle.

Patricia came up one more time for air and to gather her bearings. She had moved a good distance from the houseboat. She swam underwater to the lake's shore and bellied up onto land. She was closer to a neighbor's cabin than to Gigi's.

Patricia crept up on the land and started working her way back toward the lane that led to Gigi's cabin.

Her truck was still there; at least her pursuer or pursuers hadn't sabotaged it. She hoped whoever was on the houseboat was still there, that she had enough time to get away.

She sprinted for her truck. She got in, shifted it to neutral, and let it roll quietly away from the cabin to gain some momentum so she wouldn't get stuck in the mud, then dug her keys out of her jeans pocket, started the truck, and pulled away.

Once Patricia was up on the state route, on paved road, she started driving as fast as she dared. She turned on the heater as high as she could. She started the tape.

This time the medley of music and the rain were accompanied by Patricia's teeth uncontrollably chattering, her body violently shivering.

Chapter 24

As Patricia drove back to Cincinnati, the truck heater only partly warmed and dried her. She was still shivering by the time she stopped at the first place she passed that looked open. She slowed her truck and turned around carefully on the road, which, at that point, cut close to the Ohio River, and offered a small prayer of thanks to any God who happened to be listening that the owner of Gus's Bait Shop and Gas Station had decided to keep the shop open.

Patricia filled her truck at the gas pump, offering up another small thank you that the rain had subsided. She noted the pay phone outside by the door as she went in to pay. Inside, she heard gruff, male laughter coming from behind a partially open door behind the front counter. Patricia looked around the tiny shop and found a coffeemaker with a hand-lettered sign propped next to it: $.50 CENTS A CUP. Patricia poured one cup of coffee and drank it quickly. That partly cut the chill that covered her like another skin. Then she noticed a rack of sweatshirts inscribed GUS'S BAIT SHOP AND GAS STATION. Patricia quickly peeled off her own wet shirt, too cold and tired to care if anyone came out and briefly saw her in just a bra. Then she pulled on a sweatshirt, but left her arms free while she slipped out of the wet underwear. She quickly put her arms in the sleeves of the sweatshirt, and rolled up her own wet clothes. Her jeans and shoes were still damp, but at least her upper body was more comfortable. Patricia poured another cup of coffee and went up to the counter.

"Anybody home?" she called.

The laughter stopped abruptly. A tall man, thumbs under suspenders, came through the door. He stopped by the register and eyed Patricia suspiciously.

Patricia grinned at him. "Filled my truck, twelve gallons."

The man nodded. "Night like this, I'm not going to go out and check. I'll take your word for it." He punched in the amount, then eyed Patricia's new shirt. "And one sweatshirt, and a cup of coffee."

"This is my second cup."

He nodded again, as if somehow a thirst for his coffee made Patricia's presence less surprising. As she paid cash he said, "Lucky for you I've hit a winning streak in the poker game. I forgot to close up."

She smiled sadly. "Guess it's my lucky night, too." He gave her her change, then watched her leave.

Outside at the phone booth, she got the number from the operator for the Lake George Police Department. She called the police, anonymously reported Gigi's murder, then hung up and used the wet shirt she had just shed to carefully wipe the phone clean of her fingerprints. It was possible the police would trace the call.

She got back in her truck, tossed her wet clothes in the passenger seat, and continued on to Cincinnati, eager for home.

But then she recalled the visit she had planned to make before Gigi called her. She was weary, and yet the events of the night seemed to make tonight the perfect time to carry out the ritual she had planned to symbolically absolve herself of guilt over past choices. She drove past the turn toward her home and headed for Oaklawn Cemetery.

The gate was locked at the cemetery. Patricia took the flashlight from her glove compartment and stepped out of her truck. She climbed the gate, dropped to the other side, and started walking up the hill studded with grave markers. She used the flashlight to find her way around them.

At the top of the hill, she stopped and thought about what she looked like—a woman alone, in a city graveyard, on a dark, moonless night, visiting the grave of an old lover for the first and last time since he was buried fourteen years before—and laughed out loud. The scene was set for great drama, but Patricia could only find humor in it.

Shouldn't there at least be some lightning flashes? But no, it was an absolutely dark, moonless night, cut by just the steady beam of her flashlight, a high-quality flashlight her parents had bought to make her eleventh birthday extra special. She even knew the batteries were fresh, so she couldn't count on the light going out to add a little atmosphere to this ritual.

Patricia's laughter subsided with a sigh. She felt her weariness to her bones and longed to get her task over with so she could go home and go to bed.

She walked down the side of the hill to Bobby's grave. Although she hadn't been to it in fourteen years, she would never forget its location. She came upon it, knelt down, and trained her flashlight on it. AT HOME IN HEAVEN, REMEMBERED ON EARTH. ROBERT HARRISON. BORN MAY 12, 1958, DIED OCTOBER 2, 1979. BELOVED ONLY SON OF JAMES AND MARY HARRISON.

This was the first time Patricia had seen the marker Bobby's parents had selected for his grave. The message was more sentimental than she would have expected of them. Patricia had met Dr. and Mrs. Harrison only once, on the day of the funeral, and she remembered feeling a strong sense of condemnation toward them, for they seemed cold and distant to her, their eyes red-rimmed but their emotions held in reserve. She had wanted to lash out at them, to try in some way to blame them for their son's terrible choice. Now she thought they seemed not so different from other people she knew. Or from herself.

A large marker stood to the left of Bobby's grave. Briefly, Patricia trained her flashlight on it. It was a double marker engraved with James and Mary Harrison's names. Birth dates, but not death dates, were already carved into the marble. Somewhere, out there in the dark night, James and Mary Harrison lived on, sleeping side by side in life as they would eventually in death. A child preceding one in death was the worst pain Patricia guessed could be experienced, and yet Bobby's parents had lived on, presumably living and loving together since they had a double marker with both their names waiting for them. Was it a comfort to know they would rest, finally, by the child they had lost in one of the cruelest ways possible? Or did they barely think of it now, the knowledge only crossing their minds when, perhaps, they took his sister's children to the park to play and thought they saw, in the turn of a head or an arch of an eyebrow, something of their son in the next generation?

Patricia would, of course, never know. But mentally she thanked his parents for having placed the marker there. It was a reminder to her that life and love persevered, not in spite of, or triumphant over, death and cruelty, but along beside them.

Patricia lay the flashlight down on Bobby's grave. She took off the treble-clef amulet he had given her and held it with her left hand. With her right, she scraped back the earth, scooping out a shallow cup, and put the amulet in it. Then she packed the earth back over it.

Perhaps tears came from her eyes then. Patricia couldn't say later; perhaps her eyes were just watering from the sting of exhaustion. But in either case, she said, "Good-bye, Bobby," out loud, then stood up and headed back to her truck.

A car was parked in front of her small home when she pulled up to it.

What now— Patricia thought, then realized that it was Dean's car when she saw the flash of bright red Corvette under her truck's headlights. He had a key, which she had given him so he could get in to feed Sammie when she went away on camping or business trips.

Dean had a fire going in the fireplace. The smell of brewed coffee greeted her as well. He was asleep on the couch, a book fallen to the floor beside him.

Patricia quietly snuck back to the bathroom and stripped

out of her clothes. She took a steaming-hot shower, dried herself thoroughly, then put on her thick white terry-cloth robe and her slippers.

She walked back out to the family room, where Dean was still asleep. She knelt beside the couch and gently shook him.

When he awoke, she grinned and said, "Hi, honey. I'm home."

"Patricia! What the—" Dean sat up on the couch, rubbing his eyes. "I was worried about you."

"Oh, you know how those late nights at the office can be—"

Dean frowned. "Come on, Patricia, I was worried about you. I called you here, and then at the office. When I didn't get you after several tries, I came here. And then I decided I'd just wait for you here. I guess after our talk earlier, I wanted, wanted . . ."

"Just to say good night in person," Patricia said gently.

Dean nodded, studying her carefully, as if suddenly curious about her gentle tone. "You look like you've had a difficult night."

"It's a long story. I'm not up to telling it now."

Dean rested a hand on her shoulder. "You look like you could use some comforting."

"No." Patricia shook her head. "No," she said again. "Not comforting. Celebrating."

Dean arched his eyebrows in surprise. "Celebrating? A celebration of what?"

Patricia grinned. "Of life."

With that, she climbed up on top of Dean, then firmly began kissing him. He didn't resist.

Chapter 25

The farmhouse, a white clapboard two-story with a large front porch, looked large compared with the mobile homes clustered around it. Patricia stood by her truck, which she had parked by the sign TAYLOR'S TRAILER PARK, surveying the scene.

She walked up to the porch. A clothesline was strung between two of the porch's wooden posts. On the line hung a large, colorful assortment of what at first appeared to be doll- or toddler-sized dresses, but a hand-lettered sign tacked to a post read GOOSE CLOTHES. Patricia looked at one of the outfits hanging on the line. Inside was sewn a tag that read *Lovingly created by Naomi*. She checked a few of the other outfits; all had the same tag.

Lined up along the wall by the door were several ceramic geese, modeling outfits ranging from an apron and cap to a witch's cape and hat to a Santa suit. Naomi was apparently gearing up for the holiday season. Ceramic geese dressed in various outfits sitting out on front porches had become the suburban rage in southwestern Ohio over the past few years—the modern equivalent of hot-pink plastic flamingo lawn ornaments from the fifties. Patricia had read once in the newspaper that the goose fad got started in a suburb near Cincinnati.

Patricia had always found the dressed-up geese irritating and idly wondered once if she should launch a curmudgeonly protest, maybe calling it a campaign against goose abuse; were people really spending time, effort, and money to outfit ceramic geese?

But this morning she grinned. Somehow, the outdoor boutique of goose clothes lent the right touch of lightness and humor to the start of her day. She had awoken this morning curled up next to Dean; a lovely feeling until the events of the night before began slowly entering her thoughts. Then, in a rush, all the questions she had to answer came back to her and she had hurried off, not even pausing for breakfast, to follow up on the leads she had.

And now one of the leads had led her straight to a display of the ceramic-goose fashion industry's finest. The notion made her grin even more widely, and finally she burst into laughter. Maybe she wouldn't learn a thing here that would help her solve the case; maybe she would never be able to figure out who had murdered Jessica and then Gigi. But at least, on this morning, her sense of humor at the world was refreshed. She'd never again regard the goose denizens of suburban porches quite so critically.

Patricia went to the front door and knocked.

"Coming, coming!" she heard someone call in a cheery singsong voice.

The door suddenly opened, and standing in the doorway was the woman from Jessica's fuzzy picture, her grandmother, Naomi Taylor. She wore a housedress and cowboy boots. A few tabs of gray hair stuck out from underneath a Reds baseball cap. A calico cat, perched on her shoulder, stared at Patricia warily, but Naomi herself greeted her with a dazzlingly beautiful smile, her petite mouth full-lipped, her teeth perfectly white and even. It was the only vestige of any former beauty she had once had. Her arms and face had gone to fat now, and her face was deeply wrinkled. While those etchings showed that she'd had a hard life, her twinkling dark eyes suggested that she had probably laughed more than she'd cried about it.

Patricia smiled back at Naomi, regretting that she had to talk with the woman about her recently murdered granddaughter.

"Hello. I'm Patricia Delaney. We talked just a while ago on the telephone."

Naomi kept smiling, but a hint of pain crossed her face. "Yes. You wanted to talk with me about Jessica."

"If I could. I know it's painful for you, but it might help find out who—" Patricia started gently.

"Oh, Lordy, Lordy. Come on in." Naomi sighed. "I loved the girl. Raised her from the time she was seven, but I guess I got to her too late. She never did nothing but cause me pain."

Naomi stepped aside and let Patricia through the front door.

Immediately, Patricia could see why Jessica had become so particularly neat and organized as her office indicated. Stacks of boxes and newspapers crowded the small, front room. Even the front windows were blocked by furniture, boxes, books, newspapers, lamp shades, piles of electrical cords, old appliances, and in one corner, three televisions stacked one on top of the other.

A single path cut through the room's clutter to a doorway to the kitchen. The path wound past a couch, in front of which stood a sewing machine on a small desk. The back and arms of the couch were draped with goose-haute-couture-in-progress.

And the place was filled with cats. Patricia could smell them before she saw them; as her eyes adjusted to the room's dimness she saw at least seven cats nestled into the nooks and crannies of the room. Most of them slept; a few stared at her warily.

Patricia's heart dropped. Suppose Jessica had brought a second copy of the diskette to her grandmother's home for safekeeping? She could have tucked it anywhere in the house. It would take months to take the house apart searching for it.

"Just take a seat anywhere," Naomi said. Apparently, she was oblivious to her home's condition. Or maybe she just liked it that way.

Patricia sat down on one end of the couch. Naomi studied her as she settled in to the other. Yes, the old woman was eccentric, thought Patricia, but she was also sharp. She could see, just beyond the merriment, the discernment in the woman's dark eyes.

"You working for the woman they says killed my girl?"

Direct question, thought Patricia. A direct answer might get her thrown out. An indirect one surely would.

"Yes, I am. Except I don't believe she did," she said. "I believe someone else killed your granddaughter." And Gigi as well, Patricia mentally added.

"I read it in the papers, but I forget easily these days, what they say her name was now?"

"Gigi Lafferty."

Naomi repeated the name to herself under her breath, shaking her head. "I was pretty surprised to read in the papers this Lafferty woman used to go as Loretta King when she was girl. I knew Loretta King. Thought she was a nice girl. Never would have thought she'd turn out to be one of them high-society women." She looked back up at Patricia. "But you know, I don't think she killed Jessica either. There was something too sad about the girl when I knew her. A kind of sadness you don't get rid of in one lifetime. People like that, with that kind of sadness, ain't the kind that kills another, not so's it's purposeful."

"When you knew Gigi, as Loretta, what was she like?"

Naomi nodded. "A little bit of a girl. Sad, like I said. I could tell she was fine, though. Way she talked. Carried herself. But I never asked her nothing about her background. She never said. I just fed her good when Jessica brought her around."

Naomi paused, recollecting. "Told her once she was a pretty girl. Be prettier without all that eye stuff and rouge on her face. She just started crying. I hugged her. That made her cry worse, but it seemed to make her feel better, too."

Naomi shook her head. "Nah. I don't believe she killed my girl. Told the police that, when they was asking me questions about Mrs. Gigi Lafferty. Told 'em I didn't know no Mrs. Lafferty, Jessica never brought her around, but I knew Loretta King, and people can call themselves any number or kind of names they want, but they don't change, and Loretta King wasn't killing nobody. They didn't want to believe me. Didn't really want to talk to me after I said Jessica didn't bring her around after she came back from Vegas."

Naomi hesitated, rubbed her eyes, blinked a few times, then looked sharply at Patricia. "Don't think she killed my girl. But I'd surely like to find out who did."

Patricia nodded. "I would, too," she said. "I would, too."

A cat jumped onto her lap. Cats had a radar for her dog lover's antipathy for them, and so delighted in making her acutely aware of their presence. If she pushed it away, another would probably take its spot. She didn't want to risk a cat parade across her lap, or offending Naomi. She smiled bravely over at Naomi, who had settled into the other end of the couch, and gave the cat a clumsy pat between the ears.

"That's Mandy," said Naomi.

"How—sweet."

"You don't like cats much, do you?" Naomi grinned. "A person who likes cats would scritch them under the chin and coo at them a little. C'mere, Mandy."

The cat sauntered over to Naomi and settled on her lap. "I didn't mean to end up with so many of them, you know," she said. "But I'm a generally sociable person. I don't like being alone. I started taking them in after Jessica left for Las Vegas. She always liked cats. And I thought, when she comes back, settles down, I'll give her this cat. Then I started finding things I thought she could use. I always was a collector of things, any little thing, you know, but I'd see something, a chair maybe, and I'd think, I'll save that for Jessica. She might want it for her own place when she comes back, settles down."

Naomi stared across the room. "I didn't really think, in a way, she'd come back. I was surprised when she came back. Happy. But she didn't want nothing from me." She paused and wiped her hand across her eyes. She looked back at Patricia, a smile back on her face. "Sorry."

"That's okay. You said you raised her from the time she was seven?" The woman obviously needed to talk, thought Patricia. Maybe she'd learn something that would help her just by listening. Maybe not. In any case, she might be able to help an old, lonely woman feel a little better.

Naomi nodded. "Bill, that's my son, dropped her off here one day. Said Jerri—that was his wife, Jessica's mother— had taken off again, and he had to go find her. Don't know if he ever found her or not. Never heard from either Bill or Jerri again. Truth to tell, I never tried much to find out what became of them.

"I figured both me and Jessica were better off just the two of us, and Jessica didn't ask many questions about what had happened to her mama or papa. I reckon she also understood, in the unspeaking way children are wise, that she was better off without them around."

Naomi shook her head and sighed. "Jessica and me, we got along fine. But I never could get through to that girl that she had to work for what she wanted. She was always looking for the easy way to get what she wanted. And she was bright, too bright for her own good. She could con a kid out of lunch money just to buy herself a treat after school, and the kid would fall for it with a smile. So I guess she thought a place like Las Vegas would be the best place for her. But it ain't no school yard out there. Or anywhere, really. Jessica just never saw the danger in a situation."

"Do you think she was in danger after she came back here?"

"I don't know." Naomi stared down at the cat on her lap, scratching its side. She considered Patricia's question carefully. She looked up at her. "I think she was messing around in things she'd been better off staying out of."

"What makes you say that?"

Naomi looked suddenly, tremendously sad. Her chin quivered for a moment. "Jessica didn't come around much, after she came back here. Didn't want to stay here, didn't want any of the things I'd saved for her. She told me she'd

found herself a good job, a nice place, got some nice furniture and new clothes, and was going to make something
of her life. Some friend of hers had just the right connections, she said."

Naomi cleared her throat, then continued. "First month
or so after that, she visited me regular. Then she stopped
coming around. Then when she came back, she was brood-
ing like. I couldn't get her to open up, talk to me. Then the
last time she came, she left me this big yellow envelope.
Said if anything was to happen to her, I should give it to
the authorities."

Patricia's heart clenched at that. She told herself not to
get too excited yet. The envelope might not contain anything truly useful. And while Nancy hadn't mentioned coming out here to talk with Jessica's grandmother, that didn't
mean she hadn't. Even if the envelope contained what
Patricia hoped it did—a copy of Jessica's diskette—the police might already have it, which would mean that Patricia
would not get a chance to review it.

"How long ago did she leave the envelope with you?"
Patricia asked, forcing her voice to remain steady and calm.

"About two weeks ago. It was the last time she came to
visit."

"Did you happen to look inside it?"

"No." Naomi grinned suddenly, gleefully. "And I didn't
leave it with the police, either. I thought about it, when they
come to tell me my poor Jessica's murdered. But like I said
before, they didn't want to hear what I had to say. Didn't
ask much questions. Didn't answer many either. Just gave
me the news, went on their way. Seemed like they thought
they already had all the answers.

"So I thought, Jessica would want this to be given to
someone who'd ask questions about what happened to her.
And so I thought I'd just have some faith the good Lord
would send someone like that my way, and if no one came
in a few weeks, I'd go ahead and give it to the police."

Naomi moved herself slowly from the end of the couch
to the section in front of the sewing machine. She opened

a drawer and pulled out a manila office envelope. She handed it to Patricia.

Patricia accepted the envelope and opened it. There was a computer diskette inside. And there was something else—a photograph. She pulled it out long enough to glance at the black-and-white glossy and assess its relevance to the case. It was a photo of Allen and Gregory in Allen's office. Part of a window frame intruded on the left side of the photo; lines of open miniblinds cut across the front of the picture, and office clutter was visible behind them. But enough of Allen and Gregory showed to make the implications of their activity quite clear. They were partially unclothed, and embracing passionately.

Patricia's photography experience enabled her to know that the photo had been taken at night with a telephoto lens and, she was quite sure, without the subjects' awareness. She also knew that Jessica, who had taken such a poor-quality picture with a 35mm automatic of her grandmother, could not have possibly taken a photograph requiring the photographic skills of long-distance shooting at night through a partially obscured window. There was, however, someone at Lafferty Products who did know a great deal about photography, someone who was close to the Lafferty family, and who was known to spend time after work with Jessica. Rita Ames. The only problem was that Poppy had been quite clear that a man had accompanied Jessica to see him. Maybe the data on the diskette would help Patricia have a clearer understanding of what the photograph implied.

Patricia slipped the photo back in the envelope and clasped it shut.

"That going to help you figure out what happened to my girl?" Naomi asked.

Patricia nodded. "I think so. May I take it with me?"

"Yes." Naomi looked at Patricia, studying her again. "You know, you got a little bit of that sadness, like I said earlier Loretta had. Not all over you, like she did, but a little bit."

"Any suggestions for an antidote?"

"Love well." Naomi nodded, and repeated, "Love well. But you ain't never going to get rid of it entirely. That's okay. Kind of adds to you, you know."

"Thanks for your help," Patricia said.

Naomi pulled herself off of the couch. Patricia stood. "You figure it out, my baby's murder. Then let me know what it was about," Naomi said. It wasn't a question. It was a command.

Patricia headed for the front door. There, she paused, turned around, and looked at Naomi. She wished she could offer the old woman some comfort, tell her she knew her granddaughter had loved her dearly, tell her she knew her granddaughter had just been involved with the wrong people through no fault of her own. But the latter was not true, and Patricia couldn't speak truthfully on the former. All she could do, as Naomi had directed, was figure it out, and later, at some point when perhaps the sting would be easier to take, come back and talk with her again.

Patricia smiled gently at Naomi. "I will," she said.

Chapter 26

"Once more, from the top," Patricia muttered to herself. She pressed the keys to move to the top of the file displayed on her computer.

The data on the diskette was compatible with the database package Allen used to keep track of various aspects of the Lafferty Products business. Because she used the same database package in her office, she was able to read the data on the diskette on her computer. That, at least, was gratifying.

What was frustrating was that she was not sure how the information could be used to prove that sabotage was occurring at Lafferty Products. The data gave the names of companies that had sold supplies to Lafferty Products, a description of the supplies purchased, the date the sale took place, the amount billed for the supplies, and the date the bill was paid. All data was for the previous June. And there was nothing about it that looked unusual.

Patricia sighed as she scrolled through the data again, looking for any kind of anomaly, knowing she wouldn't find anything because she'd already gone over every bit of information on the diskette numerous times. She wanted the satisfaction of frowning at the computer screen, saying, "Something looks wrong here!" then realizing, with a triumphant *aha* what that something was.

She pushed back from her desk, crossed her arms, and stared at the computer screen. She was frowning, all right, but all it did was give her was a headache knotted between her eyebrows. Maybe, she thought, she didn't see what looked wrong because the data wasn't meant for her eyes. Jessica had tried to sell it to Gigi, specifically stating that if she passed it on to Neil, he would know what it meant. So, possibly, she could show the data to Neil and he could tell her.

But if Jessica had told Gigi about the photograph of Allen and Gregory, Gigi hadn't mentioned it to Patricia. That made Patricia believe that for some reason Jessica had not told Gigi about it. Possibly because Allen and Gregory were involved with the sabotage as well, or because Jessica had been trying to blackmail them with a combination of the diskette and the photograph?

Then, of course, there was Rita Ames. Patricia was fairly certain that Rita had helped Jessica take the photograph, or had taken it herself. Connecting her to the diskette was problematic; nothing so far would suggest that link. Yet the diskette and photographs were in the same envelope Jessica had left with her grandmother, which implied a link between them. So, possibly, if Rita knew about the photos, she might also know about the diskette and why it would prove corporate sabotage.

But since any of the four who could possibly explain the data were also involved in some way with Jessica, and thus could be her and most likely Gigi's murderer, Patricia couldn't just waltz up to Neil, Gregory, Allen, or Rita and start demanding answers.

But then, Patricia told herself, she already was in danger. Someone had tried to set her up at the houseboat. God only knew what that someone would have done to her if she had run off the boat toward the house. Possibly she could go to the police with the evidence she had, but it wasn't enough for them to solve the murders, and really, what did she have? Nothing, until she could prove that the picture and the diskette meant something.

Patricia closed her eyes and inhaled slowly, then exhaled slowly, letting the knot in her forehead relax. Focus and relax, she told herself. There had to be a way to find out what the picture and the diskette really meant without completely blundering into danger, as she had on the houseboat.

An abrupt knock came at her door. Patricia opened her eyes, startled. It was Saturday afternoon. She wasn't expecting anyone at her office.

"Who is it?" she called.

"Nancy Grey."

"Come in," Patricia said.

The door opened and the police detective entered. She shut the door and settled into Patricia's visitors' chair. "You're hard at work, I see," Nancy said.

Patricia arched an eyebrow. "Likewise, I see."

"I wonder if it's on the same thing?"

Patricia sighed. "Detective, really, I don't have time for cryptic or clever right now. What brings you to my office?"

"Okay. I can be straightforward. Seems last night the police department in Pikeville, near Lake George, got an anonymous phone call."

Nancy paused, studying Patricia's face. Patricia kept her breathing regular, but focused on it in order to keep her expression steady.

"Do you know where Pikeville is?" Nancy asked.

"I've heard of it."

"Mmm. Well, it's a small tourist town. The police there don't get too many calls, anonymous or otherwise, for much more than kids getting a little too rowdy at summer parties at the cottages around the lake. But this caller stated that they would find a body tied to a houseboat docked near a certain cottage." Nancy paused, regarding Patricia. "Pretty dramatic anonymous tip, don't you think?"

Patricia smiled evenly. "Probably woke them up."

"Actually, the police department there, though small, is quite good. The answering officer went to the houseboat, and in fact found the body."

Patricia let her smile ease away gradually. "Oh my," she said simply.

Nancy continued. "Since it was raining so hard, there

were no traceable footprints or tire tracks on the property. There were two muddy boot prints, looked like men's boots, inside the house, but it's hard to say how long the prints might have been there. Being thorough, the police there are trying to determine the size and manufacturer of the boots. And they went to the phone booth where the call was placed—they do track numbers from which incoming calls are placed—and checked for similar boot prints. They couldn't find any, and unfortunately, there were no fingerprints at the phone. None at all, which is rather strange for a public phone. Apparently whoever made the call wiped the fingerprints from the phone. The phone was just outside of a bait shop and gas station about twenty-five miles west of Pikeville. Are you familiar with the area?"

Patricia didn't say anything.

"Hmmph. Well, the store owner remembered a wet, tired-looking woman who came in to buy some coffee, gas, and a sweatshirt. Unfortunately, the owner couldn't remember what the woman was driving or if she used the phone."

Patricia rubbed her forefinger across the diagonal white scar on her chin. "That's a pretty impressive story of how modern investigative techniques are being applied even in small, rural police departments. Thank you for sharing that with me. Oh, you might ask the owner for the receipt of the woman's purchases, just in case she used a credit card." She smiled sweetly.

Nancy shot her a reproachful look. "Thanks for the suggestion, Ms. Investigative Consultant. Actually, we checked and the woman paid cash. Clever of her, don't you think?"

"Very," Patricia replied, suppressing a laugh.

"Anything strike you as strange about me telling you this?" Nancy asked.

'Well, yes. I have to wonder how you found out, since Pikeville is clearly out of your jurisdiction. And I don't imagine Pikeville and Montgomery police have that much occasion to swap stories about sharp investigative procedures."

"Good point," Nancy said. "We got a call this morning that the body was Gigi Lafferty's. Which is how we got involved. We're informing next of kin."

Patricia looked at Nancy steadily. "I'm very sorry to hear that. But of course, I'm not next of kin. So I do have to wonder why I'm hearing this from you, rather than, say, reading it in tomorrow's newspaper."

Nancy settled back in her chair and let out a long, low whistle. "I would think you'd have a stronger reaction than that to hearing about the death of a client. Especially one for whom you have gone to so much trouble."

"I'm quite sorry, of course, to hear of Mrs. Lafferty's death."

"Of course," Nancy said. "Sorry enough, I hope, that if you know anything about her death's circumstances—like who might have placed that call, or who might have known she was in Pikeville—you might share that information with us. We're treating this as murder, given the condition in which her body was found. Actually, it was tied up, as if someone—the person who placed the call, no doubt— wanted to make sure her body was found. We're assuming this is linked to Jessica Taylor's murder. Maybe Gigi had a coconspirator in Taylor's death who got nervous that Gigi would come forth, and killed Gigi, then felt a bit guilty about just leaving her body to sink to the bottom of the lake, and called the Pikeville police. . . ."

"But you're making several assumptions—" Patricia stopped herself short, took in a deep breath.

Nancy smiled. "I didn't think you'd like that theory. So I'm sure if you have any information that would help us . . ."

"I'll be in touch," Patricia said. "When and if I do."

Nancy nodded. "Very well. I'll let myself out."

Patricia watched Nancy leave, then stared for a while at the computer screen.

Fine, she thought. She'd find out the information she needed to prove that someone besides Gigi had killed

Jessica, then taken Gigi's life. The key had to be the diskette and the photograph. And she knew which of her four suspects she would talk with first, even if it was risky.

Chapter 27

This ceramic goose was dressed in a yellow-and-orange apron fringed with lace and a matching cap, in honor, Patricia supposed, of the fall season. She grinned with her new appreciation of ceramic geese, although she didn't think Rita would be the type to have a ceramic goose on her front porch. Of course, she hadn't thought of Rita as the type to have an affair with her boss, either. Or to take revealing, intimate, and very personal photos of her coworkers.

Patricia rang the doorbell and waited. Rita had been first on her list to talk with because she thought Rita was least likely to have killed Jessica or Gigi. Poppy had said a man had accompanied Jessica to visit him about finding someone to set fire to the Lafferty Products warehouse; Nancy had said a man's boot prints had been found inside the cabin at the lake. That didn't prove Rita innocent, of course. If Patricia was right, and she had taken the photographs of Allen and Gregory for Jessica as part of Jessica's blackmailing schemes, she might have killed Jessica to cover up her involvement.

Be prepared for anything, Patricia thought, taking a deep breath. She rang the doorbell again.

A young boy, about ten years old, came to the door.

Patricia smiled at him. "Hello. I'm looking for Rita Ames. Is she home?"

The boy shouted over his shoulder, "Mom!"

A few seconds later Rita was at the door. She looked surprised to see Patricia and said, "Well. I've heard of being eager for mentoring in the corporate culture, but isn't this a little overeager? It's Saturday afternoon. . . ."

"I'm not here for that. I want to talk with you. About Jessica. About a photograph of Allen and Gregory that I believe is your work. About Lafferty Products."

Rita stared at Patricia for a long moment, then said quietly, "Toby, I want you to go up to your room."

Toby, looking intrigued now by the exchange between his mother and the lady at the door, said, "I thought you wanted me to put away the groceries."

"I'll take care of it this time. You go up to your room."

"But you said, 'specially since Dad left, I had to . . .'"

Rita pointed away from the door. "Your room. Upstairs. Go. Now."

Toby heaved a dramatic sigh, but ran off as his mother had directed him. Rita watched him go, then looked back at Patricia. "Want to see how quickly ninety-five bucks of groceries can disappear into a fridge and cupboards? It's not a pretty sight."

Patricia followed her back into the kitchen. Rita dug into one grocery sack and started putting away cans of soup.

"I get the feeling," Rita said, not looking at Patricia, "that you're not just some temp hired to fill in for Jessica."

"I'm an investigative consultant. I was hired by Gigi Lafferty for some personal concerns. . . ."

Rita looked up sharply. "These concerns wouldn't involve Neil, would they?"

"Not in the way you're thinking. Gigi spent some time as a young woman as a topless dancer under the name Loretta King. Jessica knew her then, and was trying to blackmail her for it, knowing Neil would be very upset if he learned of his wife's past."

"You bet he would. Purity and chastity for everyone except for him, that's Neil's philosophy, but of course he doesn't see anything he does as—" Rita stopped, shook her head. "Sorry. So Gigi hired you to what, get Jessica off of her back?"

Patricia smiled and shook her head. "I don't do that kind

of work. She hired me to investigate her past, see whether or not Jessica could prove that Gigi had been a topless dancer. I didn't know, in fact, of Jessica's involvement or even her existence until I went to the Lafferty home to collect my payment from Gigi. What I found was Gigi gone, and Jessica's body in the swimming pool."

"Things got ugly for you, then?"

"You might say they got interesting, anyway. For various reasons, I started doing some digging. Seems before she died, Jessica told Gigi she would sell her information proving Neil's company was being sabotaged by someone who was in the company, and Jessica had proof. But somebody murdered her before she could get the evidence to Gigi."

Patricia sat her briefcase on the edge of the kitchen counter, opened it, and pulled out a manila envelope. She opened up the envelope and held up the black-and-white glossy of Gregory and Allen. "I finally found copies of what I believe was the evidence Jessica had to sell Gigi. It includes this."

Rita stared at the photo. She set a jar of peanut butter down heavily on the counter.

"I think it's your work, Rita. I think we ought to talk about it."

Rita glared at Patricia. "What a perfectly awful accusation. I have absolutely—I just—I think you ought to leave."

Patricia shrugged and put the photograph away. "All right. Have it your way. But I think you ought to know—you'll hear it soon enough on the news—that Gigi is dead. Murdered. And I believe whoever murdered Jessica murdered Gigi. And the only thing I have to go on that's concrete is some evidence Jessica left with her grandmother, which included this photograph. Which Jessica could not have taken, because she didn't have the skill. But you did. Of course, I can't force you to talk about it. For all I know, you hated Gigi. But she mentioned you to me as being her friend, at least at one time."

"My God," Rita whispered. She clasped her hands to her mouth, looking momentarily like she was going to throw up. "My God," she said again. Then she flung open a cabinet and pulled out a glass. She filled it halfway up with tap water, drank the water in one swift gulp, then filled the glass again. "Let's—let's go sit down at the table. This stuff—can wait."

Patricia and Rita sat down at the kitchen table. Patricia left the photograph lying on the table. Rita stared at it awhile longer, her head propped up in her hands. Then she looked up at Patricia. Her gaze was steady, although tears filled her eyes.

"I've always loved photography. I've always wanted to be a professional photographer. It was something I was working toward, on my own time. I'd even dreamed about opening my own studio. I never—I never dreamed, though, that I'd use my skills to invade someone else's privacy."

Rita turned the photograph over and pushed it away. "I haven't been able to even touch a camera since. . . ." She stopped and sighed.

"You did take this, then?"

"Yes. Jessica told me she'd destroyed all the copies, though, when I told her I didn't—" Rita broke off again.

"Maybe you should just start from the beginning."

Rita laughed abruptly, her laugh almost a cough. "The beginning? Where's that? When my marriage started going south, partly because I spent too damn much time at the office trying for a higher position, which in itself was partly because of my marriage problems? When Neil started noticing, coming by my office late at night to tell me what a trooper I was, how much he appreciated my extra efforts? Or maybe the first time we screwed in his office. Or the first time at his and Gigi's new house. You know, he even told me that he and Gigi hadn't made love there yet. I was, he said, helping him christen their house."

Rita shook her head. "That made me sick. I mean physically sick that night, after I got home, but at least it woke me up. I was being used. And I was using Neil, who was not only my boss but a friend's husband, because somehow I thought this would help things at work go a little better, which certainly would have been nice since things at home had gone rotten. I was betraying everything and everyone that meant anything to me.

"Then life just went into a nosedive, you know? Maybe that was the beginning. Neil broke off with me—I didn't even notice the new cute employee down the hall to figure out why—but he suddenly did. And then he promoted Gregory Finster—one of my own direct reports!—into the position I'd been at the office working late at night to get. And then my husband left me. I don't know whether or not he figured out I was having an affair. I don't even know if he would have cared, things had gone so sour between us. I think he just tired more quickly than I did of our fights, or maybe worse, our silences."

Rita shrugged and took a sip of her water. "Pick a point in that long, sad story and tell me where the beginning is."

"What do you think?"

Rita sighed. "Probably right after my husband left. Jessica came to my office. She was very direct. She knew I had had an affair with Neil. Neil himself had told her. And she figured I resented him for that, and for promoting Gregory over me. She was right. I did. I hated both Neil and Gregory. I saw my problems as being caused by them at the time. She came to me at just the right time. A few weeks earlier or later I wouldn't have been bitter enough to listen to her. But I was at the height of my hatred."

Rita fell silent and stared off into the distance as if she were mentally reliving that hateful time in her life.

After a few minutes Patricia said quietly, "Jessica had a talent, it seems, for knowing how to target people's weaknesses and profit from them."

Rita looked back at Patricia suddenly. "Yes. Yes, she did. Her proposal for me was very simple. She told me she was angry at Neil, too—she didn't say why and I didn't ask. I don't think she was, though; I think she just wanted me to feel as much as possible like her coconspirator. She told me she had a really simple plan for striking back at both Neil and Gregory, but she needed my help. One night she'd stumbled in on Gregory and Allen making love in Allen's office. They'd been so involved they didn't even notice. What if, she said, we had photographs proving their affair? We could make Gregory, or Neil, or both, pay for the photographs."

Patricia frowned. "A gay love affair isn't exactly shocking like it used to be. Who would really care if Gregory and Allen were having an affair?"

Rita gave her half cough, half laugh. "Oh, I wouldn't care. You wouldn't care. Lots of people wouldn't care. And I believe no one should care. Probably you do, too."

Patricia nodded. "Yes. Go on."

"But believe me, Neil would care. He is very, very conservative. His multiple affairs, you see, that's one thing. To him, that just proves his maleness. But his son gay? Or his wife a former topless dancer? Jessica had him figured out, all right. He'd be horrified. He'd assume everyone else in the world would be horrified, that his chances for success in business and politics would be ruined. And nothing matters more to Neil Lafferty than success."

"So what would he do if he learned these things about his wife and son?"

Rita considered the question. "About Gigi—he'd probably leave her if he had to. Take the high road, say he didn't know anything about her past, wouldn't have married her if he had, play the poor victim of a lying woman."

"He'd throw her over that easily?"

Rita looked at Patricia sharply. "You don't know Neil. Yes. He would."

But Gigi had known him that well, Patricia thought. And she hadn't quite been able to let go of the security and status he provided her. No wonder she'd gone to such lengths to find out if Jessica could prove her past.

"What about his son? Would he have disowned Allen as well?"

Rita smiled slowly, bitterly. "Everyone has a soft spot, you know. You probably see that all the time. Even Neil has a soft spot. And it's Allen. Oh, he'd have raised the

roof with Allen. Threatened to throw him out of the house.
Fired Gregory. Or paid him off to make sure he never got
near Allen again. But do anything to really hurt Allen? To
really cut him off? No way. Neil has this fantasy that Allen
is going to be just like him any day now. Want to take over
the business someday, want to rise in the limelight alongside his daddy."

Patricia rubbed her finger across the scar on her chin as
she considered Rita's comment. Perhaps either Allen or
Gregory would have murdered Jessica to keep her from
telling Neil about their relationship, to avoid the repercus-
sion Rita had described. But then why not murder Rita as
well? Why murder Gigi? If Allen and Gregory's relationship played a role in Gigi's murder, Patricia reasoned, it
had to be in connection with the sabotage Jessica had described to Gigi. And in connection with the visit to Poppy
to find someone who would set fire to the warehouse.

What if Jessica had been blackmailing Allen and
Gregory, but not for money, to keep quiet about their relationship? Neither one had enough money to satisfy Jessica.
But if they had a scheme for defrauding Neil's business in
some way, Patricia reasoned, they could have let Jessica in
on it as a form of payment for her silence, then killed her
if they thought she'd told Gigi, and Gigi later for the same
reason. For that matter, if Neil had somehow already
learned of Allen and Gregory's activities through Jessica—
maybe Jessica tried to get paid twice, once by Gigi and
once by Neil, for the same information before skipping
town—maybe he'd killed both Jessica and Gigi to ensure
that word would not get around of what was going on, in
fear that it would ruin his political chances.

Patricia looked back up at Rita. "There's something else
I want to talk with you about. Jessica told Gigi that she had
evidence someone was sabotaging Neil's company. I found
what I believe is a copy of this evidence, along with the
photograph."

Rita looked surprised. "I don't know anything about sabotage. I'm not even sure I know what you mean."

"Defrauding the company, perhaps?"

Rita shook her head. "That much I can tell you I am innocent of. And I don't know anything about it. I took the photographs for Jessica. By the next week I was sick over what I had done. I went to Jessica and begged her to give up on her scheme."

"She'd hear nothing of it, of course," Patricia said.

"Of course. So I told her I wanted nothing to do with her plans. If she wanted to try to profit from the photograph, then leave me out."

Patricia arched an eyebrow. "I can't believe she'd let you off the hook that easily."

"She didn't. She reminded me a few times that she could tell Neil at any time that I'd taken the photograph, and he'd fire me. So I'd better do her any favors she might ask in the future."

"What kind of favors?"

Rita smiled in bitter amusement. "I think she actually believed she had a future in the company, even while blackmailing people. I think there was part of her that wanted that taste of—of, what? Security and respectability and status, I guess. I think she thought I could help her get it."

"Some people might say her threat of telling Neil you'd taken the photograph would be sufficient motive to murder Jessica," Patricia said. But why would Rita murder Gigi? And she didn't really believe Rita had murdered Jessica, either.

Rita didn't look shocked or outraged at the suggestion. She sighed tiredly. "Some people might. But hell, I can't even take a naughty photograph or sleep with the boss without making a mess of it, or feeling incredibly awful afterward. Deep down, I'm a puritan. I think in a way I'd be relieved if Neil fired me. Plus, I'm a soon-to-be single mother. Even if I really wanted to kill someone, I couldn't risk what that would do to my boy, or my life."

Patricia nodded. "Maybe you could look at what Jessica called evidence of sabotage at Neil's company, tell me if it means anything to you." She got a printout of the data from the diskette from her briefcase and handed it to Rita.

Rita studied it for a few minutes, then handed it back, shaking her head. "I'm sorry. It looks to me like records of purchases of supplies from various companies."

"But nothing looks unusual to you."

Rita shook her head again. "I don't know that part of the business in detail."

"I understand," Patricia said. She began repacking her briefcase. "Thanks for your help and honesty—"

"Um, wait. What are you, I mean, with the photograph you've got, are you . . ."

Patricia smiled. "I don't know what I'm going to do with it. I may have to turn it over as evidence to the police eventually. It depends on what, if anything, I can learn about this report that might also be evidence in Jessica's and Gigi's murder. I'm not going to try to blackmail you, or anyone else, with it, if that's what you're worried about."

"Oh, no, I didn't mean—well, I guess I was a little—" Rita shook her head. "Thanks."

"You don't need to thank me. But I do want you to do me a favor."

Rita looked up at Patricia warily. "What's that?"

"You said you hadn't taken any photographs since this business with Jessica. Go take some. Of the trees turning color. Of your kid. Of the mall parking lot, whatever. I think it would do you some good. You've made some pretty big mistakes, but you can't torture yourself over them forever. Everyone's got something in their past they don't like. Get on with life."

"And you think taking a few photographs will help me do that?"

Patricia shrugged. "Maybe. I don't know. It's just a thought."

She went to the front door, traded farewells with Rita, then went back to her truck. For a while she sat, watching the quiet Saturday activity in the neighborhood, considering what to do next. She didn't feel comfortable confronting ei-

ther Neil, or Allen, or Gregory, since any of them had compelling reasons for killing Jessica and Gigi. And she didn't
feel comfortable calling Nancy Grey with what she knew,
not just yet. All she really had was a photograph, a printout
from a diskette that looked like a perfectly ordinary business report, and the stories of Naomi, Gigi, Rita, and
Poppy. It added up to a theory, but it didn't add up to
enough evidence for the police to confront Neil, Allen, or
Gregory.

Patricia started her truck. Back to the office, she thought.
It was time to put her computer to work, digging up anything she could on the companies listed in the report.

Chapter 28

Neil Lafferty sat by the pool behind his house, staring into the water. He had just awoken from an unplanned nap.

He was not at all sure what had compelled him to come back to the pool after the police had left. He had been sorry, of course, to hear of his wife's death, but almost relieved that that was what the police came to tell him. At first he thought the police had come back to ask him more questions about the afternoon of Jessica's death. He had come back to the house that afternoon, after meeting a woman from the country club during lunch—it had been almost two weeks, after all, since he had tired of Jessica and broken off with her—to freshen up and shower before returning to the office.

Neil had been shocked, even horrified, to discover first the house a mess, then Jessica in the pool. But he knew he couldn't call the police. It would look like he had killed Jessica himself. He had, in his first confused moments after finding her body, tried to clean up the spots of blood on the carpet, and since then had been angry at himself for doing so. What if, somehow, he'd left some trace of evidence of his presence in the house that afternoon by taking the extra time instead of leaving immediately?

He stared in the pool, and realized he could never swim in it again. Every time he looked at it, he remembered seeing Jessica there. It was too cold now to go swimming anyway, even if he had wanted to. In fact, it was time to have the pool drained for the year, the patio furniture put away. Allen was supposed to take care of all of that, but of course he had not. Allen would wait until his father had reminded him several times, then smile in amusement at his father's frustration with him.

Neil had only put the pool in because he knew Allen would like it. Neil did not particularly care for swimming; he always felt he was fighting to stay afloat in an element that was unnatural to him. But he loved to watch Allen swimming. The water had the opposite effect on Allen, somehow giving him added grace.

But why, Neil wondered, should he have come back here after the police left, after they informed him that Gigi had been found, drowned in a lake, either accidentally or by suicide? There were numerous arrangements to be made, as well as considerable thinking to be done about how to handle this situation with the media and his business associates, and so the natural place for Neil to go would have been to his office. Yet he had come back to the pool automatically, staring at the water until he dozed off, trying to feel something, anything, about the loss of his wife.

All that came to mind, though, was how he was going to handle this with the press with just the right mix of sensitivity and poise. He didn't want this to ruin his political ambitions. He didn't want anything to stand in the way of those.

And then he had dozed off, and dreamed something about Allen as a boy, about water, about the swim team he'd been on, and all the aspirations Neil had for him, and how suddenly Allen had lost interest and quit the team.

But why, the question came back to him persistently, why have you come back to sit by the pool?

To wait, he thought.

And the thought startled him.

To wait for what?

Someone, something . . .

The back patio door opened, and Carla, the Laffertys' maid, stepped out.

"Excuse me, Mr. Lafferty."

"Yes?" Neil said without disguising his irritation. The

woman always seemed wary of him, as if he was suddenly going to lunge at her. He had no interest in her; couldn't she tell that?

"There's a woman here to see you. A Patricia Delaney."

Neil found himself feeling suddenly relieved, and realized that he had been waiting for Allen. Allen, of course, was out who knew where, doing who knew what, but somehow, Neil had been waiting for Allen to come to him by the pool, to tell him something. . . .

Neil shook his head to clear it. "Send her back," he said.

He glanced at his watch. My God, he thought. He'd been asleep for three hours and had missed his usual time for lunch. No wonder he was feeling odd. He straightened himself up in the chair. As soon as Patricia left—and he was determined to get rid of her quickly—he'd have some lunch, then start taking care of all the arrangements. . . .

"Hello, Neil."

Patricia's voice came from behind him. Then she stepped into view and sat down in a lawn chair across from him.

"My condolences," she said.

Neil looked at her. She seemed to be waiting for a response.

"Yes," he said finally. "Thank you. As you can imagine, I have much to arrange. I was just . . . resting for a moment here. What brings you by this afternoon?" Neil smiled thinly at Patricia. "Not mere condolences, I imagine?"

Patricia arched an eyebrow. "For some people in your situation, that would be enough. But I will admit I have another reason as well. I told you, in our previous meeting, that if I found evidence of the sabotage Jessica told Gigi was occurring in your company, I would inform you."

Patricia pulled her briefcase up onto her lap, opened it, and pulled out a computer printout and handed it to Neil. He took it and glanced over it.

"Purchases of supplies for the company. Nothing extraordinary about that," he said.

"Look a little closer, Neil. I just came from my office, where I ran searches on each of those companies. I checked databases of private and public company information. I checked electronic directories of local companies. All of the companies checked out—except for three of them. Those companies have three things in common. They all have box addresses at the same private mailing service. None of them exists in any of the directories or databases I checked. And all told, they reflect about thirty percent of the purchases of supplies for that month."

Patricia paused. She seemed to be waiting for a reaction. Neil understood what she was saying, as well as what she was implying. But he found, oddly, that he did not care. He was tired. He was numb. He stared back at her.

Patricia cleared her throat. "I imagine that if I checked other months, that pattern would hold. And that your supply expenses, since these so-called suppliers started getting paid by your company, have gone up between twenty-five and thirty-five percent. And I imagine that if I took a stroll through your warehouse, I would not find anything there from these suppliers." She hesitated, then spoke her next words slowly and carefully. "I have seen this kind of pattern before, Neil. Your company is being defrauded. In a very costly way. By someone who has access to and understands your computer system very, very well."

"Thank you for your work in bringing this matter to my attention. I have the semiannual inventory of the warehouse scheduled for next month; I'm sure any discrepancies in what was purchased on paper and what was purchased in fact will show up then. And I may have my auditor take a look at this. I'm sure, though, this will turn out to be an explainable error—"

"Error! How can you be so . . . your wife . . . Jessica—" Patricia started to say, then checked herself. She smoothed her hair back from her face, composed herself, then closed her briefcase. She stood up.

"Very well," she said crisply. "I'm glad I can provide information that might assist in your inventory. I will consider my work for you done. Expect my bill, including the amount Gigi owed me, within the next few days."

Neil waited until she was gone, then looked over the report slowly, carefully. Yes, he understood what the report, what Patricia's information, implied. Understood that very well. And understood that he would take care of it in his own time, in his own way.

It was a simple matter of control, of correction. That was what his own father had always said. He had not used enough of either on Allen. He had indulged him too much. That would change. Very soon.

And yet, a few minutes later, Neil found himself standing by the pool. He tore up the report that Patricia had left with him and tossed the pieces into the water. He watched the bits of white paper floating, then taking on water, then sinking. He wondered how long it would be before the paper would disintegrate entirely.

Chapter 29

Perhaps, Patricia thought as she drove out to Lafferty Products, perhaps if she'd shown Neil the photograph, that would have enraged him enough to be more forthcoming about confirming that, indeed, his company was being defrauded. But she still was not entirely convinced that Neil was not the killer. And she did not want to reveal Allen and Gregory's affair if it was not positively related in some way to the murders.

All she could do now was try to spot check the Lafferty Products warehouse to confirm that it contained no supplies from the three apparently fake companies. Then she would go to Nancy Grey, tell her what she had learned, warn her that Jessica and a man from Lafferty Products had talked with Poppy about burning down the warehouse the next month—about the time Neil said the semiannual inventory was scheduled to occur.

Then she would have to consider her work on identifying Jessica and Gigi's killer complete. The prospect of being done with the case did not satisfy her. She still could not prove beyond any doubt whether Gregory, Allen, or Neil had killed Jessica and Gigi, although she suspected Gregory or Allen most strongly. Her only hope was that the information she could provide to Nancy would give the police enough to go on to start digging further, asking questions she could not, and elicit a confession from one of them.

Patricia pulled into Lafferty Products. The place looked nearly abandoned on this Saturday afternoon. She parked near the warehouse.

Getting into the warehouse was simple. Her temporary badge was still active, and the lone security guard waved her through. Fifty minutes later she walked out, her suspicion confirmed. Nothing from the three questionable suppliers was stored in the warehouse that Patricia had been able to find. She headed back to her truck, intending to pay Nancy Grey a visit.

Patricia got in her truck, started it, and began reaching for her seat belt. Suddenly her passenger door opened, and Allen Lafferty was in the truck beside her, with a wide grin on his face and a gun poking in her ribs.

"Gotcha!" he said, and laughed.

Patricia forced her self to breathe evenly. She would have to use her wits to get out of this situation, and get the answers she had hoped the police would work on. Consider it an accelerated schedule, with a different questioner, she told herself.

"All right," she said quietly. "What do you want me to do?"

"I want you to pull out very calmly, like you normally would. Then I want you to drive east until we're out of town. I'll direct you."

Patricia did as she was instructed. Soon they were on the state route, heading east, alongside the Ohio River. It would be a gorgeous day for a drive like this, she thought, if only she didn't have a gun poking in her ribs by someone who, after his initial bit of juvenile humor, looked deadly serious about using the thing. Get to work to make sure he doesn't use it, she ordered herself.

"You know," she said, "it's pretty hard to concentrate on driving with that gun poking in my ribs. I know you've got it and there isn't anything I can do about it. Could you just hold it a little further away?"

Allen eased the gun away from her ribs. "Sure. Wouldn't want the driver uncomfortable." Patricia glanced over at him. The gun was still directed point-blank at her.

She pressed down evenly on the accelerator.

The gun was back in her ribs suddenly, making her

wince. "Ease off, Patricia. We wouldn't want any nice officers trying to pull us over, now, would we?"

She eased back on the accelerator until her speed dipped just under the speed limit. The gun was retracted from her ribs. Allen's message was clear.

"You seem to have a very specific destination in mind."

"Yes. Very."

"You know, I wonder, over something like filching a few bucks from your daddy's company, if it wouldn't be easier to take the consequences from your father than to risk a murder rap—"

The barrel of the gun struck her knee. The truck swerved.

"Keep it steady," Allen said. "My destination for you is a while away. But I can find a closer one if you want."

Patricia drove quietly for a few minutes, catching her breath and adjusting to the throbbing pain in her leg.

"I guess I wouldn't mind a few answers," she said quietly.

Allen sighed. "You want me to talk? Fine, I can talk. What the hell. Satisfy the brave detective just before her demise, isn't that the way it's supposed to go? Satisfy the bad guy's urge to brag. Then the detective finds a way out. I'll talk. But you're not finding a way out. You're going exactly the way Gigi went."

To Lake George, Patricia thought. The night she had driven there had been dark and rainy, but she had been intently focused on the road to cope with those conditions, and so she clearly remembered parts of the route. There had to be someplace along the way where she could either get help or somehow get away from Allen. . . .

"I'll start with a little story," Allen said. "I've always wanted to brag about this one, I've just never had the opportunity before. There once was this boy named Terry."

Terry, thought Patricia. She did not know who Allen was talking about, yet the name sounded familiar. . . .

"He tried to get in my way. So I drowned him one night. It was very simple; I challenged him to a night swimming race across a lake, just he and I. He agreed to it. About halfway across, I took him by surprise. I was stronger than him. No one ever suspected."

The name clicked into place. Terry Parker, the boy on Allen's swim team from years before. Patricia had run across an article about his drowning when she researched Allen; Allen had been mentioned as one of Terry's teammates.

"Well, my dad suspected. I could see it in his eyes. He couldn't prove it, of course. And if he could have, he wouldn't have. I was his little boy, you see, supposed to grow up just like him. Be a star. Be a success. He wasn't going to risk losing that image, or his image either, for the sake of one kid drowning. But it kind of changed things between us. I could see that. He became just a little fearful of me. It was a nice switch."

Allen laughed suddenly. "That did feel good. But I am disappointed to see you don't seem shocked."

"You drowned Jessica and Gigi when you thought they would get in your way. Should I be shocked that you drowned someone else in your past for a similar reason?"

"Yes, I drowned them. Neither of them gave me much choice. Jessica found out about my relationship with Gregory. We—weren't as careful as we should have been. She took photographs of us, came to me one day, and tried to blackmail me."

So, thought Patricia, Jessica hadn't told Allen or Gregory that Rita had actually taken the photographs.

"I didn't have any money at the time, and Gregory didn't either," Allen continued. "I had just started the scheme to take money from the company, though, so I offered to let her in on it in exchange for her silence. I knew if Dad found out, Gregory would be fired, and Dad would try to keep us apart. She agreed to my offer. And she did prove useful. I knew the inventory of the warehouse would come up, and questions about the amount of supplies in fact versus the amount of money spent on supplies would come up as well. So I realized we needed to destroy the evidence before then. She took me to talk with a man she knows in Newport, who she said could put us in touch with an arsonist. I need to get back to him, in fact. . . ."

Poppy, thought Patricia. Poppy had damn near gotten her killed in a fire fourteen years before. And now someone he was helping set up a similar fire was planning to kill her by drowning her. If Allen didn't kill her, maybe the ironies of her past life overlapping into her present would.

Patricia felt her concentration wavering and ordered herself to focus. The memory of the road was coming back to her now. They should pass by Gus's Bait Shop and Gas Station on the left in about ten minutes, she thought. Just after that, on the right, was a break in the trees where the road passed right by the river. It was a risk, a big risk, but if she could manage . . .

"I didn't trust her, though," Allen was saying. Patricia refocused on what he said. "I kept a careful eye on her, and I listened in on her phone calls at home and work. It wasn't hard to tap her phones; it was just a matter of staying after hours at work, and then dropping by her apartment to talk with her about the scheme and waiting until she was out of the room for a few minutes. Jessica placed a call to Gigi one morning setting up their meeting. I went home early that day, let myself in the house without Gigi hearing me. Then I listened from another room to their conversation, and I realized that Jessica wanted to leave town fast, and that she was going to sell her evidence to Gigi.

"I confronted Jessica after Gigi left," Allen said. "I didn't even realize she'd taken one of my backup diskettes from my office. I, of course, entered all the data for the bogus companies after the official data had been entered. Once payment was made to the companies, and the checks cleared in the accounts I'd set up, I erased the data about the bogus companies from the system; it stayed in just long enough to kick out the payments. But I back up everything on diskettes. I didn't expect Jessica to be clever enough to take one of the diskettes from my office. She tried running from me, but I followed her upstairs. I snatched the diskette from her, knocked her into the edge of the dresser in Dad and Gigi's room. She was so frightened by the little bit of blood from the cut in her head that she only barely struggled when I dragged her down the steps. Then I pushed her in the pool and drowned her. Then I set it up to make it look like Gigi had left in a hurry. I figured why not let Gigi take the fall? I knew Jessica and Dad were having an affair. So I figured Gigi could be blamed for killing Jessica in a jealous rage. There. Does that satisfy your lust for confessions?"

"There are a few things I don't understand yet. Like how you knew to find me at the warehouse. Like how you knew where to find Gigi."

"Very simple. Dad told me about your visit after I came home this afternoon. Just sort of mentioned your conversation casually. That's not like Dad, giving me a little hint that I was close to getting in trouble and had better do something about it. He really doesn't want me to get in trouble, even if it costs you your life. Just think what the embarrassment of his boy in trouble could do to his aspirations." Allen sounded sad and bitter.

He continued, "I called your home and office, and you weren't at either place. I figured you'd want to check the warehouse. So I came there and waited."

"How did you know where to find Gigi?"

"Through Gregory. He was also how I learned you are actually a private investigator. You see, Gigi had been going to him for a little counseling. She wanted her own identity. Her own life. But she just couldn't bring herself to break off from the security of Daddy-o."

Much like you, Patricia thought. She kept her eyes steadily on the road curving alongside the river, her hands firmly on the wheel, forcing them not to shake, and stayed quiet.

"So she went to Gregory. He encouraged her to talk to him, of course. He knew if Dad voiced any concerns about the company to her, she'd tell Gregory. It was a way to keep tabs on Dad, making sure he wasn't getting suspicious. She told him everything. About Jessica trying to blackmail her. About you. About her little retreat at Lake George. Proved quite useful." Allen laughed. "She was so shocked when both Gregory and I showed up at her cabin. The disbelief on her face made me laugh. Gregory didn't like it, but I knew we needed to get rid of her and you; just your knowing Jessica had evidence made you too dangerous. I wasn't sure if you'd found a copy of the evidence; after all, if she was clever enough to take my backup diskette, maybe she'd be clever enough to make a copy of it. I had searched her apartment and office cubicle and hadn't found anything, but I couldn't be sure. I figured if I could make it look like you had been involved in Gigi's death, that would be enough to keep anyone from believing anything you might have to say about a scheme to defraud the company. I forced Gigi to make the call that got you out there. And then I got rid of her the way I'd gotten rid of Jessica."

"So it was you at the cabin and houseboat that night?" Patricia asked.

"Yes. Very clever how you got away, by the way. Although, if Gregory hadn't turned on the back floodlights accidentally, you probably wouldn't have. But you couldn't expect to get away forever."

They passed Gus's Bait Shop and Gas Station on the left. Now, thought Patricia. Now was the time to put Allen off guard.

"I wonder," she said, "if you've ever considered that Gregory might be using you. I mean, you obviously don't have any confidence that he'd stay with you if your father found out about your relationship. And haven't you wondered why he wanted you to defraud the company? I bet it was his idea, wasn't it?"

The handle of the gun came suddenly, sharply against Patricia's temple. She closed her eyes for just a second, then forced herself to block the pain. She only had a few minutes if this was going to work.

"Don't speak against Gregory to me! Yes, it was his

idea, but Gregory and I were going to take the money, get a fresh start somewhere else."

"Did he tell you about his past problems? His bankruptcy? His lawsuits as a psychologist?"

"I—I don't know what you're trying to do, but if I were you . . ."

There was the curve, thought Patricia, and just around it the edge of the road by the river. Her heart was pounding. "I guess he didn't. I think he was using you to get money so he could set up his own little empire again, with or without you. You don't really believe he'd stay with you if he thought his plans would be ruined."

"Look, just shut up and drive. I've told you—"

Suddenly, they reached the edge of the road. Patricia braced herself. In one swift movement she floored the accelerator, cut the wheel, and opened her door. They went flying into the air.

For just a brief second Patricia caught the look of shock on Allen's face. He wasn't braced for the sudden turn, and his head went flying into the windshield. He was knocked out immediately.

And then they hit the water, and Patricia faced another moment in which life and death seemed to hang in balance for an eternity as the universe waited to see which she would choose.

She hadn't really had the chance to make the choice for herself when Gigi rescued her from the fire fourteen years before. Now she could take herself safely to shore and leave Allen behind to drown. It was a fitting fate for him; after all, he'd drowned three people in his lifetime and planned to do the same to her. And if she tried to rescue him, there was the chance he'd come to and bring her down after all.

For a second, under the water, she thought she'd been given this choice because she had been interrupted once before while wrestling with a similar decision. But now she was making the choice over another human being's life, and that was the more terrible of choices to have to make.

Patricia pushed herself to the surface of the river, to the relief of oxygen. She broke the surface of the water for just a moment, drew in a breath, then turned and plunged back into the river.

Chapter 30

The computer printer hummed as it printed out the final page of the report, and then was silent. Patricia ripped the report off her printer, settled back in her office chair with a glass of iced coffee, and glanced through the report, soon to be filed in a blue folder labeled *Lafferty*. In Patricia's business, she kept materials for active cases in red folders; materials for closed cases in blue folders.

This case, inasmuch as Patricia had nothing left to investigate on behalf of Gigi Lafferty, was closed. But then that was like saying that the report she had just printed off gave a full, accurate rendering of the events of the past few weeks.

The report gave the facts. It summarized her involvement with Gigi Lafferty from the initial meeting in her office. It included statements about the events of the past few days since she had made the choice to haul Allen Lafferty from the river: once he was able, he had given a full confession to the police, and his confession was confirmed by a pair of his boots that matched the prints found in the cabin; Gregory Finster denied his involvement with Allen, calling Allen's assertions a "delusion," but was being investigated as an accessory to murder and to fraud; and while Allen seemed to enjoy, even revel in the media attention his confession was getting, all his father, Neil, would say was a tight-lipped "no comment."

Patricia had even received a note and some photographs from Rita. The note briefly said she had resigned from Lafferty Products and suggested lunch. Rita's photographs were, much to Patricia's amusement, of neighborhood porch geese, decked out in autumnal splendor. It made her decide that she would have lunch with Rita in the next few weeks. And next week Patricia was paying the visit she had promised to Naomi.

Patricia included in her blue folder printouts of the media reports that she accessed in the various newspaper databases she used. While those reports got a few days' worth of front-page, splashy headline treatment, equally interesting, at least to Patricia, was a news article, buried deeply in the hard-copy version of the newspaper, and barely consuming any computer space at all in the databases, about a certain Newport establishment called the Sacred Light Sanctuary of Hope. The police had raided the place and found that it was serving as an warehouse for stolen electronic goods. The owner, Joey Jones, had been arrested for trafficking stolen goods. Patricia had smiled at that. No matter what he called himself, she would always think of the odd man as Poppy.

So the report, and all its exhibits, were complete and organized and ready to archive away in a blue folder. It was a formality Patricia attended to at the conclusion of every case, one that usually gave her a sense of satisfaction.

But this time she found herself feeling more restless than satisfied. The case was neatly summarized and concluded on paper, but in real life she felt as though it would not be closed for a long time. It had revealed too much within her, of her own demons, her own weaknesses, her own fears. The revelations had strengthened her, but they would take a long time to assimilate into her approach to life.

And her sadness over Gigi's murder would linger for a long time. Patricia felt that she and Gigi were kindred spirits, more so than she and her friends. They had both tried, even to the point to putting their lives in jeopardy, to overcome the pretenses of their pasts in order to move on with their lives. Unfortunately, Gigi had done so in a way that cost her her life.

Patricia abruptly flipped off her computer and printer,

tucked her report in the blue folder, and took it to the back office where she filed it under *L*. Then she shut the filing-cabinet drawer firmly.

When she returned to her outer office, Dean was sitting in one of her visitors' chairs.

"You're a little early," Patricia said.

"Do you mind?"

"No. I'm kind of glad you're so eager to go. Is there going to be room in your car?" Patricia's truck was still being assessed by her insurance company. At least she had rescued the neon green "car phone" after her truck was pulled from the river. The phone sat on her desk now, a little reminder of the humor of life.

Dean laughed. "I haven't said I'm going to buy a computer and haul it over to the tavern today. I just agreed to look at computers with you."

"All right," she said. "Sounds like you're ready to go."

"And you?"

She grinned. "I'm ready to go, too."

Patricia and Dean left her office, and a sense of happy, quiet anticipation washed over her. It was Friday afternoon, and suddenly she could think of nothing more she wanted for this autumn afternoon than to go computer shopping with Dean. Then maybe they'd share a quiet dinner before going back to his tavern for the evening, and afterward . . . Patricia smiled to herself as she got in Dean's car. She didn't know exactly what might happen afterward. All she knew for certain was that the present felt good.